Lord Ware's Widow

by

Emily Hendrickson

A SIGNET BOOK

SIGNET
Published by the Penguin Group
Penguin Putnam Inc., 375 Hudson Street,
New York, New York 10014, U.S.A.
Penguin Books Ltd, 27 Wrights Lane,
London W8 5TZ, England
Penguin Books Australia Ltd,
Ringwood, Victoria, Australia
Penguin Books Canada Ltd, 10 Alcorn Avenue,
Toronto, Ontario, Canada M4V 3B2
Penguin Books (N.Z.) Ltd, 182–190 Wairau Road,
Auckland 10, New Zealand

Penguin Books Ltd, Registered Offices:
Harmondsworth, Middlesex, England

First published by Signet, an imprint of Dutton Signet,
a member of Penguin Putnam Inc.

First Printing, November, 1997
10 9 8 7 6 5 4 3 2

Printed in the United States of America

Dangerous Flowering

Georgiana had made the mistake of mentioning her passion for flowers to Lord Thornbury—that was all the information he needed to induce her to go with him alone to visit the conservatory by moonlight.

"I have a large greenhouse at my estate in Kent," he told her as he stood by her side gazing at the exotic blossoms. "I believe my orchids would interest you."

"Do you have a great deal of trouble growing them?" Georgiana asked. "They are quite temperamental."

His answer was quite unexpected. He tipped up her chin with one perfectly gloved hand while slipping the other around her. The lush scents that swirled around her combined with the masculine cologne he used to bewitch her senses. Never had she dreamed a kiss could be like this, so gentle yet so demanding.

Still, she imagined she was safe as he released her and said, "We must return to the party now. I'd not have anyone cast a shadow on your reputation."

Safe, that is, until he added, "But later, my sweet. Oh, later . . ."

Chapter One

The silence in the luxurious country library belonging to Lady Kenyon was broken only by the crackling sound from the pages of three-day-old newspapers from London. The July afternoon sun beamed in through the leaded windows, casting sharp shafts of light across the interior, revealing dust motes floating lazily in the air. At last, one of the two gentlemen seated near the bay window spoke.

"You really intend to pursue this, er, course, Thornbury?" Lord Musgrave asked hesitantly, peering over the top of his paper in an attempt to gauge the mood of his friend. Lowering the paper, he ran his fingers through his sandy hair, his brown eyes clearly troubled. He had somewhat the look of an unhappy beagle.

The grin that had charmed most of the females in the *ton* at one time or another slowly spread across the handsome countenance of Jason Ainsley, Earl of Thornbury. His nod was most decisive, the grin almost smug.

"Think she will come?" Lord Musgrave persisted. "Might not. Lady Ware hasn't been seen in society since her husband's death several years ago."

"She wrote a gracious letter to Aunt Charlotte promising she would be here. Today, as a matter of fact." Lord Thornbury also lowered his paper, a devilish smile crinkling up the corners of his eyes. "It is a challenge, Musgrave. To woo and win the favors of the beautiful Georgiana, Dowager Marchioness of Ware is a temptation I cannot resist."

"Might not be beautiful anymore," Lord Musgrave reflected. "Dash it all, mourning turns some females into watering pots and drabs."

"As I understand it, this was a marriage of convenience," Thornbury replied with cynicism lacing his voice. "I doubt she was overly beset with grief." He glanced at his good friend Musgrave and gave him a reassuring nod. "I shan't seduce her. I have never had to go that far when interested in a woman. They usually come to me," he finished without a trace of boastfulness.

Indeed, that was putting the matter lightly. Thornbury had been pursued by more women than he could count and could have his choice of agreeable females wherever he chose to go. He envisioned a pleasurable dalliance with the reputedly beautiful widow to enliven his visit with his aunt. The house party he had promised to attend that might have been boring now appeared most encouraging.

"Well," Musgrave said while casting a jaundiced look at his friend, "I hope she gives you your comeuppance. 'Tis time some woman did."

"I doubt it will be the meek little widow. Usually these beautiful women are not inclined to wit; charm is enough."

Musgrave's mobile mouth twisted into a rueful grin and he said no more on the matter. Silence resumed, with the crackling of the papers as the loudest sound to be heard for some minutes.

Suddenly, the sound of carriage wheels hard upon gravel came though an open window. The men quickly rose, consigning their newspapers to the floor. A look out of the bay window brought the sight of a shiny black carriage drawn by four equally black horses bowling along the avenue to the house.

"Suppose it might actually be her?" Lord Musgrave said thoughtfully with a side glance at Thornbury. The earl had dragged Musgrave to the country during the Season, albeit the last of it, on a questionable lark and Musgrave was of a mind not to wish him well in his quest.

"We shall see," the earl replied quietly, leaning against the frame of the leaded window so as to better identify who exited the carriage that had now come to a halt before the front entrance. Liveried servants hurried from the house, bustling about the carriage, letting down the step and removing a trunk from the boot while a small, drab female, obviously an abigail, popped from the vehicle to oversee matters. She carried a small case, jewels belonging to the marchioness most likely.

"The carriage is without a crest, but that means nothing. The new Marquess of Ware most likely keeps that one for his own use, giving the widow another," Thornbury mused aloud.

"I think this is a dashed harebrained scheme. Why should you think to win the old geezer's widow?" Lord Musgrave asked with a frown.

"After all these years the widow is suddenly making an entry to society. When my aunt mentioned it in her letter I couldn't resist the lure. There was a good bit of gossip when old Ware died. I've a notion to become"—he paused, giving Musgrave another of those devilish grins before continuing—"acquainted with the cause of it all."

"But he was the stuffiest old bird in the country, fat as a flawn, and nasty-tempered to boot," Musgrave muttered, moving forward so that he might also catch a glimpse of whoever next exited that carriage. "Can't think but what his widow would be an antidote. Stands to reason. Who else would have him?"

"At the time, rumor had it that she was exceptionally beautiful and very young and had been forced to wed him," Lord Thornbury replied softly.

"You mean *she* was the bride whose husband died in bed on his wedding night? Died of joy, some said," Lord Musgrave added with a chuckle.

"The one and the same," the earl replied, drawing in a breath at the sight of the young woman who exited the carriage. She glanced up at the house, revealing a face of exquisite beauty above a form that even in her traveling clothes looked more than adequate. Her blue twilled silk pelisse with its puffed oversleeves flattered her slim figure. Gloved hands dealt with a blue parasol and a cream scarf with graceful gestures. A gust of wind tore the delicate hat from her head and a footman dashed after it.

With practiced appraisal both men took note of the raven hair softly curled about her head and the pure line of her profile. Even at this distance there was little doubt that Georgiana, Dowager Marchioness of Ware was a very beautiful woman.

"Am I right?" Thornbury said softly.

Lord Musgrave gave a low whistle while exchanging a meaningful look with his friend. "I see what you mean, old chap. Quite a story there, what?"

"And I mean to be the one to learn the whole of it. Those lovely lips look made for kissing." The devilish gleam had returned to the earl's eyes. "I cannot wait to begin my voyage of discovery."

"Don't know about that. Doesn't look like a fast female," Musgrave said reflectively. "Be interested to see what she looks like close up."

The earl gave his friend a curious glance, then turned again to the window where he could see the traveling coach heading off to the stables. The widow had entered the hall and been lost to view. "You may have a point, but mark this, I *shall* have the lovely widow. I intend to change for dinner and look forward to our introduction."

Lord Musgrave watched as his good friend left the library. "I hope you know what you are doing, dear chap," he muttered.

Charlotte, Lady Kenyon swept forward to greet her most welcome guest, Georgiana, Dowager Marchioness of Ware. Although the marchioness was much younger, they were both widows. Charlotte had visited Georgiana the previous summer to inspect the Ware rose gardens. She had been much struck with the lovely and charming young woman, resolving to do something for her when she could.

"My dear, how fresh you look. I wish I might appear to that advantage after a fatiguing journey." She tucked Georgiana's arm in her own and slowly walked with her up the curving stairs to the next floor and along to the west wing.

"I have a well-sprung coach and John Coachman insists upon pampering me by stopping early each day," Georgiana replied with a smile.

"It pays," Lady Kenyon said with a nod. "Now—all the single ladies are in this west wing, while the bachelor gentlemen are off to the east wing, with a few married couples to each side."

"There are quite a number gathered here for your party?" Georgiana asked hesitantly. For this, her first foray into polite society, she had hoped to find a smallish group and was dismayed to detect the hint of large numbers.

"Not really. And regardless of how many attend, my house parties are always those sort where everyone goes their own way. There is tennis and fishing, riding and shooting for those who enjoy those sort of things. Billiards and cards for rainy days and evenings, of course. My late husband had an excellent library and we gather there if it should rain. Come evening we meet in the ground-floor drawing room before dinner, which is at five of the clock. It will be casual, my dear. Just the thing for you to test the waters. I mean to bring you into fashion, you know," Lady Kenyon said with a twinkle in her eyes.

Georgiana took a bracing breath, then smiled at her friend. "I shall take each moment as it comes, Lady Kenyon."

"Charlotte, dear girl. And I shall call you Georgiana if I may." At Georgiana's demure nod, Lady Kenyon gave a satisfied smile. "I shall leave you to freshen up; then please join us downstairs."

Closing the door behind her pleasant hostess, Georgiana bit her lower lip, wondering again if she had done the right thing in accepting this invitation. No matter how delightful the older lady might be, there were others at this party who could have long memories and might treat Georgiana with suspicion at best and rudeness at worst.

Not permitting herself to dwell on possibilities, she greeted her abigail when she entered from the small dressing room adjacent to the bedroom. "Is all in order, Perkins?"

"Nice place with proper wardrobes and good beds." When they traveled Perkins always made it a point to test the beds for comfort—not that they traveled frequently.

Georgiana glanced about the room, noting the exquisite canopy covered in the same blue damask as the bed beneath it. The same fabric made up the simple panel draperies that hung at the two windows from which she could see a lake sparkling in the late afternoon sun. "I believe I shall enjoy rowing on the water again," she murmured, half to herself, as she admired the view.

"Where shall I put your drawing equipment, my lady?" the abigail inquired with a fond look at her talented mistress.

"That little table near the door ought to do for the moment. I had best change and join the others. I think I should like to be among the first to go down."

"Ah, yes, that can be an advantage," the abigail said with a sage nod of her head. "And you had best wear the rose gauze with your pearls. First impressions are so important, as you well know."

So it was that within a half hour Georgiana braved the charming stairs that curved down to the ground floor. In the newer fashion of the day, the house had been built so one might have instant access to the gardens. From the drawing room the rose gardens for which Lady Kenyon was justly famous might be sought through French doors. The enormous conservatory filled with exotic plants from around the world was just off the dining room.

Upon entering the drawing room Georgiana found that she was one of what seemed at first sight to be a vast number of people, all of whom were unknown to her. She felt rather shy and resolved to limit her conversations to a select few.

"Hello, my lady."

Georgiana whirled about at the rich sound that met her ears, rather like the deep purr of her favorite cat. She inspected the gentleman who had entered the drawing room with a wary eye. Much taller than she, handsome as might be, and possessing a gleam in his midnight gaze she had seen all too many times in the past three years, he would be one to avoid if possible.

The need to introduce herself was circumvented by Lady Kenyon's hurried approach.

"Dear Georgiana, I want you to meet my nephew." She made the introductions with the grace of a skilled hostess, then turned to greet several others who had come in from the garden.

"I see you admire the garden," the earl said politely, standing at her side while she gazed out at the beds of roses—masses of red, pink, white, both Chinese and French varieties.

"Roses are a favorite with me," she admitted in a soft voice.

"I always like to see how the beds have been set out and discover which sort are grown."

"Is that what has kept you occupied and away from our company this past year or so?" He fingered the seal that hung from its chain at his waist below a deceptively simple ivory marcella waistcoat.

She gave him a look that told him he had overstepped the boundaries of good taste with his question. Nevertheless she decided to give him a partial answer, for she sensed he was one of those who persisted until he learned what he desired to know. There was something about his stance, the way that corbeau coat fit his broad shoulders, the precise folds of his snowy cravat, the manner in which he wore the biscuit pantaloons that spoke of a supremely confident man. She would hazard a guess that he rarely put those patent-sheathed feet wrong. That he may have in this instance she had no intention of revealing in so many words.

"I have always enjoyed gardening. When I was widowed I found it a great comfort in my solitude. If you will excuse me, my lord." She gave him a bland look, then crossed the room to join her hostess.

The earl stood where she left him, a bemused expression on his face that had Musgrave most curious when he joined his friend.

"Met the widow?" Musgrave asked when unable to contain his curiosity any longer.

"Indeed. This may offer more challenge than I expected." Beyond that, Thornbury revealed no more, to Musgrave's evident frustration. "She certainly is a beauty. That rose gauze brings out warm tones in her skin and the pearls add to the impression of luminescence. Rare beauty, indeed."

Musgrave failed to reply, realizing that none was required.

It was not long before Georgiana had made the acquaintance of all those in residence. There was only one who truly made her feel ill at ease and that was a pity, for he was Lady Kenyon's nephew. There might well be nothing to worry about, but her senses had picked up on something in those eyes of his that rang warning bells.

Before her year of mourning was over she had been subjected to all manner of subtle and not so subtle attempts on her virtue by married relatives and acquaintances of her late husband. Marriage, brief though hers was, had not much to recommend itself in her estimation. The odious Lord Ware was almost enough to turn her from male society forever. She had decided to test her susceptibility to the male sex by attending this house party. It was to be hoped she had not made a mistake.

Gazing down at her with a most inscrutable and polite countenance, Lord Thornbury presented his arm to Georgiana when dinner was announced, escorting her to the dining room with great seemliness. He was proving to be all that was proper. Perhaps she had only imagined that predatory gleam in his eyes?

"I imagine you look forward to viewing the roses by the morning light. I understand that is when they are at their best," he offered after seating himself at her side.

Flustered at this polite attention Georgiana agreed. It was a relief to have such a blessedly neutral topic to discuss.

"Indeed, my lord. I intend to make good use of my time while here. I have my drawing materials along and plan to inspect each and every bloom in Lady Kenyon's rose collection. I understand she has some fine specimens."

"Like most young women today, you do watercolors?" His manner was casual, verging on bored.

"Well, no, actually, I do careful drawings, then make etchings from them. I make precise notes regarding color, then tint the etchings at my leisure."

Georgiana tasted her food hesitantly, noting Lady Kenyon had an excellent cook.

There was a pause while they were served with a remove of turtle soup; then the second course was brought in from the kitchen. Lord Thornbury politely carried on a brief conversation with the lady seated to his left, a flirtatious woman named Selina Woodburn, Georgiana recalled.

There was no doubt of the invitation in Mrs. Woodburn's saucy hazel eyes. Georgiana wondered if the earl was prey to such blatant attention very often. It was something she'd not considered before, a gentleman being opportuned by a lady. It undoubtedly revealed her naïveté that she had no idea how much of that sort of thing went on. She had been so shocked when male relatives and the friends of her unlamented late husband had implied they would be more than happy to assuage her grief she hadn't considered there might be a reverse position to the matter.

Seated to her right, the very quiet gentleman, a Lord Musgrave and apparent friend to Lord Thornbury, ventured into speech. "You like the roses in the garden, Thornbury tells me."

"I do very much. And what pastime do you enjoy while in the country?"

Her question seemed to surprise him, for at first he had no answer. Then he grinned and replied, "Don't know. Seldom come out. Daresay I'll fish and do a bit of shooting. You play cards?"

"Tolerably," she replied, echoing the terseness of his speech.

"Good. We could be partners this evening—if you don't mind, that is."

Finding much to like in this unassuming and most unthreatening man, Georgiana agreed immediately.

At the conclusion of the dinner Lady Kenyon rose to lead the ladies into the drawing room, leaving the gentlemen to their port and spicy conversation. Georgiana's cousin had once eavesdropped and informed her that it was not fit for a lady's ears, being one outrageous story after the other.

Feeling shy, Georgiana drifted over to the fine pianoforte to seat herself with the thought of playing quietly for the group. She began with a simple arrangement of a Haydn piece, then continued into a Mozart sonata of which she had imperfect mastery but liked anyway. When she finished, she discovered the earl had taken a place behind her. It surprised her that she hadn't sensed his presence, he was that sort of man.

"I've not heard that piece played quite that way before," he said with the glimmer of amusement in his words.

"Yes, well," she said with a shrug, "when I do not quite know the music, I confess I fudge a bit. I very much doubt that anyone—other than you—noticed the difference."

He looked about the room and agreed. "I daresay you have

the right of it. Would you like to see the roses by moonlight? I'm told that we might be in for a special treat as well. Aunt Charlotte suggested you might enjoy it."

With her hostess implying that it was safe for Georgiana to go with her nephew, there seemed to be little she could do but agree. "I should like that. Some roses are extra fragrant in the night air, I have heard."

She placed her hand lightly upon his proffered arm, wondering what it was that seemed so dangerous about this man. There appeared to be an aura about him that attracted her even as she felt something cautioning her, warning her.

They slowly strolled up and down the neat paths softly illuminated by the full moon and aided by fairy lights hanging from several pergolas. The day's warmth combined with the evening dew to bring forth a heady fragrance. She breathed in deeply, reveling in the lushly scented air. When she returned to the dower house she must seek her own rose garden in the evening. She had been missing a treat.

"Come," the rich and very male voice at her side urged. "I believe the surprise may be found now."

She permitted him to lead her down to the bottom of the garden. There, dancing like so many magical lights, were glowworms flitting delicately on the soft night air. They seemed to execute a complicated minuet of their own and so she whispered to her escort, her voice reflecting her delight.

"I am pleased you like them. Aunt Charlotte thought you might." He retained a light hold of her hand with his other hand, but it didn't precisely threaten her. It did send tremors through her and she couldn't understand why.

Georgiana was enchanted by the glowworms with their mystical dance of blinking light. However, she discovered she was far more conscious of the man at her side, one she had at first dubbed a philanderer and a flirt. It seemed she must revise her opinion, for he was all that was polite to her. And to her amazement and ultimate chagrin, she found a wistful longing to know just what his attentions might be like.

Of course, she added to her mental wanderings, it could be that she had no appeal for the gentleman. In which case she was utterly safe in his company, she attempted to assure herself.

Eventually they returned to the house where the group was settling into foursomes for playing cards. She excused herself from Lord Thornbury and joined Lord Musgrave at the table where he had saved a place for her.

Although he was not directly in her sight, Georgiana found she had developed an awareness of Lord Thornbury's whereabouts. He joined Selina Woodburn and her husband Marius at their table, with Lady Kenyon making up the fourth.

Georgiana considered herself a competent player at best and was not terribly surprised she made a few errors. Lord Musgrave was the best of partners, smiling and excusing her so that she lost some of her nervousness. She soon found she was able to watch her cards and follow the conversation.

"Did you enjoy the roses on your little walk?" Lady Pickering asked, a coyness in her manner.

"Actually, Lady Kenyon has the right of it," Georgiana answered with more composure than she'd have thought possible. "There are a number of varieties that have marvelous scent at night. It makes for a very romantic walk," she concluded without thought to her words until she saw the malicious gleam in Lady Pickering's eyes.

"Well, if a lady strolls the paths with the dashing Lord Thornbury I daresay that most anything might seem romantic."

Her ladyship tittered a little laugh that was likely intended to sound like a tinkling bell. It didn't. Her laugh seemed forced and Georgiana, having endured far worse in her days, merely smiled and agreed politely. "I found his lordship to be quite civil," she said with as bored an air as she could manage.

Lord Musgrave choked on a mouthful of wine and Lord Pickering had to thump him on the back before all was calm again.

"I say, dashed if I don't think Lady Ware and indeed, the rest of us, could do with an early night of it," Lord Musgrave said when he could speak again. "Traveling, you know. Hard on a person. Country air and all that as well. I mean to rise early and see what I can do with a fishing pole."

Georgiana put down her cards with a grateful sigh. Lord Musgrave must be reading her mind, for she had been longing to escape the group and seek her bed.

As she ascended the stairs she found Lord Thornbury coming to her side, handing her a night candle should she have need of it.

"You enjoyed your evening, I trust. I have always found Aunt Charlotte's gatherings most relaxing and pleasant." He gazed down at Georgiana with an expression in those amazing dark eyes that she couldn't begin to discern.

Her own gaze twinkling with amusement, she nodded politely and said, "Indeed, I did, my lord. Glowworms are an unusual treat, even for a country woman."

She left him standing in the hall. Lighting her way with the candle, she walked swiftly along the corridor until she reached her room. The door closed firmly behind her before she yielded to the urge to chuckle.

"You enjoyed a pleasant evening, my lady?" her abigail said with fond regard.

"Well, Perkins, I am not certain what I expected when I came, but I think it was not what I have found. I do not quite know what to make of it all," Georgiana concluded, thinking to herself that Lord Thornbury was the most enigmatic man she had ever met. But, she decided, she had found a way to perplex him—treat him like her nephew Pip. It seemed to her that her somewhat cavalier handling of him had literally stopped him in his tracks.

Allowing Perkins to remove the rose gauze and put away the pearls that had been a bride gift from her elderly husband, she donned the sheer muslin nightrail she preferred for the warmth of summer nights.

Secure in her bed she considered the hours since her arrival at Kenyon Hall. Surely meeting Lord Thornbury had to be the highlight. Well, on the morrow, she would concentrate on her drawings and let his lordship conduct a flirtation with the more than willing Selina Woodburn.

In the east wing of the house Lord Thornbury entered his room to find Musgrave awaiting him along with Martin, Thornbury's estimable valet.

"Clever bit of a girl," Musgrave said without preamble. "Don't think this is going to be the piece of cake you believed."

"That is an insufferable grin, Musgrave," the earl replied, looking as out of sorts as he felt.

"She informed us that you were most civil to her," Musgrave continued, undaunted by the look in his friend's eyes. "Egads, Jason. Civil?" A whoop of laughter followed this conclusion to the speech.

Jason motioned toward the door with a jerk of his head.

Musgrave rose from the comfortable chair near the window and sauntered toward the doorway with a wicked light in his eyes. "What do you plan for the morrow? More civility?"

Jason glared at his friend. "It just so happens that civility is most disarming. Put her at ease, you suggested, I believe? Well, she quite enjoyed watching the glowworms and considered the scent of the roses to be enchanting. I believe the saying is that Rome was not built in a day, is it not?"

"Agreed," Musgrave replied, reaching for the doorknob. "Pity it would not be the thing to place a little wager on the outcome of your attentions. Wouldn't do that to a nice person like Lady Ware. But it ain't going to be a snap, my friend." Musgrave chuckled, then let himself out before a well-aimed shoe hit the door behind him.

Martin eased Thornbury from his corbeau coat so lovingly crafted by the master hand of Weston, then helped remove the cravat with equal care.

Jason strolled to the window, gazing blankly out at the moonlit gardens below. He fingered the seal on his watch chain while thinking furiously. Civil! She had declared him to be civil? Those were challenging words. Come morning he would seek her out, perhaps be a trifle more than civil. No matter how Musgrave might chuckle, Jason felt that a cautionary approach to the wary widow would be the most productive. That she was as fetching a piece as he recalled seeing in a long, long time was added incentive.

He fully intended that soon, quite soon, the wary widow would be his!

Chapter Two

Georgiana paused, pencil in hand, as she considered the matter that troubled her. It *must* have been her imagination. It had to be. Save for the moment she thought she had seen the familiar predatory gleam in Lord Thornbury's dark eyes, he had been the perfect gentleman. Merely because he stirred her emotions was not reason to cast aspersions at the poor fellow. It was scarcely his fault that she responded to his presence as she had to no one else. Perhaps it explained in part why he was considered a bit of a rake. Women found him irresistible and she could well understand that.

She recalled how he had led her up and down the various paths, maintaining the proper decorum and conversing in a most unobjectionable way. How could she possibly think such a fine gentleman had designs on her virtue—as had too many of her male relatives and those pompous old men who declared themselves close friends to Lord Ware? She shuddered at the memory of those questing hands, avid eyes, and suggestive remarks. Lord Thornbury simply did not fit the mold.

Resolutely, she turned her full attention to her drawing of a fine old French rose, no doubt a descendant of one of the damask roses from Asia Minor. Its vibrant pink hue vied with the strong fragrance, giving credence to its cultivation for attar. She refused to dwell on her silly imaginings, giving herself an admonishing sigh.

"Are you chilly, Lady Ware? Perhaps you would welcome this shawl?" Lord Thornbury, as though conjured up from her muddled mind, stood a few feet away holding a lovely shawl, just the weight to take a slight chill from a body.

"What a thoughtful gentleman you are," she exclaimed, thoroughly disarmed. She held out a hand to receive the covering and found instead the gentleman preferred to drape the fine wool over her shoulders. His hands did not linger nor did he bend to murmur an eloquent little bit of flattery in her ear. Georgiana was impressed.

"That is a remarkable study of this rose," he commented quietly, as though reluctant to disturb her work. "You truly are quite gifted."

"Thank you," Georgiana said, thinking that this was one of the more sincere compliments she had received in some time. She bestowed a bright smile on him, at which he pretended to blink, causing her to chuckle. "You, sir, are what I fear is called a complete hand by my nephew."

"Nephew? You scarce look old enough to be blessed with such a connection." His reply was smooth, but she could hear genuine surprise in his tone.

"My eldest sister is married to Lord Cathcart and their little boy is most precocious. I have Pip to visit whenever I can." She looked away toward the lake in the distance, thinking wistfully that if things had been different she might have had a little boy of her own by now.

"You like children, then?" He gave her an odd look, as though he expected her to prattle on about them.

"Most of them," she admitted. "Although there are others who are truly odious creatures. Which may be said of a goodly number of adults as well," she added thoughtfully.

He laughed at that remark, then looked at her drawing again. "You would not care to take a rest from your work and accompany me for a leisurely boat ride?"

She considered the diffidently phrased invitation and immediately accepted. Since he appeared not to be the slightest bit anxious for her company, she would gladly go with him. Stuffing her pencils into a small case and setting it aside, she smiled up at him. "That sounds lovely. The wind may come up later but the lake is quite peaceful now."

"You do not seem worried at my skill with the oars," he remarked, assisting her from the stool where she had perched while at her drawing.

"Lord Thornbury, I believe there is little that you cannot do should you put your mind to it." Gazing at the path to the lake, Georgiana missed the fleeting look of surprise that crossed his lordship's face.

His hand on her elbow as he guided her along the pebbled path to the ornamental lake made her feel strangely warm, yet secure. What an odd mixture of emotions—that surging warmth that did the most peculiar things to her insides combined with the certain knowledge that he would not abuse the trust she placed in him.

To conceal this internal conflict she chattered about the scenery and the fineness of the day more than she might have normally. He did not appear to notice anything unusual. But then, he did not know her well, did he?

Like all else at Kenyon Hall, the rowboats were in excellent repair, mute testimony to a good steward, she'd wager. She accepted his lordship's assistance to enter the little boat, then seated herself in the stern with as much grace as she could manage, gathering her skirts modestly about her.

"Perhaps you might be so kind as to hold my coat for me? Coats are not designed for anything more strenuous than slight movement, such as assisting a pretty lady into a boat." Without awaiting her agreement, he peeled off the fine blue coat, shook it out, then dropped it on her lap.

Georgiana was speechless, clutching the coat as though her life depended upon it. The coat held the warmth of his body and gave an unexpected feeling of intimacy. More than that, she caught the faint hint of eau de cologne, just as he'd worn last evening when he had walked with her. Why this faint perfume should affect her so, she couldn't imagine. More than all else to stir sensibilities was the sight of this gentleman in his shirtsleeves!

Merciful heaven but he was an exceptional man: finely muscled, lean, powerful looking, and amazingly graceful. It was pure poetry to observe him drop the oars in their locks, then seat himself to commence rowing. Would that she had the ability to capture that grace on paper!

It took more resolution than she possessed to look elsewhere when she could feast her eyes on those rippling muscles only slightly concealed by the fine cambric of his shirt as he gently propelled the boat along the shore. What a blessing she was not some flibbertigibbet schoolgirl who would giggle and blush and probably upset the rowboat in the process because of her maidenly embarrassment.

"Lovely day," he observed with an amiable smile at her.

"Indeed," she managed to reply, untangling her tongue with difficulty. "This is my favorite time of year. The roses are in bloom, the entire world is lush and green. The birds have settled down to tend their young; indeed, all the young animals are on display for us to enjoy."

"There speaks a country woman, if I do not miss my guess." He gave her an indulgent look and she bristled.

"Is that so very bad?" she responded consideringly.

"London ladies would not care much for the beauty surrounding us. They are more caught up with fashions, gossip, the ins and outs of the *ton*."

"Well, I have never been concerned with fashion, despite your aunt's insistence that she means to bring me into fashion. Why? I am content as I go now." But even as she spoke the words Georgiana realized they were no longer true. A discontent had crept over her in the past two days—a realization that she was missing something essential and not merely fashions and gossip.

Lord Thornbury's companionship had made her aware of her lack. The matter of love had not worried her overmuch until now. Her family had derided the silliness of love as foolish sentimentality. She had accepted their decree. But now? Now she began to wonder if she hadn't neglected a serious matter of great importance in her life. Not having known love in her short span of years, she wasn't certain what it might be like. Yet the thought intrigued her.

Certainly her sister Amanda in her marriage to Lord Cathcart hadn't engendered anything that appeared to be love. They were as distant as two people living under the same roof might be. Their marriage seemed sadly flat to Georgiana, as did her own life, come to think on it. Roses were all well and good, but you couldn't take them to bed with you.

"Are you truly content?" he asked politely, but there was the merest hint of disbelief in his voice, one that Georgiana could not dispute for she was far too honest to pretend to be happy if she wasn't.

"Well, perhaps not," she admitted in a burst of candor. "I confess that lately I have found that something may be lacking in my life. Perhaps I need to travel a bit more," she concluded thoughtfully.

"You have not given any consideration to remarriage?" Jason watched her most expressive face to gauge her reaction to his words. Had he overstepped his bounds again? She might be a wary creature, but she was oddly open in her speech. She was *not* given to roundaboutation. And while the topic of marriage was one he usually avoided like the plague, he suspected that the last thing on the mind of this woman was marriage, especially to him. He was utterly safe.

"I suppose that is what is expected of a young widow." She flicked a glance at him, then looked across the rippling waters. "However, I do not find much to recommend that state to me."

"You prefer single blessedness? If there is such a situation," he added reflectively. He pulled on the oars at a leisurely pace, allowing the boat to glide along the shore in stately progression.

"I cannot say I prefer it. Let us agree that I am reasonably content with my life. And you, my lord? Are you content with your life?" It was a bold query, most likely beyond the bounds of convention, but this conversation had strayed from those confines. She smoothed the fine fabric of his coat in her lap with one hand, intent upon his reply.

Jason dropped his gaze to where his hands clasped the oars rather than meet her disconcerting appraisal. Was he content with his life? Of course he was. What a silly question from the very woman he hoped to seduce given time and patience.

"Well?" There was a hint of challenge in her gentle tone.

"I enjoy my life," he said at her prompting, aware he had been silent too long while he considered her unusual question. "I have many friends, enjoy my pursuits."

Georgiana almost asked him about those pursuits, then realized it would be highly improper to probe into activities that were none of her business. She said, "While I have few friends—for living remotely restricts one's associations—I treasure those I have." She thought of the poor governess at Ware Court, wondering how long she would survive in that dangerous household. Georgiana and she had developed a bond of sorts—fear of the same man. "I should enjoy a visit to London at some point, I believe."

"Do consider it."

"Perhaps I shall. At least I would be spared the knowledge I need find a husband—as so many young women must. I trust my visit might be quite pleasant." Georgiana was proud of the casual glance she bestowed on the gentleman, sure she gave not the slightest hint that she found him the least fascinating. "I doubt our paths would cross, although it is always agreeable to see a friendly face in a crowd." There, if that did not make it clear that she had no intention in his direction she didn't know what would.

His expression was almost comical, one of affront that quickly changed to relief. Georgiana supposed that he was more accustomed to having a woman flirt with him rather than make it apparent she had no interest in him.

"Should I discover you to be in London, you may be certain that I would seek you out. There are too few originals in the city, and you are most certainly that," he concluded in a preoccupied way. "I predict you would take London by storm." Then he looked surprised as though wondering what had prompted him to give voice to those thoughts.

Georgiana gazed into the intense deep blue of Lord Thornbury's eyes and felt the world spin about her. It would take very little effort on his part to sweep her off her feet. She must guard her heart.

"Thank you," she said simply, then turned to look across the lake at a flock of birds on the wing. "It is too fine a day to be so serious, my lord. Can you think of something utterly frivolous to discuss?"

"Well, I believe we are to indulge in a jaunt to view some scenic ruins this afternoon. Does that please you?"

"I shall take my sketching pad and bring home a memory of the day. Gothic ruins are just the thing, are they not?"

Jason forbore mentioning his memories of this day, which

would include those sparkling blue eyes as she posed her daring question earlier.

The remainder of their boat ride was quite tranquil. Georgiana commented gaily on the bird life, identified the plants that grew along the shore, and avoided any topic remotely personal in nature.

When Lord Thornbury assisted her from the small craft, she thanked him politely, then held out his coat. "I suspect you may need help with that," she said, unable to resist a chuckle at the flash of annoyance that crossed his face. He folded his coat over one arm and offered the other to her. She placed a slender hand on his arm covered with no more than fine cambric.

He accepted the truth of her words with a smile and nod. "We are creatures of vanity, I suspect. Do you wish to resume your sketching? Or do you intend to seek the luncheon set out in the dining room?" They strolled up the path from the lake until they reached the spot where he had found her. Here, they paused.

"All this fresh air has made me utterly famished. Food is a welcome notion. I shall perhaps see you later, my lord?" she said before turning aside to gather up her sketching pad and case of pencils.

Jason could scarcely contain his astonishment. Unless he was much mistaken, he was being politely dismissed. This was a state of affairs to which he was utterly unaccustomed. Before he could think of something to say, she turned around to give him a curious look. He waited to see what she might possibly say next.

"Thank you again for your friendship. I have never had a gentleman friend before and I shall treasure it, believe me." She smiled in a most endearing manner before adding, "I am not one given to flirting; Mama did not approve of such behavior."

She dipped a charming curtsy, then slipped past him and disappeared into the house before he could find the words to express whatever was floating about in his mind.

"Something the matter with your coat, old chap?" Musgrave asked as he ambled up the path.

"What? Oh, no. Nothing at all. Went for a ride in the boat and took it off. Can't row in the blasted thing, you know." Jason strove to collect his senses.

Musgrave nodded solemnly. "Weston would have a fit if he thought you were doing anything so mundane as using your muscles."

"Hungry?" Jason hooked his coat over two fingers, slinging it over his back until he could find his valet.

"Don't mind if I do have a bite to eat. Your aunt provides an excellent table." The two men walked slowly toward the house with the intent of finding the dining room and a tasty repast.

"How was fishing this morning?" Jason remembered to ask.

"Tolerable," Musgrave said. "Not that I am any judge, but your aunt's man said my catch was a fine one, whatever that means."

"Someday you are going to have to admit that a few of the pursuits in the country are not so dreadful," Jason replied with a grin.

"How did you make out with the wary widow?" Musgrave asked in an undertone.

Thankful that for once his friend had the sense to keep his voice low, Jason shook his head in caution. "Tell you about it later. Sufficient to say that I believe I made progress."

Musgrave appeared skeptical at those words but didn't argue the point.

Up in her room Georgiana discarded her drawing materials on the small table, then drifted across the lovely carpet to gaze out of the window. It had been pleasant to spend some time with a gentleman who appeared to have little interest in her. She assured herself that his diffidence was most proper. His civilized behavior was most refreshing after her past experience with the opposite gender. There had been no flirting, no innuendos, no offers that could be construed as suggestive. She sighed, not knowing why.

"Milady, you wish to change for the afternoon? Following the luncheon there is to be an expedition. I trust you intend to go along?" Perkins said with her usual understanding of Georgiana's moods as well as desires.

With a nod, Georgiana put aside her thoughts regarding

Lord Thornbury and prepared for a delightful afternoon inspecting a ruin, whatever period it might be from.

When she came downstairs attired in a pretty blue pelisse of fine cotton over a paler blue dress and a chip bonnet tied with matching blue ribands, she felt ready to face most anything. She turned at the bottom of the stairs, almost colliding with Lady Kenyon. "So sorry," Georgiana apologized.

"Nothing to it, dear girl. Are you enjoying yourself? Saw you with my nephew out on the lake. Lovely day for an outing on the water. He makes a most pleasant companion, does he not?" Her ladyship gave an affectionate glance toward the dining room where her beloved nephew was presently to be found.

"Indeed, ma'am. Most pleasant. I cannot thank you enough for including me in your party. As you have said, it is time for me to get out and about. I find it quite to my liking."

"Enough to join me in London next Season?"

"Well," Georgiana temporized, "that is some distance away. We shall see how I get on in the meantime, shall we?"

"I mean the invitation, you know. Wouldn't do for a young widow like you, beautiful and a prime target for fortune hunters, to set up a household on her own. It would be quite proper for you to reside with me and I would so enjoy your company. You must confess being a widow has its lonely moments."

"With that I can agree. I promise to consider your offer," was all Georgiana would say, "and we shall correspond between now and then."

"Do eat a bite to sustain that charming figure, then join the group for our little jaunt to the ruins."

In the dining room Georgiana found Lords Thornbury and Musgrave in close conversation. On the far side of the table Lady Pickering lectured the shy Miss Russell. This young lady had played the harp last evening, but avoided conversation with one and all and was now being taken to task by the Pickering woman. The luscious Selina Woodburn was not to be seen and Georgiana wondered if she had left her bed yet. The thought of that woman simpering and fluttering her lashes at Lord Thornbury was enough to make a body grind one's teeth.

Lord Thornbury looked up to discover Georgiana hovering

near the long table, wondering where she ought to sit after filling her plate from the sideboard.

"Allow me, Lady Ware." Before she could protest, he popped up and had her seated next to him in a trice. Lord Musgrave smiled at her across the space before Thornbury returned to his place.

She was almost self-conscious at the amount of food she had heaped on her plate but it was the first time for some months that she had felt utterly ravenous.

"See, Musgrave? A pearl among women—one who actually consumes food!" To Georgiana he said in an aside, "You cannot know the number of chits who appear to exist on butterfly wings for all they eat when at table."

"So I have heard. I fear I am most unfashionable there as well, my lord. Your aunt may well have second thoughts about having me join her in London next year should she see this plate of food—or worse yet, the emptied plate."

"You contemplate a visit with my aunt in London? That would be enjoyable for you, I suppose. Do you not mind being around a few older folk?"

Georgiana gave him a naughty glance, then said, "Why, sir, I find you and Lord Musgrave perfectly charming company."

Lord Musgrave again choked over his beverage. When he was to rights again, he leaned forward to smilingly scold Georgiana. "If you must say something outrageous, please do wait until I have swallowed. It is dashed miserable, let me tell you."

"So sorry, my lord. Lord Thornbury has a way of provoking me."

Musgrave subsided into silence while Lord Thornbury made the effort to chat about unobjectionable topics, leaving alone the matter of Georgiana's possible visit with his aunt in London.

Surprisingly she enjoyed an excellent meal, considering the effect of the man at her side. Perhaps he merely stimulated her appetite.

They all left the table at once when the footman entered to inform them that the landau was ready.

"I am glad to see that you ate well. You are a slim bit of a girl," Lord Thornbury remarked approvingly.

"Perhaps our sparring stimulated my appetite," she said innocently, then wondered why he developed a sudden bout of coughing.

The ride to the ruins was accomplished amid much laughter on the part of Georgiana and Lord Musgrave, with Lord Thornbury joining in at times. Miss Russell remained shyly silent seated next to Georgiana in the landau while Lady Pickering and her husband, the Woodburns, and Lady Kenyon followed in the next carriage.

They arrived at the site of the abbey and mingled together before setting off on an exploration. Somehow Selina Woodburn managed to clasp Lord Thornbury's arm when she abruptly twisted her ankle. That injury miraculously improved when it appeared his lordship would heartlessly abandon her for the others exploring the ruins.

"I trust your husband will know precisely how to care for that damage to your ankle, Mrs. Woodburn." With that brief statement, he handed her over to her spouse, then took off after his friend and the incomparable Lady Ware.

Selina's complaints drifted across the grounds of the abbey ruins as Georgiana picked her way across the grass to the opening of what once must have been the entrance to a medium-sized abbey.

"What a splendid place this must have been at one time," she said after looking about her. Arched overhead were the remains of the roof of what she was certain must have been the cloisters. It was possible to tell where the refectory had been. "I suspect the chapter house was located here," she pointed out to Lord Musgrave as they slowly walked around the tumbled stones. "And do you think the main church could have been over there?"

"It was a small abbey as abbeys go," Lord Thornbury interposed after catching up with the pair.

"That would appear to have been the abbey garden over there. Look, an apple tree and an old rose still grow in the sheltered corner between the cloisters and what may have been the infirmary."

"What makes you think an infirmary was there? Not but what I believe you have the right of it," Lord Thornbury said.

"Well, it was a goodly sized building a little set apart from the others and located close to the river that runs along one side of the ruins. I have read that the monks were far more advanced than we regarding the use of water and cleanliness. Look, that must have been where the kitchen was."

"What would you know about kitchens, Lady Ware?" Selina Woodburn said in a silky voice. "I am certain a marchioness has no contact with such a humble room."

"On the contrary," Georgiana replied, giving the other woman a steady look. "I was taught that any *lady* who expects to capably manage a large household must know how things are properly done—else how can you explain to the cook or housekeeper what you wish?"

"Do not tell me that you could cook a joint of beef! I'll not credit it," the woman said lightly with a laugh.

"I could," Georgiana said. That woman would catch cold if she thought to bait Georgiana with her words.

Lord Thornbury elected to show Mrs. Woodburn how cleverly the river was dammed and the pretty little waterfall that remained after all these years.

Georgiana looked after them as Selina chattered on in her high-pitched voice about the delights to be viewed in Brighton.

"Daresay she must be a trial to her husband, what?" Lord Musgrave said in an undertone to Georgiana.

"Possibly." She cast a glance at the couple who stood on the riverbank by the waterfall and wondered what would happen should the annoying woman lose her footing.

"And you truly know how to cook a joint of beef?" Lord Musgrave inquired, finding he was continually astonished at this young woman.

"Well, of course I do, not that I have actually done such a thing. But I understand the process and that is what matters. If something is wrong with the food, I can hazard an intelligent guess as to what caused it."

"Amazing."

"Yes, well, let us join the others, shall we?" With that, Georgiana sailed ahead along the rubble-strewn path, skirting lichen-bedecked rocks. She came to where an old rose struggled to survive and studied it. Thinking that Lord Musgrave was still at her side, she said, "Thorny old thing, is it not? Mrs. Woodburn had best stay clear or she will likely have another accident."

"Mrs. Woodburn is safely in the care of her tolerant husband at the moment. Do you wish a cutting from this rose?" Lord Thornbury said, surprising Georgiana into whirling about, whereupon she found herself smack against that magnificent chest she had so admired this morning. The proximity rendered her speechless.

"Lady Ware, are you all right?" his rich, melodious voice said from somewhere over her head.

She stumbled back a few steps, hand to her throat in dismay and thought she probably looked like an idiot. "Yes, er, that is, I believe I would like a cutting if it might be managed. It would be interesting to try to cross it with a French rose, or perhaps that damask red that I have at the dower house."

He reached out to steady her, which only served to unnerve her further. "You live in the dower house and not at Ware Court?"

"The present marquess is in residence with his young wife. We are of an age and it would cause complications were I to intrude upon them." Not to mention the anger of a plain but wealthy wife whose husband eyed his stepmother with less than motherly regard. "I am quite content at the dower house with my pretty little rose garden. Believe me, it is a charming place."

Feeling that she had babbled quite enough, Georgiana was most gratified when Lord Thornbury merely took a knife from his pocket, cut off a portion of the rose, then called a footman to place it in moist dirt until they reached his aunt's home.

"Thank you, my lord," she said, grateful that she could now escape to the harmless company of his aunt and her friends.

"Anything for you, my lady."

"Oh, dear," she whispered as she hurried along the path to where Lady Kenyon stood. Was it necessary to revise her opinion of Lord Thornbury? He had seemed so safe. Then she thought of that magnificent torso, those manly arms, and the effortless grace with which he had propelled the boat this morning and decided perhaps she ought to rethink things very carefully indeed.

Chapter Three

Upon returning home from the ruins, the remainder of the day had been most unexceptionable. Georgiana had encouraged Miss Russell into pleasant conversation while they explored the print room, then joined her in the music room where they spent an agreeable hour practicing a duet for harp and pianoforte. Of Lord Thornbury she saw nothing.

Dinner was to be at six-thirty, a more fashionable hour, and Georgiana found she had to marshall her sensibilities before entering the drawing room where the group would assemble. She spotted Lord Thornbury at once. He was impossible to miss dressed in his black pantaloons and white marcella waistcoat topped by a midnight blue velvet coat to match his eyes.

He was deep in conversation with his friend. Georgiana wondered briefly what topic might be so absorbing, then dismissed them out of mind when Lady Pickering bustled up to ask about the duet Miss Russell said they had practiced.

"Are we to be entertained with the results, dear Lady Ware?" she twittered like a sparrow with a crumb.

Since Georgiana had heretofore experienced barbs rather than buttering up from this quarter, she was quite startled. Glancing at Miss Russell, who stood in mortified silence, Georgiana nodded graciously and agreed. "If it is agreeable with Miss Russell, I believe we shan't disgrace ourselves." Actually, practicing the duet had been fun and she looked forward to playing providing the shy Miss Russell didn't turn tail and run.

Everyone was more formally dressed this evening and it was with pleasure that she placed her hand on Lord Thornbury's velvet-sheathed arm to join the procession to the dining room. He was without a doubt the most handsome gentleman present, which must lend a certain cachet to her appearance. Judging from the glances darted her way from the lushly endowed Selina Woodburn, Georgiana had risen in estimation since last evening. The silk jaconet gown she wore enhanced her bosom; it was a particularly lovely shade of celestial blue and trimmed with blond lace and delicate embroidery.

"You enjoyed the outing to the ruins, Lady Ware?" Lord Thornbury inquired, just as though he hadn't unsettled her with his words and attitude earlier.

Well, if they meant nothing to him, she could play the same game. "Perfectly charming, my lord. It is most agreeable to explore new areas, see new sights."

"Have you spent much time in London?" he asked with that casual charm that was such a part of him.

"I have never been there. It was not deemed necessary for me to go when my future was arranged and I had no need to enter the marriage market. But I believe I shall accept your aunt's kind invitation, at least for a short part of the Season," Georgiana concluded pensively.

"Not been to London?" he said, fastening on the one thing that he could not credit. "Whatever was your family thinking of?" Then, seeming to realize that he had again been intrusive, he apologized, "Forgive me, but you are such a beautiful woman, it should have crossed their minds that you might have made a far better alliance than with an elderly peer."

Georgiana tossed him a speaking look, but replied mildly, "You forget the old adage, sir, an old bird in the hand is worth two fledglings in the bush, if you follow my reasoning. Besides which, my parents had no desire to counter Lord Avon's wishes. My uncle rather rules the family."

She could feel his astounded gaze on her. His comment was mild, however. "Does he still control you?"

"No," she said with a happy shrug. "Once I married, no matter that it was brief, I became my own woman. I cannot begin to tell you what a relief that is. Not but what I still receive missives from him informing me what he thinks would be an excellent path for me to take. Now I am able to ignore them."

"The delight at that turn of events is evident in your voice," Lord Thornbury replied.

Not caring to respond to that comment, she turned to answer a remark from Lord Musgrave and the remainder of the dinner passed in trivial conversation.

The duet went off better than she had hoped. It seemed that when Miss Russell played her harp she was able to forget the rest of the world, even gentlemen.

Again Georgiana partnered Lord Musgrave at cards. There had been no charming walk in the garden to savor rose scent, nor a second glimpse of the glowworms performing their irratic minuet. The ruins might never have been.

She retired following the late supper, not exchanging another word with Lord Thornbury.

Jason watched her chat briefly with his aunt, then leave the drawing room with Miss Russell at her side.

"How goes the pursuit?" Musgrave said jovially. "You seemed in good form at those dashed ruins we stumbled around this afternoon."

"I play her like a fish," Jason said, but with no sign of glee in his voice. He was having doubts about his little game with the widow. She was not what he had imagined. While he might enjoy the pursuit of a beautiful woman, he did have a conscience.

"How is that?" Musgrave said with a frown.

"Attention, then backing away, just like playing a fish on the line. Now she wonders if she imagined the looks, the promise in my voice. Tomorrow I shall prepare to reel her in, as it were." But to himself, he added a maybe to that claim. For the first time he could remember, he was unsure how to proceed. Yet she had responded so well to his charm, turned into his arms so neatly. No, he assured himself, she would welcome his attentions. He was certain of it.

Come morning when Georgiana joined Miss Russell in the breakfast room she found the sideboard groaning with every sort of bread imaginable, pots of tea, chocolate, and coffee plus anything else one might wish to consume at that hour.

"It looks to rain before long," Miss Russell offered after staring out of the window for a time.

"Hardly surprising, I suppose," Georgiana replied with a sigh. "It would be too much to hope that we might have a week of sun."

"Good thing we viewed the ruins yesterday," Lord Musgrave said, entering the breakfast room in time to overhear their words.

Georgiana made no response to that remark. She had yet to understand Lord Thornbury's behavior. That he should be so ardent one moment, then return to distant politeness the next was greatly confusing. She surmised her lack of comprehension could be traced to her want of social polish. She didn't know all the rules for flirting.

"It has begun to rain," Miss Russell observed while helping herself to another cup of chocolate.

"Dreary day. Either of you ladies play billiards?" the irrepressible Musgrave asked.

"I have always wished to learn," Georgiana admitted. "What about you, Miss Russell?"

"I as well. Would you consider . . ." she began with a look at Lord Musgrave, then stopped, blushing furiously.

"I should deem it a rare pleasure if you would allow me to show you a few pointers on the game," Lord Musgrave said most handsomely.

"What game?" Lord Thornbury inquired as he strolled into the breakfast room looking like a fashion plate in a corbeau coat over buff pantaloons and cream waistcoat.

"Aim to teach the ladies how to play billiards," Musgrave said in reply, quite as though daring his friend to argue with him on the matter.

Lord Thornbury paused in the act of piling food on his plate to stare at his friend. Georgiana thought all that was lacking was a quizzing glass for that stare to squelch pretensions. "You don't say?"

"Care to join us?"

Lord Thornbury glanced at the rain-streaked windows and said, "Sounds like a most agreeable pastime."

So, following the conclusion of a hearty breakfast, the four sought the billiard room, where Lord Musgrave promptly began to instruct the prettily flustered Miss Russell about the intricacies of the game. He selected a cue from the rack, arranged some balls on the table, then commenced to demonstrate the correct way to position her hand on the cue.

Georgiana eyed the closeness of the two and wondered how she would cope should Lord Thornbury follow suit. He didn't, precisely. Rather, he handed her a cue, set out three ivory balls at the opposite end of the table, then directed her attention to them while wrapping his arms about her in a most familiar way, unlike the more proper Musgrave.

"Sir, I protest," she whispered as loud as she dared without calling the attention of the others to his scandalous behavior.

The look he gave her was one of perfect innocence. "I assure you, Lady Ware, that this is the best way to demonstrate how to hit the ball. There are so many angles, you see."

Georgiana didn't. See, that is. It was all she could manage to handle the sensations of being crushed so close to this handsome gentleman. And angles? What sort of angles did he have in mind, pray tell?

He demonstrated. She learned how to rest the cue precisely where it should be, her hand arched so the cue would sit on the proper place between her thumb and forefinger. He covered her arm with his, guiding her hand, placing the cue where it ought to be, all but caressing her arm as he instructed her. All this while he murmured in her ear, his voice purring, his body seeming to touch hers at far too many places. It was a wonder she didn't melt from the heat she felt. But she would never let him know how his closeness affected her. Somehow she sensed this would not be the thing to do, even had she no experience in this sort of flirtation in the least.

She found out the proper point at which one hit the ball to make it go where one wished. The central stroke was exactly centered on the ivory ball. Other points of contact made the ball do the most amazing things, like jump or twist. Again, he guided her arm, never changing his position. He was almost plastered against her and the worst of it all was that she welcomed his touch! He was, she reflected, most skilled in teaching billiards. It must be something he did often, to be so proficient at it.

The concentration required to absorb Lord Thornbury's instruction was daunting, but she was not about to give in. She had more stamina than that.

At long last he removed his arms from about her, resting his hands on either side of her to effectively trap her against the table. Hesitantly, she half-turned to gaze up at the man who churned her insides into a whirlpool.

"I wonder if I shall ever learn all the intricacies of the game, sir?" she said, hoping her cheeks were not as flushed as they felt.

"I am certain that you are capable of learning the intricacies of any game you so choose, Lady Ware." His voice held a husky intimacy. Then he bestowed one of those bone-melting smiles on her that she could feel all the way to her toes, and she wondered if she would recall anything of his instruction other than the feel of him against her body.

"Perhaps we should test my skill?" She desperately strove for a calmness she didn't feel.

"I have the utmost confidence that you will do well. After all, I am your teacher." His eyes held a twinkle that seemed rather disarming, not predatory as might be expected given the circumstances.

"I suspect you have had a great deal of practice at this sort of thing. You do it so well." His expression changed rapidly from suave tenderness to one that might have been chagrin.

"I must confess I enjoy teaching."

"I can see that; it appears to come naturally to you." She looked to the other end of the table, where Lord Musgrave had Miss Russell in giggles and looking far more at ease. "Perhaps we could have a rudimentary game?"

Was that a sigh of resignation she heard from behind her? Well, as a flirt, she did not do very well. On the other hand, she wasn't certain she wished to polish her skills in flirting. It all seemed rather superficial. Besides, that art was for catching a husband and she did not wish to be married again. Once was more than enough.

By concentrating on the small ivory ball and the position of her cue she was able to block out the disturbing male presence at her side. Lord Thornbury made little comments under his breath, but she ignored those as well.

"Dash it all," Lord Musgrave said at last, "either you are a better teacher than I knew or Lady Ware is a natural at the game."

"I told her she could master it if she chose. Lady Ware could do well at any game she pleases. She has an incredible gift of concentration and an excellent memory."

Georgiana turned to face Lord Thornbury at last and met his gaze square on. Smiling, she said, "I give leave to doubt that, my lord. But I confess I find the challenge irresistible."

"Two of a kind," murmured Lord Musgrave.

"Challenge is what adds spice to your life, my dear Lady Ware," Lord Thornbury replied, taking Georgiana's ungloved hand in his and placing a kiss dead center, while casting a provocative glance into her bemused eyes.

That kiss on the hand, directly on her tender skin, was like nothing she had ever experienced in her life. Tingles danced along her arm, disturbing tremors shot through her entire body. Good heavens, if she reacted like this at a mere kiss on the hand, what would happen should he kiss her lips! It did not bear consideration.

The moment was lost when Lady Pickering floated into the room, chattering away to Mr. Woodburn as they entered. She paused, looking at the four gathered about the table and slowly smiled.

"What a charming tableau you make. Are you prepared for the evening? Lady Kenyon just informed me that since the rain has abated we shall have the pleasure of attending the assembly in Cheltenham after all."

Since Georgiana hadn't known about the projected assembly expedition, she could scarcely have been concerned one way or the other. "I wasn't aware such a delight was contemplated."

"I trust you have included a suitable gown in your wardrobe.

One must always be prepared for balls and the like when attending a house party, country pastimes being what they are." Lady Pickering gave Georgiana a patronizing look, then selected a cue from the rack. "May we join you for a game?"

"I believe that Miss Russell and I must consult with our abigails regarding our attire for the evening. Excuse us, please," Georgiana said smoothly. It was a distinct relief to escape from Lady Pickering and her little barbs, not to mention the men.

"How well you do that. I fear if I were left to my own devices I would have remained to listen to more of her little pointed shafts at my inability to converse," Miss Russell said regretfully.

"The trick in conversation is to persuade the other person to talk about him or herself. I have always found that most useful," Georgiana confided, while walking up the stairs to the bedroom floor. She resisted the urge to look behind to see if Lord Thornbury had followed them from the billiard room. What he did was his own business.

Ambling along the path of the conservatory Jason ran his hand through the carefully casual curls his valet had arranged this morning. Musgrave at his side was equally morose, his eyes again those of an unhappy beagle.

"Dandy morning, what?" Musgrave offered after a bit.

"I almost had her if that blasted Pickering female had not joined us just then. I could feel her weakening. Nothing like a slow kiss on the hand combined with a soulful look in the eyes to soften their resolve."

"Is that so?" Musgrave mused. "Must remember that."

"Yet I wonder if I am doing the right thing," Jason continued. "Still, after her marriage and the years that have followed, she must be up to snuff."

"Thought the old gaffer died before anything interesting happened," Musgrave pointed out.

"So I have heard. But can you imagine any red-blooded male allowing that woman to go untouched?"

"Can't say. Depends on how she denied him, don't it? Might have been violent," Musgrave reasoned.

Jason shot his friend a look of disbelief, then went off to

consult with Martin regarding his own attire for the coming assembly. He must look close to perfection to aid in his capture of the beautiful widow.

Several hours later the party assembled in the drawing room, all garbed in fine clothes suitable for a country assembly. Georgiana was gratified to see that her own gown of silver tissue over pale blue silk faille was not the least out of style compared with what the other women wore. She fingered the pearls at her neck with her gloved hand, recalling the touch of Lord Thornbury's lips on that hand not so long ago. She fancied she could still feel the imprint of his warm and sensuous touch on her skin.

At dinner she found herself seated between Mr. Woodburn and Lord Pickering with Selina Woodburn and Miss Russell the recipients of attention from Lords Thornbury and Musgrave. It was pleasant to enjoy her dinner with the need to ask but a few questions of the gentlemen at her side to carry her through the meal. She avoided gazing at Lord Thornbury, who showed to great advantage in his splendid deep wine velvet coat worn over a white marcella waistcoat and black breeches and hose. The man was perfection from his tousled hair *à la Brutus* to the refined cravat with a blood-red ruby nestled in its folds.

There was no time permitted the men to sit over their port following dinner. Rather, they all rose to gather in the entryway while the several carriages awaited without.

Georgiana made certain that she had Miss Russell at her side when it came time for them to enter the landau. It seemed to be taken for granted that Lord Thornbury and Musgrave would drive with them. The evening was cooler than previously and she was grateful for the light wool shawl Perkins had insisted she take with her.

"I am delighted to attend a Cheltenham assembly," Miss Russell said with a touch of daring.

"I have not danced these past years," Georgiana admitted. "I suppose I shall be a trifle rusty and I have yet to learn that dreadful new dance, the waltz. I doubt it will be played this evening, however. Country people are always a bit slower to accept foreign things and this dance comes from France, I believe."

"I understand there have been similar dances for ages in Germany *and* France. Actually it is the Germans who have introduced a modified waltz into court life," Lord Thornbury ventured to say with a look at Georgiana that she wished she might see better. The moonlight offered a bit of light, the coach lamps a little more, but most everything was in deep shadows.

The assembly rooms were brightly lit without and within. The carriages clattered along the cobbled streets, making a fearful racket before coming to a stop at a covered entrance.

"My, what splendor," Georgiana whispered to Lord Thornbury as he assisted her from the carriage.

"It is no more than you deserve, my lady. You should always be treated like the queen you are."

"Doing it too brown, my lord," she whispered again, glancing at him with a mischievous sparkle in her eyes.

"Are you always so difficult to divert, madam?" he replied, his mouth close to her ear.

"I know a Banbury tale when I hear one," she said with a chuckle.

"Egad, woman, you cut me to the quick," Lord Thornbury said, again keeping his voice low so that none other might hear their exchange.

"May I suggest you behave yourself," she scolded lightly, thinking again of her nephew Pip.

"I intend to behave just as you deserve, Madam Flirt."

Georgiana had no chance to reply for all the carriages had arrived and the group made their way into the assembly rooms. Lady Kenyon had taken care of arrangements so that all that remained to do was remove their wraps, check a mirror, and enter the spacious rooms to mingle with those already in attendance.

It was immediately apparent that the local inhabitants of Cheltenham were more than a little impressed with the group from Kenyon Hall. Georgiana surmised that having an earl, two barons, a dowager marchioness, and dowager countess at one time was not a common occasion. Their gowns were examined minutely by interested ladies and the gentlemen inspected the deft design of the cravats with an eye to duplicating them if possible, she was certain. She could see avid glances at the earl. Lord Thornbury, if aware of them, took not the slightest notice.

"There are some very pretty girls here this evening," she murmured as he adjusted her shawl—most unnecessarily, it seemed to her.

She might have thought his gesture unnecessary, but his tender smoothing of the shawl made it quite clear to all the gentlemen attending that she was Lord Thornbury's particular interest and should be treated with all due respect. Even in Cheltenham, the earl's reputation as a premier gentleman of the *ton* was known.

Georgiana accepted the earl's hand for the first dance and did not sit out even one for the remainder of the evening. Contrary to her fears, she had not forgotten the steps, complicated though some were for the country dances. She had loved dancing and missed it greatly in her self-imposed exile from society. Perhaps she would enjoy London more than she thought if she were treated to such events as this.

"It is truly lovely, is it not, Miss Russell?" Georgiana said when a break came while the orchestra sought a bit of refreshment.

"I confess that I have enjoyed this more than I expected and it is all because of your advice," Miss Russell confided in return.

"My advice?" Georgiana queried, trying to recall what she might have offered.

"I ask the gentleman something about his interests and all I need to do is prompt him with more questions. It is amazingly simple." Miss Russell gave Georgiana a wide-eyed stare that contained a hint of mirth.

Georgiana laughed. "How clever you are. I believe you are as fast a learner as I have seen." Not that she had seen all that much, but Miss Russell need not know it.

"Mama was to come with me but my little sister became ill just before we were to leave and she'd not deny me this chance to improve myself because of Sukey's sniffles. Lady

Kenyon has been most kind and I have appreciated your taking me under your wing, Lady Ware. Mama will be in alt when I tell her that the beautiful Lady Ware told me just how to go on. She will think, perhaps, about my come-out in London."

"Good. Every girl ought to have a London come-out if at all possible. Although Bath is not to be despised, I understand," Georgiana concluded, not knowing the financial standing of the Russell family.

"Mama said house parties are most helpful, that oftentimes they prove to be excellent means for fixing a gentleman's attentions. I doubt Lord Musgrave is the least bit interested in that sort of thing at this moment, but he has provided a very nice diversion. I shall tell Mama that it has been a learning experience. And who knows, when I do make it to London, it may be very nice to have met him for he seems to have excellent connections."

"I notice you do not aspire to Lord Thornbury," Georgiana said dryly.

"Heaven forbid," Miss Russell whispered. "He frightens me witless. I suspect he does not find me nearly as entrancing as you, Lady Ware."

Georgiana merely smiled at this bit of nonsense. She had little reason to think that Lord Thornbury's interest in her was more than a light flirtation. If he thought to go further, he would be far off the mark.

The musicians struck up a lively tune preparatory to a country dance and Lord Musgrave sought her hand. Gladly accepting his, she gracefully rose and joined his walk to the dance floor.

"You are the focus of attention this evening, my lady. I misdoubt that Cheltenham has seen such beauty in a long time, if ever."

"What charming flummery, my lord. No wonder Miss Russell claims you are a very admirable gentleman."

"Admirable, madam? *Admirable* seems a dashed mild word." Lord Musgrave grinned at her in his pleasant manner.

"A true lady dare not express anything warmer."

"Does a lady ever admit to a *tendré*?" he queried casually.

"Of course, but I suspect most women are hesitant before

offering their hearts on a platter, so to speak. It must be dreadful to be rejected."

"Not tried it, myself."

"Nor have I," she admitted. "Since my marriage was arranged and to a gentleman unknown to me, I had naught of the usual flirtations, you see."

"Pity. Understand a nice flirtation can be a bit of fun."

"Nice? Oh, Lord Musgrave!" She gave him a mischievous look before twirling away in the pattern of the dance.

After the dance he escorted her back to where Lady Kenyon sat chatting with her nephew.

"My dear girl, you are the belle of the ball. Thornbury just told me so." Her ladyship patted Georgiana on the hand, then turned to her nephew. "What time do you think we ought to leave?"

"Certainly not before I claim my second dance with Lady Ware."

Georgiana obediently offered her hand only to find him drawing her close to his side as he led her onto the dance floor.

"You must allow me to guide you in this dance, my lady. I believe you will find the steps quite simple. There is a pronounced rhythm in the music that impels the feet to do as they ought. You, my dear, are going to learn how to waltz."

The softly spoken words struck horror in her heart. "Learn a strange dance in the middle of a Cheltenham assembly, my lord? You must be mad." Georgiana backed away from him slightly, as far as his hold would permit.

"We shall begin over here to one side of the room, the area that is least populated. If I know you, we shall be circling the room in a trice. You have natural rhythm, dear lady, and appear to learn new things most rapidly."

Somewhat mollified at his flattery, she decided she was better off having him teach her than causing a scene should she try to leave him. She turned to face him, lifting her chin, challenging him with her eyes. "So be it."

The lilting music stirred her to sway in his arms. Indeed, she so concentrated on the measure that she scarcely noticed his light clasp at her waist, nor his hand warmly holding hers. She half-closed her eyes, feeling the rhythm of the music, allowing herself to be swept around in a circular pattern, resting her hand on the soft velvet of his coat with hardly a recollection of what was within that garment.

"Ah, as I suspected, you do very well." His husky voice rumbled somewhere above one ear.

She stumbled at those words. "So sorry, my lord," she said when she had recovered her poise and balance.

He had predicted rightly, it seemed. They soon circled the room, one of the few couples who dared the new dance that had set London on its ear.

"It does not seem too dreadfully wicked," she began. Then she at last realized how intimate they were—his hand fit so snugly at her waist, his other hand holding hers in such a tender manner, and his proximity positively daunting.

"Oh, mercy," she whispered. "On the other hand, perhaps they have an excellent point."

He chuckled, the very sound overwhelming her further. "My dear lady, we have just begun."

Chapter Four

The following four days brought confusion to Georgiana. It was not that anything was truly amiss; it was merely that life, particularly Lord Thornbury, was not going forth as she thought it—and he—ought.

He and Lord Musgrave disappeared in the morning to fish or hunt or whatever gentlemen did when off on their own. He appeared in time for a late luncheon, then in the afternoon he wooed her. That was the only word she could think applied to his behavior. She might have likened his behavior to an attempt at seduction, but she felt that Lord Thornbury was above that sort of thing with a young and likely vulnerable widow.

She had heard a good many pretty speeches in the past three years not to mention a number of near ravishments. What a blessing that Bel, her uncommonly large and quite ferociously protective cat, had neatly foiled each assault. It seemed her male relatives discounted the effectiveness of a cat as a protector, no matter that Bel looked tigerish and most fierce. To add to her amusement, as well as relief, evidently not one of them had mentioned Bel to any other, for none of her so-called suitors had thought to bar the cat when he besieged her, resulting in each one being nastily scratched and bitten by an angry Bel. Perhaps it insulted their dignity to be thwarted by a mere cat. There was nothing "mere" about Bel in the least.

As yet, Bel had not approved of one of the men who had called on Georgiana and she could not help but wonder how Bel might react to Lord Thornbury.

All of which returned her attention to the gentleman at hand again. Had she really conceived a fondness for him? It must be confessed she had, and for that matter, she had even contemplated what it might be like to be captured in his arms—as she had been with the more persistent of her "suitors."

Somehow she suspected it would not be as disgusting as when, for example, her stepson had crushed her in his manly embrace and forced his brandy-scented mouth upon hers. It was difficult when one's stepson was a good deal older and wiser in the ways of the world, not to mention well along the path to emulating his father in girth and prosiness. He had not taken kindly to her rebuff and Georgiana had felt it prudent to move to the dower house as quickly as possible. Then Bel had sauntered in, taken charge of the dower house, and life had improved considerably. There had been no repeat of her stepson's assault.

On the other hand, it seemed that Lord Thornbury intended to go just so far with her and no further. He certainly confused her. He flattered, smiled those bone-melting smiles, strolled along the paths with her to smell the roses, and did the many little things Georgiana understood were done when a gentleman was courting a lady.

Only, he *couldn't* be courting her. She had made it plain she had no desire to wed. So, she supposed she ought to merely accept his attentions as something with which to pass the time and set her confusions aside as Miss Russell did.

"La, Lady Ware," the ingenuous miss declared one morning over the billiard table where the two of them practiced their shots, "Lord Musgrave is a very nice man, and he flirts beautifully. I doubt, however, if he sees me as more than an agreeable way to pass the hours."

Could Miss Russell be less than three years younger than Georgiana? Seventeen? The very age at which her family had wed her to an elderly peer? Georgiana felt twice her years in many ways, yet Miss Russell was surprisingly wise regarding men, of that there was little doubt.

"There you are, Lady Ware," the velvety voice belonging to Lord Thornbury suddenly purred from behind Georgiana. "I thought perhaps you might enjoy an inspection of the rose garden this morning. That French rose you hoped to see bloom has at last unfurled a bud and I believe you will agree it lives up to all expectations. Come," he beckoned with an imperious hand.

"Enchanted, my lord," she hastily replied, setting aside the cue to go with him after an apologetic glance at Miss Russell. "Would you care to join us, my dear?"

"I shall see it later, perhaps." She made a shooing motion, then returned to studying the ball on the table.

"Aunt Charlotte says this is the finest rose in her collection. She is so pleased it deigns to bloom while you are here." Lord Thornbury gently pulled Georgiana along with him in what she thought to be a delightful show of enthusiasm. She had longed for someone to share her enjoyment of roses. It seemed his lordship did.

The bloom was truly magnificent, well worth waiting for in Georgiana's estimation.

"It is one of the Damascus offspring, I believe." Creamy white petals showed a rich gold at the base with a fragile veining of delicate rose on the outer side of the ruffled petals. "One of the more exquisite roses I have seen," she said while bending over to determine its particular scent.

"You will wish to capture this beauty on paper, no doubt?" He turned to snap his fingers to where Perkins had lingered in the background holding Georgiana's drawing pad and case of pencils. Behind Perkins came a footman with a neat little stool just right for sketching.

"You leave nothing to chance, do you, my lord?" Georgiana said with delight.

"I try to cover all points, Lady Ware," he murmured with a provocative twist of his sensual mouth.

"It is very bad of me to ignore you to concentrate on a mere rose, sirrah," she said with a hesitant smile.

"I promise to demand payment for services rendered later on, dear lady, should your conscience trouble you," he murmured as he assisted her to settle on the stool.

Tossing an arresting glance at him, Georgiana promptly forgot him in her close attention to her drawing. She must capture every little vein, ruffle, and gilt-encrusted stamen of this magnificent rose before it faded.

"Oh, I almost forgot," Lord Thornbury said before departing, causing Georgiana to glance back at him. "I persuaded my aunt to give you a cutting from this rose so that in future years you may enjoy its heavenly scent in your own garden."

Her heart swelled with gratitude at his thoughtful gesture. "What a lovely thing for you to do, my lord. I am extremely grateful to you . . . and your aunt, as I shall tell her later on."

He looked vaguely smug, as well he might, Georgiana reflected. He had accomplished a very noble deed in her eyes. How he thought she might repay him bothered her a bit. He would never look to monetary reward and what else did she possess?

Setting that niggling thought aside, she turned her attention to the rose, her pad, and pencils. Perkins brought her a roll and tea an hour later, for Georgiana refused to leave her spot until the drawing was complete.

When at last she felt she had done the magnificent rose justice, she stretched her arms, arched a tired back, and rotated her head to work the stiffness from her neck.

"Time for a leisurely stroll in the garden, perhaps along to the lake," Lord Thornbury said, surprising Georgiana, who had believed herself to be alone among the roses.

"Gladly, sir. The sun is most pleasant, yet the few clouds keep it from becoming too warm—perfect for a walk." She set aside her pencil case, carefully covered the drawing of the unusual Damask rose issue, then rose from her stool.

"What? Am I not to see the drawing after all I did? *That* is my demand, Lady Ware, that I see the results of my scheming."

"What a bit of nonsense, my lord." But she picked up the tablet upon which she had recorded the image of the rose and meekly handed it to him. Could it be that he intended to make that his claim, his prize, as it were? Viewing her drawings was scarcely what she would call a reward for such efforts as he had made, but it was a relief.

He studied her work in silence.

"Perhaps you would care for one of the etchings when I have completed this series? It is little enough with which to repay you."

"But this is incredible, far beyond what I suspected you

might do," he declared, sincerity ringing in his voice. He carefully replaced the covering, then set the tablet on the stool before summoning a footman. "See to it that this is given to Lady Ware's maid for safekeeping."

Then he offered his arm to Georgiana with a respectful bow. She found herself charmed by his words and attitude. Respect and charm did not often come her way from a polished gentleman—particularly the respect.

"You play the pianoforte with zest and originality, you draw superbly, waltz divinely. What other charms do you possess, Lady Ware?"

"You, sirrah, are a tease of the first water, but a most delightful one, I must say. Any other talent I own would have to be my gardening. There are long hours in the winter when one cannot garden and then I either put my roses into an etching, or work one on canvas. You found a path to my esteem with a gift of a rose."

Feeling that she was too forthcoming, Georgiana hastily turned his attention to the flock of ducks on the lake, then to the matter of the ball that was to bring the house party to a conclusion.

"I should have been resting to prepare for the ball this evening, I suppose," she mused, kicking a leaf from her path. "Am I correct in thinking there are many others who will attend in addition to those who have been visiting these past days?"

"My aunt has invited all the neighbors in the surrounding area. We shall be a jolly group this evening. You look forward to it?" He placed a hand over hers where it rested on his arm, a gentle, warm touch that did not threaten her.

Georgiana gave that hand a look, then turned to gaze off at the lake. "I do. And yet I don't, for it means the end to a very pleasant interlude."

"You intend to return to your dower house on the morrow?" His voice softly encouraged her to share her thoughts and plans with him.

"As soon as may be. I miss my cat and the roses and my etchings."

"A cat? You are becoming a confirmed widow with her cat, then?" He sounded vastly amused at her life.

"Indeed, sir." She smiled in reflection. "I am fixing to buy most extravagant caps and give no thought to remarriage—as I thought I said." She chanced to glance up to see a pleased expression on his face, quite as though she had answered an unspoken question for him.

He guided them back in a circle and into the house, then to the foot of the stairs. "I imagine I dare not keep you from your room. Your maid will come searching for you should I selfishly keep you at my side any longer. I have observed that no lady likes to be rushed when preparing for a gala event such as a ball."

"You are correct," she said, flashing a smile at him and feeling in high spirits. "I shall see you at dinner, no doubt."

"And we shall waltz this evening if I may demand two dances in advance?" He refused to relinquish her hand, seeming determined to hold it until she agreed.

"You have my word, sir," she said before withdrawing her hand from his and sedately walking to her room. Not that she wished to be sedate. She knew a strange urge to dance along the hall, about her room, with the happiness that bubbled within. Was she in danger of forgetting her determination to remain single the remainder of her days?

"My gown, Perkins, is it ready?" Georgiana cried as she closed her bedroom door behind her. Sinking down on the pretty little chair before her looking glass she studied her flushed cheeks, sparkling eyes. Had she ever been in such looks before?

"Indeed, my lady," her soft-spoken abigail said. "I also ordered your trunks brought up. So often there is a delay when many are leaving at once. This way I can pack your gowns at my leisure and all will be in readiness when you choose to leave."

"Ah, Perkins, how glad I am that you came with me when I left Ware Court." Georgiana gave her maid a fond look.

"Had I not gone with you I would have sought work elsewhere, my lady. I had no wish to be given a babe by his lordship." Georgiana caught Perkins's gaze when she turned to stare at her usually reserved maid.

"It seems we shared his lordship's interest. How democratic of him, to be sure," Georgiana said in a voice tight with irony while she rubbed the little finger of her left hand. It still ached from time to time. His late lordship had broken it during their last heated argument. Then she looked across the room to her trunks, one large, one small. "It is a good idea to have all things packed and ready to leave. I wish to be home as early as may be, perhaps tomorrow if the roads cooperate."

She smiled, then turned her attention to removing her garments. She'd rest a bit, then prepare for the ball.

Jason lazed back in the tub he had ordered. Water sloshed to the floor as he soaped his body, then rinsed off. All had gone superbly well, today and before. Tonight the widow would be his. Usually he was not driven to such lengths, but the beautiful widow was wary and unaccustomed to dalliance, he could see that. His conscience twinged a bit, but he squelched any thought of wrongdoing on his part. After all, she had smiled at him, encouraged him, walked out alone with him. She had said she'd no wish to marry, but the smile she'd offered left no doubt of her desires.

Yes. It was a matter of hours and she would be in his arms, his bed. His body responded to the very thought of such delights and he congratulated himself on his patience. She had been a wary one, unsophisticated, unused to the ways of the *ton* and stylish widows. But she was surely worth his wait. Oh, yes, he had no doubts but what the delightful and talented widow had gifts in other areas as well.

When Georgiana swept down the stairs she knew a satisfaction that she looked well. The local mantuamaker had outdone all her previous efforts with a copy of a gown that had been in a recent issue of *The Monthly Museum*. Spider gauze was deftly draped over a skirt of finest Florence satin in an especially pretty amaranthus color. And that color was echoed in a dainty arrangement of tiny pinkish-purple silk flowers in Georgiana's ebony curls. The same silk flowers had been tucked here and there along the hem of the gown, caught up in scallops of fabric. Georgiana felt quite nice.

"Lady Ware, how charming you look." Lord Thornbury advanced upon Georgiana with a smiling face, an arm outstretched to offer as support.

There was definitely more noise in the house this evening. She tensed, not liking to meet strangers. Then she mentally reprimanded herself. She must get over her silly starts. The Cheltenham assembly had gone well. This ball would too.

The drawing room was abuzz with additional guests invited for dinner. Yet even more would come later for the ball. Georgiana looked about her, then saw Miss Russell. That dear young lady appeared as uneasy and lost as did Georgiana, never mind that Lord Thornbury offered the service of his arm.

Georgiana felt the security of his well-clad arm beneath her trembling hand. To find a gentleman who did not immediately jump to the conclusion that a widow was fair game was not only novel, but to be cherished. Dare she open her heart to him? She had kept that heart well locked away, fearing to expose her emotions.

Yet here was a man who shared many of her pleasures—music, roses, not to mention charming walks among the ruins. Oh, he could not be untrustworthy! Surely a gentleman who had behaved so admirably could be depended upon to act with refinement and sensitivity?

"I would join Miss Russell. She looks a trifle bewildered. I would wager she has not often been in such company. At seventeen there is so much before one."

"And you are such a very great age," he mocked.

"I may be but twenty, but I feel more like fifty, I vow." Georgiana slanted a smile at him, then greeted Miss Russell, who wore a simple white crepe gown. "How lovely you look!"

"Thank you, ma'am. May I say that you look like a princess this evening?" The girl blushed prettily, giving Lady Ware a very nice curtsy before returning to her previous occupation, fiddling with her fan.

"Nicely done, my dear," Georgiana said quietly.

"I shall die. I know it," Miss Russell muttered.

"Nonsense. Here is Lord Musgrave to join us. Ah, do we go

into dinner so soon?" Georgiana turned in surprise, for the butler had summoned the guests to dinner when it seemed they had barely assembled.

"My aunt wishes all to eat well in advance of the others who come later. The table must be prepared for the supper to come," Lord Thornbury said close to her ear.

"Naturally," Georgiana replied, feeling foolish that she had not thought of such practicalities. But then, she had attended few balls in her life and certainly never given one.

They swept into dinner, after which all was a haze for Georgiana. Had she thought the offerings during the past week were elegant, they paled into insignificance with the dishes presented this evening. Exquisite course after course with elegant removes were whisked to the table, followed by pastries fit for a king. With a feeling of unreality she joined the women when Lady Kenyon led them to the drawing room.

"Have you attended many dinners like that one?" Miss Russell whispered as they walked across the entry to the drawing room.

"Never. I daresay you have as much experience as I, for I have been living secluded in the country these past three years."

"Ever since your . . . er, that is, how sad," Miss Russell floundered.

"Do not concern yourself. I have determined that I must find my place in society, no matter how modest it might be. Time and enough that I have buried myself here in the rural charm of the country. Perhaps it *is* time for me to sample the delights of London."

"London," breathed Miss Russell with all the reverence due to a sacred place.

Georgiana was spared having to explain that she suspected that London was only wonderful when one had money and connections, both in much abundance, when the gentlemen joined them.

Before long the remaining neighbors arrived and the ball began.

When the music began for the first waltz, Lord Thornbury presented himself to Georgiana to claim his promised dance.

"By all means, my lord. I always keep my promises," Georgiana said with a sparkle in her fine eyes.

The dance had not lost its power to enchant her since last she performed it with Lord Thornbury. Lady Kenyon had called him Jason, but Georgiana dared not think of him that way lest she forget herself. To say his name would be far too familiar; it simply was not done. But she did like it.

It was heaven to be held in his arms, his eyes gazing down at her with such tender regard. Although of little experience, Georgiana fully believed that he had begun to care for her as she had for him. She could not imagine what the future might hold in regards to Lord Thornbury, the handsome and dashing gentleman who had taken over her dreams, but she had begun to hope. And that was more than she had done in a number of years.

It was after the second waltz that the warmth of the room began to oppress her. She prepared to find a glass of lemonade when Lord Thornbury anticipated her need.

"Allow me to attend to your wants, Lady Ware," he said in the seductive purring voice he had used before. Its husky quality sent tremors through Georgiana and she berated herself for being a silly and rather green goose.

Instead of simpering or flirting, she merely accepted the drink, then strolled to the windows that overlooked the rose garden.

"I would suggest a walk in the garden to cool us, but it looks as though it might mist. May I offer my company for a pleasant diversion in the conservatory instead?"

Happy to be with a gentleman she could trust implicitly, Georgiana agreed at once. "How lovely that sounds. Your aunt raises the most extraordinary plants in that place. Someday I should like to have such a facility in which to grow exotic plants."

"I have a large greenhouse at my estate in Kent. I believe I have begun a respectable collection of orchids you might enjoy," Jason said, then wondered why he had told her that. He'd not intended to invite her interest.

"Do you have a great deal of trouble growing them? I understand orchids are a trifle temperamental."

He maintained a polite and neutral conversation about plants and flowers until they were at the far end of the conservatory. And then he calculated the moment was right. He turned to face her, tipping her chin up with one perfectly gloved hand while slipping the other around her. The conservatory was in darkness save for a small lantern at the opposite end of the room. He had checked on that earlier in the day, satisfied his stage was set.

"Georgiana, I cannot resist your appeal, your beauty. I must . . ." and he did not wait for a reply, but seized the moment. Drawing her most tenderly into his arms, he proceeded to use every ounce of his considerable skill to charm the beautiful widow. His kiss, he felt, sizzled the widow's nerves to a nicety.

Georgiana did not even attempt to deny him. While she had fought the attentions of every man who had tried to kiss her before, now she was only too eager to accept Lord Thornbury's kiss. The lush scents swirling about her combined with the masculine eau de cologne he used to bewitch her senses. Never had she imagined that a kiss could be like this, gentle yet demanding, experienced yet seeming to acknowledge her innocence.

His lips released hers and she knew bereavement at her loss. Held close to him, she cherished what his kisses might lead to. That it would be proper she had no doubt. Merely because she had strolled with him while leaving her maid behind was no reason to expect anything less. He had always treated her with courtesy.

"We must return. I'd not have anyone cast a shadow on your reputation. But later, my sweet. Oh, later . . ." His lips captured another kiss even sweeter than the first, then he guided her dazed and breathless person back to the dining room. Here he collected a plate and placed several dainty tidbits on it for her.

She had not the least notion what she ate. Nor did she pay a great deal of attention to the dances that followed. That is, until the genial baron who lived on the estate bordering Kenyon Hall chanced to trod on her hem.

"Bother," she muttered as she whisked herself off to the room set aside for repairing such minor disasters.

The hall was a trifle dim and she observed that several of the candles had blown out, as though someone had opened a door causing a gust of wind to work its will.

Inside the small chamber she found needle and thread and a maid who was immediately sent to have a footman light the candles once again. The window in this room was open and she went to close it when she heard voices outside, one of which she knew extremely well. Lord Thornbury's rich tones could not be mistaken, nor could Lord Musgrave be missed. She did not like to eavesdrop and went to latch the window when she heard her name and paused. Bearing in mind the old adage about listeners, she nevertheless found herself rooted to the spot.

"It is all but accomplished," Lord Thornbury said quietly, blowing a cloud of smoke into the soft evening air.

"You are so certain?" Musgrave replied in equally soft tones.

"Lady Ware responded so sweetly to my overtures that I chanced to proceed further. I promised to come to her later and she did not deny me." There was the merest hint of triumph in Lord Thornbury's voice now.

Georgiana froze, unable to move. What had she promised? She certainly did not remember saying anything that would give his lordship cause to speak thus. She recalled that he had urged they return to the ball for he did not want anyone to think ill of her. He was protecting her, she thought. He had murmured something about later, but at the time she hadn't the foggiest notion as to what he had meant by that. Now she very much feared that she did.

It was as though a veil had been removed from her eyes, enabling her to see matters more clearly. That blasted man intended to seduce her! Why had she been so blind? How could she have trusted him so? What a foolish little country idiot she was, to fall for the honeyed words of a rake, even if he was Lady Kenyon's nephew.

Not bothering to close the window, Georgiana tiptoed from the chamber to hurry along the hall. She had the good fortune to find Lady Kenyon crossing the entry hall on a minor errand.

"Dear lady," Georgiana said, hoping she sounded as calm as she felt, "I find I must leave as soon as may be. A crisis has arisen at home." She went on to thank her hostess profusely for the charming visit, then explained she must complete her preparations for departure.

"Surely it could wait until morning?" Lady Kenyon said, much perplexed and feeling there was more to this than was being revealed.

"I fear not. My household is in an uproar and I just learned of it," Georgiana said in reply, thinking that if it wasn't at this point it soon would be.

Satisfied that it was an imperative matter to demand such immediate action, Georgiana was sent on her way with the promise of a light repast to be packed and placed in her coach. As though she felt like eating another bite!

Hurrying to her room, she found Perkins putting the last of her gowns into the large trunk.

"Here, put this dress in as well," Georgiana said while pulling the flowers from her hair. "We are leaving at once. Something has come up and I cannot remain another minute."

Her change of clothing was accomplished in lightning speed. Georgiana penned a couple of lines to Miss Russell, promising to see her in London. Then, after a last look about the lovely room she peeked around the door. Finding the hall silent and empty, she swiftly made her way to the back stairs, down and out to the stable area. While her horses were put to her traveling coach, she supervised the speedy interment of her trunks in the boot, then urged Perkins to join her in the coach.

"I am breathless, my lady."

"Thank heaven you are no more than that, Perkins."

"What happened to your lovely evening, my lady? You had so looked forward to it," the abigail ventured hesitantly.

"I found a man I trusted wrongly, Perkins. He was no better than the rest of them. I *cannot* bear to face him again. So I flee," she concluded bleakly and stared out into the night as the coach rumbled away from Kenyon Hall and the perfidious Jason Ainsley, Lord Thornbury.

Chapter Five

Dawn glimmered in the sky when they made the turn to the avenue leading to Ware Court. Shortly after the turn, and long before the Court might be seen, they reached their destination. Never had Georgiana been so thankful to see the dower house as this morning.

Perkins roused from her slumber as the coach pulled to a halt. With a sleepy-eyed shake of her head, she assisted her equally drowsy mistress from the carriage.

"Get some sleep before all else," Georgiana ordered John Coachman, concerned for the older man who had driven through the night in Georgiana's furious flight.

"Aye, milady," he replied with a tired doff of his tall hat.

The cook was moving about in the kitchen when Georgiana and Perkins quietly let themselves into the back entrance.

"My lady!" the good woman cried in puzzlement. "You are home beforetimes." She cast an anxious glance at the stairs that led to the upper floor, then stood wringing her hands.

Georgiana surmised that something was amiss, but was too tired to wonder overmuch about it. The house seemed blessedly quiet, normal, and free of arrogant gentlemen who thought they could do as they please with young widows.

"We shall have something to eat before taking a nap. Our night was somewhat disturbed. Nothing can compare to a sound sleep in one's bed," Georgiana said while fighting the urge to yawn and losing.

"Indeed, my lady," the cook replied with another anxious glance at the stairs, quite as though she was listening for a sound from above.

"Is all well? Did anything of interest occur while we were

absent?" Georgiana casually inquired, pausing at the open door to the hallway.

"No—that is, yes, milady," the cook replied, looking quite as upset as she sounded.

"She means that you have been invaded by a female seeking shelter in the one place your stepson is not likely to search," came a sweet, high voice from the first-floor landing.

"Miss Pettibone!" Georgiana cried, rushing along the hall to the bottom of the stairs. "What has happened?"

"I daresay it is something you must be most familiar with, since you left the Court so hastily and put his lordship into a fit of the dismals at the same time."

Miss Elspeth Pettibone, erstwhile governess to the unruly Ware hopefuls, clutched her faded blue dressing gown about her thin figure and carefully picked her way down the stairs until she stood facing Georgiana. "*I* refused to stay there one moment longer. *He* refused to give me a reference. How I am to obtain employment without such is beyond me. Forgive me for seeking refuge here, but I had no notion of where I might flee. I thought you might offer some sensible advice."

Georgiana thought quickly, then said, "You did the right thing, of course. Please dress and we can discuss all this at the breakfast table. I need to freshen up as well. Shall we say thirty minutes?"

At the suggested time the two women sat down to well-filled plates, cups of piping hot tea, and questions suspended in the air.

"What was the final straw, if I may ask?" Georgiana asked hesitantly.

"Two of the maids left and he had no one else to torment with his attentions. Really, one would think Lady Ware would suspect something was amiss. First you and Perkins, then the two maids leave. If he does not mend his ways, there will be naught but men willing to work at Ware Court."

"Or a certain sort of female," Georgiana said wryly, exchanging a look with her unexpected guest.

Miss Pettibone was of the gentry, like many a governess required to find work when the family coffers emptied. Had circumstances been different, Georgiana might be in the same position. Her heart went out to the proper and really quite charming woman. She was perhaps five years older than Georgiana, her slight frame accentuating the fine bones of her face. Her delicate features were highlighted by her unusual gray eyes and the soft blond hair that crowned her head like a spun silver halo.

"Of course you may stay with me as long as you please," Georgiana decided upon reflection. "It has bothered me not to have a companion or chaperone when I go about, as on the visit to Kenyon Court. In fact," Georgiana said, thinking swiftly about Lord Thornbury and his possible fury at being thwarted, "I believe it to be of utmost importance that I acquire someone of impeccable reputation to reside with me. I can think of no one who fits that description better than you, dear Miss Pettibone. Should my stepson dare to inquire, we shall give out that I begged you to come with me to lend me countenance on my trip to . . ." Georgiana thought wildly. Where could she go to escape her home, the Ware family, and Lord Thornbury—in the unlikely event he came charging after her? "Sidmouth," she decided at last. "Indeed, we shall go to Sidmouth, for I believe the sea air would be most beneficial to my health." And the *ton* would likely follow the Prince to Brighton. She would be free to enjoy a holiday at the seashore without having to face society or encounter Lord Thornbury.

Miss Pettibone smiled at that bit of nonsense, for if any woman looked in the pink, it was Georgiana, Dowager Marchioness of Ware. "As you wish, my lady."

Georgiana took a reviving sip of tea and mulled over their respective situations still further while she partook of her food. Neither of them had reason to wish to be at the dower house at the moment. While it was unlikely that Lord Ware would purely out of spite accuse Miss Pettibone of absconding with the family silver, he might. And he could make things unpleasant for Georgiana at the same time.

The notion that Lord Thornbury might follow her was laughable, yet she suspected that it was not only a woman scorned who knew fury. Men might as well.

"I think," she mused slowly, "we shall proceed to Sidmouth at once. As soon as John Coachman has had a nap and Perkins can repack my trunks we shall be on our way to the south coast. Does that meet with your approval, my new companion?"

Miss Pettibone gasped, then used her linen napkin to dab the corners of suspiciously bright gray eyes. "Thank you, my lady. You are most kind."

"I also think that I should very much like to have a friend. I have no one I may trust, other than Perkins, and I find you eminently trustworthy. We share the same dislikes, after all." She also knew that Miss Pettibone had brought impeccable references with her and came from a perfectly fine, if poor, family. "Do you think you might forget 'my lady' and call me Georgiana?"

"If you wish, my lady—that is, Georgiana. Goodness, when I fled Ware Court, I had no notion I would land on my feet in such an agreeable manner." Elspeth bestowed a watery smile on her benefactress.

"By the way, you are acquainted with Bel? We shall have to take him with us. I am enormously fond of the cat."

"He slept at the foot of my bed last night, evidently thinking I might need his protection," Miss Pettibone said with a wry shake of her head.

"Good." Georgiana rose from the table. "I shall put our plans in motion, then. As soon as we are packed, we shall depart."

It was actually six hours before Georgiana entered her traveling coach with Elspeth at her heels, followed by an unruffled Perkins who took all the changes in her life with calm certitude. Georgiana suspected that Elspeth possessed nothing but the most dreary of bonnets, so begged her to take one of Georgiana's bounty.

"No, do not deny me this pleasure," she insisted when she saw how well the chip straw with the pink and gray knots of ribands became her new friend. Georgiana decided that when they reached Sidmouth they would seek the services of a mantuamaker and outfit Elspeth in attire suitable for a companion. When she informed her new friend of her fate, Elspeth objected.

"My dear, what is proper for a governess is not necessarily

so for a companion. I'd not wish to be thought niggardly, you know. And I find the prospect of buying things that make you look pretty quite to my liking."

Elspeth sank back against the cushions with a dazed look on her face that lasted for some hours. She sat, her hand threaded through Bel's thick coat, absently staring out at the scenery quickly moving past them.

Georgiana elected to overnight along the way so she might have her own horses once she reached Sidmouth. So it was that the journey south was far more leisurely than the bolt from Kenyon Hall had been. It suited the ladies to a tee.

Jason searched the ballroom for the beautiful widow and concluded at long last that she had gone to her room to prepare for their romantic interlude. Feeling in prime form and eager to begin what he felt would be a splendid association with the widow, for he was certain she would not bore him for some time to come, he marched up the stairs and along the hall to where he knew her room to be with an air of expectancy perhaps heightened by the wine he'd consumed.

He rapped softly on the door.

Silence reigned within.

At last, puzzled at her coyness, or whatever possessed her not to respond to his impatient knock, he turned the knob to enter the room. It lay in darkness with only dim light from the grate and the moonlight without to aid him.

Puzzled still more, he fumbled with lighting a candle from the coals in the grate. He rose to look about him, holding the candle high. It was then he realized she could scarcely have answered him when the room was empty! The wary widow was not here.

At first he could scarce take it in. He checked the wardrobe to find it devoid of garments. She had left the house! He espied the folded note, then picked it up to read the contents. It was addressed to Miss Russell, declaring that Lady Ware looked forward to seeing her in London but no word to give a clue as to the reasons behind her rushed departure.

He tapped the folded note against the desk. Lady Ware had seemed receptive to his advances. He would stake his reputation that she welcomed his ardent kiss earlier this evening. What had happened? Why had she not the courtesy to tell him to his face that she did not wish his attentions? He was not a brute that he would force himself on an unwilling partner. He might have been disappointed, but, egad, he was a gentleman after all. No matter how he longed to know the widow's charms firsthand, he'd have accepted her refusal . . . reluctantly.

Dousing the candle, he quietly slipped from her empty and silent room and returned to the ball. He sought out his aunt and pretended a disinterest in the widow.

"I see Lady Ware is not about. Has she the headache and sought her bed?" He thought he sounded commendably concerned.

"T'was the oddest thing. Dear Georgiana spoke about a sudden need to return to the dower house, some calamity having occurred that required her immediate attention. I cannot think what that might have been and she gave me no chance to inquire further. She's a very private person, and one dare not intrude on that retiring nature."

Jason thought back to the quiet conversation while they had floated along the edge of the lake in the boat, how open she had been—quite as though she trusted him. What had happened to her regard for him? He wanted to know.

"She has left?"

Lady Kenyon glanced at the longcase clock that stood by the door. "I should say that she departed about an hour ago. Most considerate girl, wanted no fuss, merely slipped down the back stairs and out to the stables. Gone in a trice."

Jason mulled over this information while seeking out his friend, Musgrave.

"You look rather down for a chap soon to be in the beautiful widow's embrace," Musgrave commented while staring discreetly off into the distance.

"She decamped. Tell me, am I such an ogre that she needs flee in the night from my presence? I had thought," Jason said, sounding more aggrieved by the moment, "that we were getting along famously."

If Lord Musgrave thought that Lady Ware ought to be congratulated upon giving his friend a royal comeuppance, no sign of it appeared on his face. "Pity, that," he said with some sympathy in his manner.

"You know, I quite enjoyed her company. I looked forward to spending some time with her, learning to know her better, taking pleasure from her wit, and admiring her talent. I do not understand it."

Most likely thinking that this must be the first time in his handsome life that the earl had not been given his way, a small smile fleetingly touched Lord Musgrave's lips. "Perhaps you should visit the lady to learn what it was that upset her. That way, you could avoid committing the error in the future."

That Musgrave had not the slightest idea his suggestion would be acted upon was evident when Jason gave him an arrested look, then nodded decisively. "We shall do just that. I must remain here another two days, but then we can happen to pause at the dower house at Ware Court, perhaps even say hello to her stepson. I confess I am curious to see what manner of man he is. You will go with me?"

Musgrave shot his friend an incredulous glance, then nodded his agreement to the proposal.

So it was that three days later the earl's splendid equipage tooled along the avenue leaving Kenyon Hall in a southerly direction. Not in a mind to rush, Lord Thornbury took his time, using the silence when Musgrave dozed off to consider possible reasons for Lady Ware's decamp.

Nothing made sense to him. Her passionate response to his kiss in the scented darkness of the conservatory had seemed genuine to him. Since she was an intelligent woman, he doubted she misunderstood his oblique reference to his joining her later in the privacy of her room.

Yet, the reverse might be possible, he supposed. Given her background, she may have not realized his intent. Whatever the reason was, he jolly well intended to find out.

When they at last arrived at the dower house to one side of the avenue leading to Ware Court, he discovered that Lady Ware was not in residence. Not only that, her employees refused to give so much as a hint where she might be found.

Such loyalty was to be commended, except when he was desirous of information.

He was totally thwarted in his quest.

He did take time to inspect the rose garden of which Lady Ware was rightly proud. The gardener unbent sufficiently to inform his lordship that the cuttings brought from Kenyon Hall had been properly tended to and looked as though they would grow.

"Let us pay a brief call on the Marquess of Ware, Musgrave," Jason murmured to his friend. "I am curious about this chap. If he cannot tell us of his stepmother's whereabouts, he certainly will provide a bit of history on the lady."

The pompous butler who admitted the two gentlemen to the impressive interior of Ware Court led them along to the principle drawing room, having gauged their importance to a nicety.

The marquess proved to be a younger version of his father—plump, prosy, and quite full of his own consequence.

"Lord Thornbury, Musgrave, what may I do for you? On a tour of the Cotswolds, perhaps? Ware Court is of significance, of course. We have a rather fine collection of paintings and tapestries, not to mention the rose gardens which are at the height of flowering at the moment."

"Just passing this way," Jason said, thanking his stars that he was not obliged to spend any time with this chap. "I am most fond of rose gardens. My aunt, Lady Kenyon, has a particularly splendid collection. Perhaps you may have heard of it?"

"The rose beds were not my idea," the marquess confessed reluctantly. "My father's second wife oversaw much planting and enlarged the gardens already here."

"Ah, yes. We chanced to meet the dowager while visiting my aunt recently. I wanted to see if she had made the return journey without mishap. However, she does not seem to be in residence." Jason's words hung in the air, awaiting a reply for some moments while the marquess studied him through narrowed eyes.

"You have met her?" The marquess leaped to bold conclusions, mostly based on his own thwarted aspirations in regard to the beautiful widow. "She is a lovely creature, is she not?

No doubt she lured you on, then refused you. I washed my hands of her some time ago. Made it plain that I would not tolerate such wanton behavior in this house. Since her removal to the dower house, I have permitted no contact. I'd not wish to corrupt the children, you see."

"Naturally," Jason replied. Knowing Lady Ware, he was more inclined to believe her innocence than this windbag with the unpleasantly moist lips.

"Now she has lured our governess down the same wayward path. Woman hared off to the dower house the other day. Hope they enjoy one another." The marquess bared his teeth in what he seemed to believe to be a winning smile.

Musgrave winced and turned his attention to the view from the window.

"I should enjoy viewing your roses," Jason said, wanting to see what he could, then be off.

The marchioness chose that moment to join them, simpering her greeting and settling her plump form opposite them on one of the upholstered chairs.

If this was what the marquess had to gaze upon every day Jason could understand why he might look in the direction of Lady Ware, but it didn't excuse his behavior.

Impatient to be gone, Jason rose to his feet, thus compelling his host to do the same. "He wants to see the rose garden, Prudence. Order drinks."

"Yes, Augustus," she said with another simper.

Jason darted a disbelieving glance at the woman, then followed his host out the door and down the steps to where the rose garden spread about them in neat beds.

He thought he could detect Georgiana's influence, but knew better than to suggest something that indicated too close an acquaintance with someone he supposedly did not know well. He bent to sniff a rose here and there and murmured suitably vague comments, for he guessed the marquess took little interest in one of the prime glories of his stately home.

At last they managed to work their way through a pathetic excuse for drinks and were able to take their leave without being the wiser as to where the Dowager Lady Ware might have gone.

"She has vanished, Musgrave," Jason announced with justifiable ire as they returned to the main road and headed to the south and the coast.

"Are we bound for Brighton?" Musgrave asked hopefully.

"Actually, I have a vacant property elsewhere that I ought to check. My agent wrote some nonsense about smugglers using the lower end of the land for storage, but I cannot imagine they would be so bold."

"Smugglers? Well! I should say that it wants looking into. Where?" Musgrave said, sitting up a trifle straighter and for the first time looking quite alert.

"Sidmouth. Are you game? Do you mind missing the delights to be found with Prinney's crowd?" Jason inquired, wryly referring to their esteemed Prince Regent.

"Since they are vastly overrated, my answer must be yes, I am game, and no I shan't miss Brighton and our fat prince."

"The marquess looks as though he intends to rival him in girth, would you not agree?"

"Indeed, I'd have to agree with that. Chap's a prosy bore. Didn't know a blessed thing about his rose garden. Wager he hardly knows the gardener."

Thus dismissing the Marquess of Ware, the two gentlemen tooled along southwardly to the coast at a leisurely pace, for Jason wished to keep his own horses. Those job ones could be a dashed pain.

It was nearly a week following his departure from Kenyon Hall that the two men rattled into Sidmouth. The sleepy little fishing village had grown considerably these past years what with society wanting a summer retreat and the prince spending some time here before settling on Brighton as a summer residence.

"Quite a few people choose to visit this little town, now," Jason explained to his friend. "Since I doubt my property is in any condition to be lived in, I suggest we repair to the Royal York Hotel. Then, once I have looked the situation over, we can decide what to do."

"Sounds most agreeable to me," Musgrave said bracingly, looking about him with interested eyes.

"There is Wallis's Marine Library on the Esplanade. He has a splendid site and offers fine billiards in addition to his shop. Pity Miss Russell is not here so you might continue her education."

"Miss Russell will do nicely on her own, I believe."

The Royal York Hotel being reached at this point, they handed over their equipage to an ostler, who led it around to the mews at the rear of the building while the men entered the front of the hotel.

The proprietor was all smiles and bows for the elegant guests who had arrived without advance notice. Fortunately, he had rooms just vacated he was able to offer them, rooms with a fine view of the coast.

Since the earl was a property owner in the village, albeit one who rarely came, he was accorded a measure of respect not granted to mere visitors.

"Anyone of particular interest in town at the moment?" the earl chanced to ask while they walked along the hall to his rooms, Musgrave following discreetly behind.

Eager to please his noble guest, the proprietor said with pride, "The Dowager Marchioness of Ware is residing in the hotel at present along with her companion and maid. I believe she intends to fix her residence here for the remainder of the summer."

It was a good thing that Jason was not in the process of consuming liquid at the moment, for he would have likely choked. He gave the man a wintry smile and nodded. "I am slightly acquainted with the lady. I look forward to seeing her again. Does she dine in her rooms?"

"Indeed, milord. The lady is most particular about her privacy." It didn't seem to occur to the proprietor that offering her whereabouts to a gentleman might be construed as a violation of said privacy. Jason was not about to enlighten him.

"I suppose she frequents Wallis's?"

"The very first place she explored. I directed her to our finest mantuamaker. Her companion had a dreadful accident to her luggage. Her trunk fell off the coach and into a river, ruining everything in it. So our fine seamstress has the pleasure of whipping up an entire wardrobe for the charming and most proper lady."

"Proper lady, you say?" Musgrave ventured to say, likely thinking it was wise to divide the questioning.

"Miss Pettibone is the most proper lady I've yet to see. She and Lady Ware seem to be good friends as well. Nice when a widow can acquire a genteel companion who is pleasant to boot. I have seen some tartars, I can tell you." He seemed suddenly aware that he was rattling on and returned to a more seemly and remote attitude. "Gentlemen?"

They had a suite of rooms, a bedroom to each side of a central sitting room. While the rooms were not large, the view was exceptional.

Once the proprietor had departed and their luggage brought up, the two men gazed out of the window at the splendid view.

"I should like this even if the widow were not in residence," Jason said with an encompassing sweep of his hand.

"You mean to confront her, then?" Musgrave asked with a hint of disapproval in his voice.

"Not in the least," Jason denied. "However, should we happen to bump into one another, say upon entering Wallis's establishment, why who knows? I believe I shall tell that prosy proprietor that I wish to be unknown as far as the lady is concerned—since she desires her privacy, you know."

"Egads, you are a one, Thornbury."

"I am glad someone appreciates that fact"—Jason said, grinning—"besides Martin—who ought to be along soon. Ought not take him long to fetch additional clothes." He glanced down at the street below and whistled softly. "Look what I see."

Georgiana took a deep breath of the invigorating sea air and gave her new friend a satisfied smile.

"I really ought to protest, my, er, Georgiana," Elspeth said fondly. "What a bouncer, to tell the landlord that my trunk fell into the river and all was lost. That poor mantuamaker believes me to be near standing in my petticoats."

"And so you are. You deserve clothes that will show you to advantage."

"I cannot say why, as I have no prospects in the least. Should you marry, I will possess a bountiful wardrobe and no employment."

"Not to worry. I have no intention of ever marrying again," Georgiana said as they entered the Royal York Hotel. She paused at the desk to give instructions for tea, to be followed by a lovely dinner for two in her rooms. Perkins preferred to eat in the dining room, saying the food was fine and she learned a good deal about the other guests that way.

The women walked briskly along to their rooms where Georgiana dug out her key from the depths of her reticule while returning to the subject of Elspeth's wardrobe.

"I hope she can finish a day dress and pelisse for you quickly. The other solution is to persuade you to use one of my gowns. We are of a height and I do believe you would look quite nice in that blue muslin. Think about it. I'd not insult you with castoffs, but I wish you to look nice, not governessy."

"I wonder if your obnoxious suitor ever came to the dower house to look for you," Elspeth said, ignoring the topic of gowns for the nonce. Georgiana had confided most of the disastrous visit to Kenyon Hall to her friend. Elspeth had been suitably horrified.

"I hope he was furious," Georgiana declared militantly. "As furious as I was when I overheard him speak of seduction with such a casual air, quite as though it were nothing more than an invitation to tea. Why all men should think so ill of a poor widow is beyond me."

"Perhaps it is the same feeling they have toward a governess who is not a platter-faced dowd," Elspeth said.

"Men truly are a dreadful lot," Georgiana mused.

"They have their uses, I understand," Elspeth retorted, a twinkle in her pretty gray eyes, as she scooped up Bel to pamper him with a bit of attention.

"Yes, well, the less said about that, the better."

Elspeth paused by the window where she never tired of gazing at the seashore she had not thought she would ever view. She glanced down at the street below and frowned. "There is something impressive about that particular male down there.

He walks as though he owns the town." She held the cat below her chin, her eyes narrowed in consideration.

Georgiana hurried to see who it was that impressed her friend so greatly, but missed this sight for the man had turned to go up Fore Street.

"Most likely headed to The Old Ship," she commented, referring to the oldest of Sidmouth's buildings, rumored to be a haunt for smugglers. She crossed over to the door to let in the maid with their tea and added, "Perhaps he has business there."

"One of the *gentlemen*? Oh, dear," Elspeth cried, scandalized at the thought of a gentleman—for there had been no mistake in the man's bearing nor the cut of his coat—who consorted with infamous smugglers.

Chapter Six

Elspeth twitched the skirt of her new Gros de Naples pelisse into place, then joined Georgiana at the door to their suite, first taking care that Bel was content. Casting one last glance at her reflection in the looking glass, she shook her head in bemusement.

"You do not approve the new you?" Georgiana said with a hint of amusement in her voice.

"I cannot believe it. Should anyone give leave to doubt in miracles, I shall be the first to convince them otherwise. I scarce know myself." Elspeth pulled on a glove, slipped the cords of her new reticule over her wrist, then opened the door.

"Perkins is a dab hand at cutting hair. You now look as angelic as your nature with that halo of delicate curls about your face. Of course, it does not hurt that you wear celestial blue. You should wear that often. It becomes you vastly."

The two ladies, chatting pleasantly, made their way down to the ground floor, then out to the walk of packed sand and dirt that went from one end of Sidmouth to the other, paralleling the shoreline. The Esplanade now was the scene of leisurely strolls enjoyed by the visitors to the seaside town.

"I see there are several bathing machines. Shall you attempt a dip?" Elspeth asked in a near whisper, quite as though a sea bath was excessively daring and not something enjoyed by at least half the ladies who came to the shore.

"I believe we both will benefit from a refreshing sea bath. I understand it is most invigorating. And . . . there is no place for men to ogle the women being dipped as there is in Brighton, a vastly superior arrangement." She exchanged a look with Elspeth and both women chuckled.

"Well, I suppose if I cannot face the thought of that chilly water, I could always try the indoor Seawater Baths. Although I must say, I find they have dubious appeal," Elspeth said, wrinkling her dainty nose in consideration of something she did not consider a treat. "One would only hope that the salt is sufficiently rinsed off, for just think of that salt clinging to the skin."

"Wretched, indeed," Georgiana murmured while searching the vicinity for a glimpse of the man Elspeth had described the afternoon before. She inwardly admitted to a curiosity regarding a man who walked along as though he owned the town, not that Sidmouth was much to own. But still, that carriage bespoke position and rank. There were not that many men in this world who would assume such an attitude.

"I do not see him," Elspeth said in an undertone, for they were close to two somewhat elderly ladies coming from the other direction.

Georgiana gazed ahead, pink staining her cheeks, making an effort to be nonchalant. "I merely wished to know how many men in this world could lay claim to such grand manners."

She noticed a hunched octogenarian being pushed toward them in his wheeled chair with every evidence, in spite of being muffled to the ears, of enjoying his outing.

"Well, that is one man we may cross off our list," she said with a glance at her friend.

"I am so pleased you invited me to join you. Think what I might have missed!" Elspeth said with a most charming little giggle.

"It would be wonderful if we might find an eligible gentleman who would carry you away with him," Georgiana mused, hunting in her reticule for her change. She wished to subscribe to the circulating library when they reached Wallis's and it would not do to have forgotten her money.

"There he is," Elspeth breathed.

Georgiana forgot about her money and looked up and about. "Where? Are you certain?"

"I could scarcely forget such bearing and assurance, believe me. He is driving that Stanhope gig coming our way."

A dog went dashing into the path of the oncoming carriage

and the driver skillfully avoided disaster with superb control of his horse.

Georgiana held her breath. Did her eyes deceive her? Surely fate would not be so cruel. Then the driver turned his carriage up Old Fore Street and was promptly lost to view before she might obtain a better sight of him.

"Gracious, Georgiana, you look as though you have seen a ghost." Elspeth gave her benefactress an anxious glance, then took a comforting hold of her arm.

"How silly of me. For a moment I thought I knew him and I do not know all that many men. I thought"—she dropped her voice to a whisper when the elderly gentleman was pushed past them—"it might be Lord Thornbury."

"No! Goodness me," Elspeth declared, making no effort to keep her voice subdued.

They reached Wallis's Marine Circulating Library and ascended the steps to the porch that was fitted out with wooden benches. Several fashionable ladies sat chatting in its shelter. Inside they found three gentlemen engaged in discussing the latest news from London—which meant something that had occurred three days past, for that was how long it took for the papers to reach Sidmouth.

"Do you know," the man who served them said, "we had a well-known authoress visit Sidmouth some years ago—Miss Austen," he concluded importantly. "She spent time in Lyme Regis as well. We have a goodly number of interesting people come here from time to time. Even our Regent has deigned to visit our fair village."

Georgiana had read something of the sort and forgotten this tidbit of news. "How nice," she murmured politely.

"Fashionable gentlemen as well. Surely you ladies will attend the assemblies at the London Hotel on Fore Street. It is quite the thing to do of an evening, if I may say so."

"Fore Street," Elspeth said. "That is the first turning off the Esplanade going west from the Royal York Hotel, is it not?"

The clerk assured her that she was correct.

The two ladies selected their books, then slowly walked from the library, down the steps to retrace their path.

"He might have been going to the assembly, not meeting smugglers at The Old Ship," Elspeth ventured at last.

"If he is as you described, I would wager he went to meet smugglers. He sounds too lofty to attend a rural assembly," Georgiana said, thinking of Lord Thornbury.

"Well, in a place as small as Sidmouth, we are bound to cross his path sooner or later," Elspeth said in an attempt to console Georgiana for missing the sight.

"I believe we ought to have a cup of tea," Georgiana declared, determined to set the image of his lordship from her mind.

"It is a healing brew," Elspeth agreed.

Upon entering the Royal York they were greeted by the proprietor and invited to take tea in the pleasant room set aside for this occasion. "We have found the ladies rather enjoy a shared tea as an opportunity to become acquainted. Most are in Sidmouth on an extended stay," he explained.

It was all most genteel. Dainty white cloths covered small tables. Maids brought in pots of tea and plates of delectable tidbits. Lemon curd, clotted cream, fresh strawberries, and tiny chocolate cakes soon adorned their pretty flower-bedecked china.

"I see women are not the only ones who enjoy this. Witness the gentlemen who have just entered," Elspeth said softly.

Georgiana casually turned her head just enough to notice the pair who paused inside the door. She stiffened, quickly returning her gaze to a distant point out of the window.

"I was correct earlier. It *is* Lord Thornbury. How on earth he came to this place is beyond belief. I cannot accept that any of my staff would have revealed my whereabouts. It must be a cruel twist of fate," Georgiana said bitterly.

"Who is the handsome man with him?" Elspeth said with an overly casual manner. "His face seems vaguely familiar."

"Lord Musgrave. The baron seems to be a good friend of Lord Thornbury's."

"I knew him many years ago," Elspeth whispered, more to herself. "That was before my father made all those unwise investments and I had a future before me. His family home is not so very far from where we once lived. He has changed most agreeably."

"Oh, I am sorry if the sight of him distresses you," Georgiana cried softly. "Painful memories seem to be our lot today. Do you wish to leave, go to our rooms?"

"If you can manage the thought of facing Lord Thornbury after all that has passed between you, Lord Musgrave and my past are nothing." Elspeth exchanged a concerned look with Georgiana, then slid her gaze to the two men who approached their little table.

Georgiana froze, thinking this must be a nightmare. Things like this simply did not happen to her in broad daylight.

"Lady Ware, what a surprise," Lord Thornbury said in that warm voice that had so charmed her before she knew better what manner of cad he was.

Should she give him the cut direct? She was sorely tempted. But, suddenly aware there were any number of interested viewers to this little scene, she dare not succumb to her desires. Instead, she gave a stiff nod, not meeting his gaze.

"Lord Thornbury," she offered in a rigid manner, her words seeming to freeze in midair. "May I present my friend Miss Pettibone? We have come to Sidmouth to enjoy a respite from tedious company." She did not wish him to think she sought to renew their acquaintance and hoped to discourage any attempt on his part to further it.

"Miss Pettibone and I have met before," Lord Musgrave said, speaking for the first time. "I had not realized that the Elspeth I knew had become such a beauty." He bowed and lifted her unresisting hand to almost touch his lips, as was most proper. "I trust we may be able to renew our old friendship. I have not seen any of your family for some years—since you moved, in fact."

"What a fortuitous circumstance, Musgrave and I both chancing to meet old friends." Lord Thornbury sounded as though he was not only pleased at this encounter, but truly thought to pursue it. Wicked, wicked man, to lie so.

Georgiana bristled visibly at this fabrication. She took a reviving sip of cooling tea and merely inclined her head a notch. "If you say so," she intoned frigidly.

"You plan to attend the assemblies, of course," Lord Musgrave insisted.

"We do," Elspeth said at the same time that Georgiana said, "Not really."

Lord Thornbury chuckled, an insinuating little sound. He looked enormously amused when Georgiana flashed an indignant glance at him. Wretched man.

"I feel certain that you will wish to join everyone else who is in town," he quickly said, meaning all those fashionable people who sought a holiday at the shore away from the noise and crowds at Brighton.

"We shall see. I understand there is no Master of Ceremonies. I fear that could lead to unpleasant circumstances. One would not wish to be opportuned by a less than desirable creature. I feel sure you take my meaning, sirrah." Georgiana turned a beseeching gaze on Elspeth, begging she understand.

"I would venture to say you could hold your own with no difficulty," Lord Thornbury said, his amusement gone and now sounding quite wintry.

"It is always difficult for a woman alone, without the protection of a husband or male relative to lend her countenance. I should imagine it would be easy for an unscrupulous man to gain her confidence and then betray it and her," Elspeth said hesitantly, with an apologetic look at Georgiana for possibly revealing more than she wished.

Lord Thornbury stood silently for a moment, then bowed. "I see you will guard each other without assistance. Good day, ladies." He turned and left the room at a lordly pace with Lord Musgrave following unhappily in his wake.

"Good heavens, Elspeth, what a fine speech you just gave. I vow I could not have done better had I mulled it over for a week," Georgiana said, placing a comforting hand atop Elspeth's.

"Yes, well, I am right, you know. After what you confided in me, I could not help but think that dreadful man thought he could waltz in here and take up where he had left off. Unconscionable. Handsome devil, I must say," she added in an afterthought.

"Thornbury or Musgrave?" Georgiana demanded, her sense of humor reasserting itself.

"Oh, both, I daresay. Bennett, that is, Lord Musgrave has matured nicely. I will admit it is a trifle heart-wrenching to see him and remember all I have lost. But," and she brightened, "thanks to you, my dear Lady Ware, I have a chance to taste a bit of that now. I refuse to allow any megrims to take residence in this poor head."

"How wise you are, Elspeth. I cannot begin to assure you how happy I am that I persuaded you to join me. I feel as though we have known each other for ages. It is an enormous comfort to me to have your company, worth far more than I could ever pay you."

Elspeth cleared her throat, then gestured to the maid. "Our tea has grown cold. Please bring us a hot pot."

They finished their tea in relative silence, each absorbed with the implications of the confrontation that had occurred minutes before.

When at last they left the little tearoom, Georgiana sought out the proprietor. "I should like to see a land agent if you have such hereabouts."

"You wish to rent a house for a time? I may be able to help you. Oftentimes, someone of consequence will confide to me that he wishes to find a responsible person to lease his residence for a time. I happen to know that Rose Cottage, a charming and centrally located house, is empty. The owner was obliged to return home at a death in the family. Might you wish to view this place? It is not overly large, but newly built with every convenience and a charming design, not to mention a splendid view."

"It sounds like the very thing I need as long as the owner does not object to a cat. By the way, does Lord Thornbury stop here long?" Georgiana asked while the proprietor wrote down the direction of Rose Cottage.

"His lordship owns property in Sidmouth and has come to inspect it. I believe there is some problem, but I could not say what it might be."

The man handed Georgiana a key to the cottage that was found only after some digging about in his desk. "Here, this ought to do it. Should you be wishing to rent, let me know and I shall contact his solicitor on your behalf. We shall be sorry to lose you, my lady."

"Thank you, sir. I find I would like a bit more space and privacy. And my cat will be happier there."

"I understand."

Georgiana made her way from his desk and up the stairs to their suite in silence. Once the door was behind her she burst forth, "Oh, the irony of it all. I seek to put that man as far from me as possible and here he is literally on my doorstep. I am certain that the proprietor learned of the words exchanged between his lordship and me. That is why he graciously offered this information on a suitable cottage. No doubt he decided that a percentage of that rent is better than having me move to another hotel."

"Is there an acceptable one?" Elspeth said.

"I suppose there must be. I fear I am becoming overly suspicious of motives, thanks to our rakish lordship. I wonder, does he still think I would welcome him to my bed?"

"Somehow I strongly doubt it!" Elspeth replied.

"The widow has turned to wintry ice from a warm spring bloom. I simply cannot understand it," Jason said to his good—and long-suffering—friend.

"Could she have misunderstood your intent?"

"We have discussed this before and I still do not know. I gather I rushed my fences."

"Not like you in the least, old boy," Musgrave said with a grin.

"I would have sworn that she welcomed me. She certainly did not refuse my kiss."

Yet, when Jason thought back on it, he recalled there had been a certain freshness to her response, an untutored and innocent—if you will—reaction to his touch. Perhaps he had been mistaken as to her level of experience. If so, it had been a disastrous error, for he found his thoughts fixed on the beautiful Georgiana, finding that he missed her company greatly.

"What about your house? Learned anything more?"

"I drove over this morning to see what I might find," Jason

replied, wrenching his thoughts from the widow with difficulty. "My agent may be right, there certainly seems to have been something odd going on. You see, all the lots on that end of town are exceedingly long and narrow until you come to mine. I own a fat, pie-shaped acreage through which runs the Peak Hill road. Because I have beach frontage, albeit quite steep, and direct access to Peak Hill road, it would be a prime area for smugglers to work."

"They could haul the goods up the cliff, then to the road and away," Musgrave said thoughtfully. "And who would be the wiser? After a look at that road, I doubt if there is much traffic on it."

"A more winding and hazardous stretch I cannot imagine," Jason agreed. "I have been told that track goes back into dim reaches of history, perhaps before the Romans occupied this country. There is a beacon on Peak Hill to raise an alarm in the event of a French invasion. 'Tis used by the Sea Fencibles," he explained, referring to that group of fishermen and boatmen who manned the battery at Fort Field as well as the beacon.

"So—what do you plan to do?"

"We shall wander down to The Old Ship and keep our ears open. I suggest we not look too lordly."

"Right," Bennett replied, his expression aptly conveying the unlikelihood that his friend might look less than he was.

Some hours later they ventured down the stairs and out the side door. It did not take them long to settle into a dim recess at The Old Ship with a tankard of ale in hand. The dark-beamed, low-ceilinged place had an L-shaped room with benches and settles for seating, with crude tables set about. Although there were windows, not much could be seen through them.

"I suspect that the best we can do this evening is to listen carefully and take note of anything we might hear."

Musgrave nodded in agreement.

They sat there for some time, having a second tankard and nursing that along as best they could. At last, Jason requested a glass of brandy.

"There is no doubt it is fine French quality," Jason murmured to Musgrave in a barely heard undertone. "The chance that it is anything else is unlikely. But how to learn who is behind the smuggling?"

Musgrave sipped his fine wine and agreed.

"Shame it has to be like this; desirable fine wine and high duty make the profits irresistible."

They sat for a while longer, but learned nothing useful. Jason surmised that they would have to become regulars before anyone let their guard down sufficiently to speak within their hearing.

"Come, we may as well go see if Lady Ware and Miss Pettibone attend the assembly this evening."

"Is there a possibility she might take flight again before you learn the truth of her departure from Kenyon Hall?" Musgrave inquired while they walked back to the Royal York.

"I cannot say. Perhaps if I play my cards most carefully she will think I no longer have an interest in her and relax her vigilance." Jason rubbed his jaw in frustration. He had never in his life encountered such an exasperating woman. She was beautiful, talented, desirable, available, and yet had turned her back on him in no uncertain terms.

"Perhaps were I to renew my friendship with Elspeth Pettibone I might learn something from her?" Musgrave offered in a most casual manner.

"She seems a charming young woman. Fancy you knowing her." Jason shook off his irritation with Lady Ware to grin at his friend. "Somehow I suspect that your action would not be overly painful."

"True. I knew her as a child and always enjoyed her company. Knew her older brother better, but since we lived so close, I met the entire family. Father was a nodcock if there ever was one. Thought he was such a downy one and he was fleeced instead. Invested in every daft scheme that came along."

"A South Sea Bubble sort, eh?"

"Indeed," Musgrave replied while following Jason up the stairs to their rooms.

Within an hour the two gentlemen, suitably attired and looking as though they were to enter a London gathering, came up the stairs to the locale of the Sidmouth Assembly Rooms on the upper floor of the London Hotel.

The musicians played a sprightly country dance and the group in the line looked to be enjoying themselves immensely.

"I believe she is at the far end of the room," Jason observed to his quiet friend.

"As is Miss Pettibone. She *certainly* has matured well," Musgrave observed.

"So often when one knows a woman as a child, it is a disappointment to see her as an adult. You are fortunate she is quite charming and presentable."

"Thornbury, should you have the rattlebrained notion that I do this solely for your benefit, do so abuse yourself of that idea," Musgrave said irritably.

"Well, well," was Jason's only comment.

"I intend to dance. Do you prop up the wall or join me in my pursuit?"

"Indeed, but not the widow tonight. I shall seek safer quarry. I saw a fine pair of eyes at that tearoom at the hotel and I believe that is her in the pink gown if I make no mistake. Since there is, as Lady Ware so nicely pointed out, no Master of Ceremonies to provide an introduction, I shall make my own way."

"You always do," Musgrave said with a slight smile.

By the end of the country dance, Lord Thornbury had presented himself to the older woman who was at the side of the pretty young thing with the attractive pair of green eyes flashing out of a winsome face framed with an abundance of auburn hair. Her gown was acceptable even by London standards, and he thought her an agreeable introduction to local society.

Musgrave found his way through the gathering until he reached Elspeth's side. "At last. There must be well over sixty people here this evening."

"Since they present assemblies only on Wednesday evenings—as does Almack's, I understand—those who enjoy dancing are sure to be here. How are you?" she inquired. "And your family? I have heard nothing from anyone regarding the Musgraves."

"All in good time," he said, taking her arm while he guided her to a set that was forming. "I insist upon a dance before we commence on past history. I have just as many questions about you and your family, you know."

Elspeth paled, but valiantly tilted her chin and offered her hand for the dance as they began the first pattern.

Georgiana watched the bit of byplay and surmised that Elspeth would have mixed emotions regarding conversation with Lord Musgrave. Looking about to see if his friend deigned to attend a modest, though pleasant, assembly it was not long before she saw him guiding a pretty young thing in pink through the intricacies of a cotillion.

He danced well. He looked even better, drat the man. Garbed in a corbeau velvet coat, his pristine white marcella waistcoat must be the envy of every man present, and as to the fit of those biscuit-colored breeches above white-stockinged legs. Well! *Why* must she be attracted to a man like him! She turned her face away from that distraction to welcome the older gentleman who had presented himself shortly after she and Elspeth had arrived.

"Major Deane, what a nice evening this is."

"Would you join me in a glass of punch? 'Tis not the best, perhaps, but not to be despised, especially since it is becoming warm in here."

She accepted his offer and went along to the area where a splendid punch bowl was set out with dishes of little cakes. She sampled one and thought the attendees at Almack's, were tales she had heard true, would envy her, for the cakes were excellent.

"I understand you plan to stay here some time, Lady Ware."

"Word travels fast," she commented with a nod. "I do plan to make Sidmouth home for a number of weeks, although I am not sure precisely how long. The seaside is offering more diversion than I had expected. This is a charming assembly."

"Dance floor is said to be one of the finest around; excellent spring you may have observed."

She glanced back and had the misfortune to espy Lord Thornbury performing an elegant chassé in fine form. "So I have," she said, feeling oddly neglected. It was utterly absurd.

She did not want Lord Thornbury's attentions in the least, yet when she saw him with that chit in the pink muslin she felt almost hurt, abandoned.

"Would you do me the honor of accepting me as a partner, my lady?"

"I should be pleased, Major." She set down her glass, then placed her hand politely on his proffered arm and walked at his side to a newly forming dance. She quickly discovered that her nemesis was to be part of the set of two couples. What odious proximity!

Jason watched Lady Ware join him and his partner and stifled a smile with difficulty. Oh, how she hated this. She would in the course of the dance be required to take his hands when they did the last figure, holding them while they made it around a circle. But he had to admit she displayed elegant carriage and he had no doubt that when she reached the *hands across* point that she would look him in the face as demanded by the dance. Not only that, but he'd wager the woman would not reveal by so much as a twitch of a muscle how she detested touching him.

He looked forward to the dance exceedingly.

It was as he had predicted. Lady Ware, or Georgiana as he had thought of her when thinking at all, was truly an elegant dancer, holding her arms high and graceful, making every other woman in the room seem clumsy by comparison.

True, she made not the slightest effort to say a word when they waited while the others took their part. But neither did she shrink from his touch. And that made him smile.

And then it was time to depart.

There were quite a number of folk ambling back the short distance to the Royal York following the conclusion of the assembly. With the difficulty of stabling and most carriages off at the mews, few sought to bring their equipage out for the matter of a few yards. Flambeaux led the way and a number of ladies complained a little about the effect of the dirt on their slippers.

"I shall see you on the morrow, Elspeth," Lord Musgrave insisted when he left her at the door to the rooms she shared with Lady Ware.

She promised nothing, only waited for Georgiana to unlock their door.

Georgiana had tried to avoid Lord Thornbury on the walk back to the hotel but the man proved impossible to shake.

"Shall I see you as well?" he murmured.

"I think not, my lord. I shall not see you *later*. We shan't be here." With that pithy remark she unlocked her door and whirled inside.

Chapter Seven

"Now that we have viewed it, I am persuaded that the removal to Rose Cottage will be far better all around. Think how Bel will enjoy being able to roam at will." Georgiana fondly cuddled her pet, scratching him under his chin until he closed his eyes in a blissful purr.

"Yes, milady," Perkins agreed with a fervent nod of her head. Since it was her responsibility to take the cat out for a walk of sorts twice a day, she welcomed the change as much as the cat.

"He is an amazing animal, I must say that for him," Elspeth said. "You will have to cage him in order to persuade those men to gather our belongings for our move. Bel quite terrified the lad who came up earlier," Elspeth said with a grin.

"All will be in order. Bel understands me when I tell him to cease."

"If you say so," Elspeth replied, sounding unconvinced.

"Did you enjoy your first assembly here?" Georgiana asked casually, walking to the window while still cuddling the cat. She wished to see if that certain lordly gentleman was afoot this morning before she took her leave.

"I certainly did," Elspeth said with a soft look entering her eyes, one that quickly disappeared. "However, I am certain that Lord Musgrave wishes no more than to have a neighborly chat about our mutual relatives. I must recall my position, Georgiana."

"Are you trying to convince me or yourself?" Georgiana took note of a particular gentleman striding away from the hotel and relaxed. She turned to face her friend while depositing Bel on the padded wicker basket she'd found to suit him.

"Both, I suppose. When do you plan to leave here?" Elspeth asked, gathering her shawl from a chair.

"Immediately, if not sooner. Perkins, are the trunks packed? If so, call the men to come for them. John Coachman should be here shortly. I sent word earlier that I required him. Fortunately we can make arrangements to stable the carriage and horses here even after we move."

Elspeth gave Georgiana a puzzled look, then went to her room to see if any bits and pieces of her few belongings remained. Perkins had been most thorough. Not even a riband lurked undetected.

The removal went smoothly. The proprietor assured Georgiana that he would welcome her to join them for tea anytime she wished. And he hoped she would enjoy her visit to Sidmouth. No doubt he also hoped she would either write others to join her, or sing the praises of this pleasant little seaside village to her friends. If he only knew.

If one thought that Rose Cottage was a simple little place, cozy and small, one would be far off the mark, Georgiana thought consideringly as they drove up the well-groomed avenue to the house. It was a large house with a thatched roof and romantic Gothic windows. Five dormer windows peeped out from beneath the thatch. Two of the six chimneys had smoke trailing up from them in a sort of friendly welcome. As they drew to a halt before the front entry, she glimpsed the extensive gardens behind the house, the main point that had been in its favor. There were simply gorgeous roses in bloom.

Elspeth shook out her skirts while surveying their new home. She glanced at Georgiana and picked up a small case to carry into the house.

Georgiana followed with Bel in her arms.

"This is far enough removed so that we shall not feel as though just anyone may drop in on us," Georgiana said with great satisfaction.

"I trust you mean Lord Thornbury?"

"Well, he shan't be coming across us at the hotel, will he? On the other hand, if Lord Musgrave has any brains at all, he will find you here."

Elspeth sent her new friend a conscious look, then confessed, "I did chance to meet him in the hallway when I was on my way to the carriage. It happened I mentioned we were removing to Rose Cottage. I trust this was not dreadfully forward of me."

Unable to scold Elspeth for wishing to see her old neighbor again, Georgiana shook her head. "Of course not. And as to Lord Thornbury, I very much doubt if he intends to seek us out after last evening. Why, he scarcely looked at me, even when we were obliged to clasp hands in that last dance." She ignored his comment about seeing her today.

If Elspeth thought that Georgiana sounded a trifle piqued, she certainly didn't give voice to it. Exchanging a glance with Perkins, she merely took her small case and asked which of those bedrooms was to be hers.

"Take any you wish," Georgiana said vaguely. "They are all of a muchness. Carry on, ladies. I am going to inspect the gardens."

With Bel padding along at her side, Georgiana headed for the lure of the rose gardens, intent upon inspecting them as well as the other exotic specimens said to grow here. What a good bit of luck that the owner had to be absent just when she needed a retreat. Perhaps, if she might do so without endangering the health of the bush, she might even gather a slip from a particularly nice plant.

The unexpected shriek was enough to cause a body heart failure. She and Bel quickly moved around the corner in the garden to encounter a pair of peacocks who immediately took umbrage with Bel. Tails fanned out, indignant sounds issuing forth in great volume, they challenged Bel to a duel for property rights.

"Nasty birds," Georgiana shouted, "be gone with you." She gathered Bel in her arms, more to protect the birds than him. "You would make mincemeat of those creatures, wouldn't you dear Bel?"

"I'd not count on that. Peacocks are not the mildest of birds," a familiar voice said over her shoulder.

Georgiana took a deep breath, then slowly turned around to face him. "Good day, Lord Thornbury. Are you not a little out of your way here? And, by the by, my Bel can well take care of himself."

"Musgrave wanted to see Miss Pettibone. I came along for the drive." He leaned upon an elegant walking stick with a clouded amber head and looked perfectly at ease—just as he had at Kenyon Hall while engaged in the slow but effective process of seducing her. Or trying to.

"Oh." She felt rather put upon. Cuddling Bel until he protested, she gently placed the enormous cat on the ground. Here he studied Lord Thornbury with a disconcerting stare and twitching tail that had put lesser men into a quake.

"That is a rather *large* animal. You are certain it is a mere cat?"

Perhaps something in Lord Thornbury's voice irritated Bel. Georgiana always maintained the cat understood every word that was said and that the use of the word *mere* upset him. There was nothing *mere* about Bel. At any rate, the creature launched himself at his lordship, all four paws with claws extended for battle.

"What the—" His lordship lost his balance and tumbled ignominiously to the grass, quite stunned with surprise, the cat atop him shredding that exquisite marcella waistcoat to bits. In spite of flailing arms, Bel then took a swipe at the biscuit-colored breeches and for good measure dug a series of channels in one of the perfectly shined Hessians.

Horrified, even as she wanted to laugh at the sight of his helpless lordship, Georgiana called Bel to rights. Offering a hand to Lord Thornbury, she apologized for her pet. "Naturally I will compensate you for the harm done. You have but to present me a bill. I fear he simply does not like men. He adores Elspeth and Perkins and has been my most devoted shadow ever since he walked in and took charge of the dower house."

"You let *him* take control?" he said with an aghast look at the smug cat that now sat cleaning its paws.

"Consider trying to change his habits, sirrah," she said in reply with a fond look at the cat. "He has been most helpful in times past. My protector, as it were."

Lord Thornbury glared at the cat that looked back at him

with equal loathing. "How you can like such an impossible beast is beyond me," his lordship muttered while assessing the damage to his person; ruined waistcoat, his breeches likely beyond mending, and as for his boot—he doubted even the estimable Martin could repair those scratches in one of Hoby's finest. Jason was lucky to have his coat undamaged, although he suspected there would most likely be grass stains on his elbows.

"We have much in common. Only Bel is able to give vent to his feelings more easily than I." She looked away from Lord Thornbury, not wishing to see what might be revealed in her face.

"What happened, Georgiana?" he said after a moment of strained silence.

"I have not given you leave to address me so, my lord. And as far as I know, the cat took a dislike to you. He has impeccable taste in people." With that, Georgiana curtsied gracefully, then sailed to the house without a backward look.

"I didn't mean the cat, drat it. I meant you!" Lord Thornbury took after Georgiana, swinging his stick with each angry stride.

Since the arched French windows opened directly from the drawing room onto the gardens, it was a simple matter to go straight in where he might confront her again—keeping a safe distance from the cat, of course. Although upon reflection there was little more harm the cat might inflict.

"Good grief, man, what happened to you?" Musgrave said with a start when he caught sight of his friend.

"Watch out for that cat. It ought to be declared a weapon of war. Perhaps you might train it to battle the Frenchies." Lord Thornbury stalked over to a comfortable-looking sofa and without a by your leave dropped down on it to glare at Georgiana.

Elspeth rose as though to leave, with Musgrave joining her.

"Pray do not feel you must withdraw," Georgiana said urgently, her voice sounded strained. "Lord Thornbury and I have nothing to discuss—that you could not overhear at any rate. I have offered to make amends for Bel's damage. I expect a sizable bill, my lord, and I shall be vexed should you think to spare me."

Lord Thornbury rose and slowly walked to tower over Georgiana. She refused to back away from him, glaring right back in his face. Seconds ticked past. Not a sound could be heard save an annoyed peacock in the distance.

"Spare you? My dear, I have no desire to spare you a thing." He stood, fists clenched while he gazed at her with an exasperated expression before turning to leave the house as he had entered.

"I shall see you later, Miss Pettibone. I had better go. 'Tis his carriage." Musgrave hurried after his friend, looking as though he would cheerfully throttle both him and Georgiana, not to mention Bel, the cat.

Georgiana stood in the spot where Lord Thornbury had confronted her for some moments before turning aside to collapse on a convenient chair. "Merciful heavens, if you could have but seen him when Bel knocked him down. I'll wager nothing of that sort has happened to him before, nor will again," Georgiana began. Then she put her hand to her mouth and her shoulders began to shake.

"Georgiana, dear, I feel sure everything will be all right," a distressed Elspeth said worriedly.

At this bit of comfort, Georgiana burst into giggles, which soon became helpless laughter. "If you could have seen him," she gasped. "His expression was beyond price. And his poor waistcoat was utterly shredded. That dreadful cat deliberately took a swipe at his breeches as well as that boot. It was as though Bel sensed my anger and in his own way paid Lord Thornbury in kind, so to speak."

Her laughter subsided, she then turned to Elspeth. "I am sorry we interrupted your time with Lord Musgrave with our little contretemps."

"I believe he intends to rent a carriage of his own and call for me to go for a drive, if that is agreeable with you. I suspect he doesn't trust Bel."

"Odd, Bel never gave him so much as a glance." Georgiana frowned, giving the cat a curious look where it now curled up in the padded wicker basket. "Distinctly odd," she said before rising to find her room and a change of clothes.

Jason ignored the scandalized looks that came his way when he entered the hotel to go to his rooms. Martin was another matter entirely.

"My lord," he said with a shudder, "that was one of our favorite waistcoats. I doubt a tailor can repair the breeches, but I shall try. As to that boot! What sort of battle were you in, pray tell?"

"A fierce wild animal attacked me without provocation." Jason pulled off the offending waistcoat, dropped it on the floor, then followed suit with the boots and breeches.

"A cat belonging to Lady Ware took exception to his presence," Lord Musgrave interpreted for Martin's benefit, not wishing for him to be so grossly misinformed. "I don't think it appreciated the cut of the waistcoat."

"I trust you will locate a decent tailor for me, should I run out of waistcoats? Perhaps you had best take one of my good ones to show as a pattern? I may need them before this is over."

Martin nodded discreetly, gathering the ruined garments, while taking note that the lining of the waistcoat was still intact and like new, possibly usable as a pattern.

When the valet had assisted his master into clean clothes and removed the others for possible repair, Musgrave leaned against the window and studied his friend.

"You don't think you have had enough punishment? You want more?"

"I asked her what happened and she fobbed me off with some blasted nonsense about that miserable cat. The more she evades a reply the more I am determined to find out the truth of the matter. You heard her tantalizing little squib last night after the assembly, didn't you? She said, and I quote, 'I shall not see you *later*. I shan't be here.' "

"I heard," Musgrave admitted. "But I fail to see the connection."

"Her look was significant. There was a slight emphasis on

the word *later*. Then to say she wouldn't be here was a definite connection. I am certain of it. But the *why* eludes me."

"What do you intend to do about your house?" Musgrave questioned, seeking to turn the topic to something other than the differences with Lady Ware.

"I instructed my agent to busy himself with completing repairs. I believe we could move in there by the end of the week. There is a bit of painting required, but we can live with that if necessary."

"Shall we go out and mingle with the locals? I suspect that is the best way to learn anything about the smuggling going on about here," Musgrave offered.

"No doubt. I heard the name Jack Rattenbury yesterday when a clerk thought I was not paying attention. I recall hearing or reading that name elsewhere. The connotation was such that it drew my mind to the smuggling."

"I know it is against the law, but when I think of the poor beggars who earn a few shillings bringing the stuff ashore I cannot help but think it is harsh to send them to prison. Some of them look near to starvation. It's the man financing the effort who needs to be caught."

"Do you think there is anything to the story that gold is being smuggled out to help Napoleon?" Jason asked as they left the rooms to find their way to High Street.

"I hope not," Musgrave replied fervently.

The two men ambled along the various streets, pausing to look over the fine church and yard, then on to the top of the street before retracing their steps. Rather than return to the hotel, they walked on to survey the river Sid.

"Not a very grand sight, is it?" Musgrave said.

"There is a ford farther up. With only one bridge a good deal inland, it is nice to have a shorter way to cross over, should one wish."

"Chap mentioned there is a fine view of the bay from atop the hill."

"You could see my piece of land from there, I expect. Want to drive up there for a look?" Jason asked, hoping to find something other than the smuggling and Lady Ware with which to occupy his mind.

Within a short time, the horse had been put to the leased gig and the two men set off to see the view to be had from Salcombe Hill.

Jason had brought his glass with him so that when they at last reached the peak, he was able to pick out his property with ease. Then he moved the glass to the left. Now he could see the coastline where, if so inclined, smugglers would bring cargo ashore to be hoisted up, then taken away to Peak Hill road.

"It is possible the smugglers operate here," he said, handing the glass to Musgrave, who put it to his eye so he might evaluate the scene for himself.

"What I'd like to know is how a few men can be tied up in this scheme without more people knowing. Although I have heard of villages where the entire population is involved."

"Find out what sort of fabrics that local seamstress has in stock. Miss Pettibone ought to give you a pretty good account since she has spent some hours at the place. French silks and laces should be simple to identify."

"Elspeth said the woman feeds a family of four on what she earns. Her husband was killed in battle on the Peninsula. I'll not turn her in, should I discover anything amiss."

"You sound like a Whig."

"Maybe I do," Musgrave said, then walked along the ridge to stare down at the waves breaking on the shore below. When he sensed Jason had joined him, he added, "There is something wrong with financing war after war with money wrung from these poor devils. Bad enough we send them off to fight. To take the bread from their mouths is worse yet. The Corn Laws which are supposed to help them only make their existence worse."

"But smuggling is against the law," Jason argued, mostly to see what his surprising friend would say to that.

"There are times when the law becomes insupportable," Musgrave replied before turning the topic to the house and the repairs needed.

The day was well advanced when they brought the gig back to the mews. Rather than enter the hotel, they returned to High Street and the dubious charms of The Old Ship.

The interior was hazy and dimly lit. Men stood grouped in clusters, deep in conversation while the curls of smoke from their pipes rose lazily to the dark beams above. Jason ordered brandy as did Musgrave. They found rough-hewn seats in shadows and again settled down to sip and listen. Eventually they rose and made their way back to the hotel.

"Martin will have to air my coat for a day after that," Jason said with a wry grin at his friend.

"Mine as well. I trust you felt it was worth the time, however." Musgrave gave Jason a quizzical look.

"Indeed. Those scraps of conversation we overheard made it plain that a shipment of brandy is expected soon. Precisely *when* depends on the weather and possible appearance of a preventative officer," Jason said, referring to the customs official.

"Are you going to notify that gentleman?" Musgrave asked tersely, frowning at his friend.

"How can I? I don't know who the bloody chap is," Jason replied irritably. "I may elect to keep an eye from near the beacon on Peak Hill."

"I've a mind to visit Elspeth this evening."

"Fine. I'd as soon go there alone. Don't want you involved more than necessary in the event something might go wrong."

"Any chance it might?"

"Who can say?"

Musgrave walked up the stairs to their rooms with a thoughtful expression on his face while Jason mentally prepared himself for an interesting evening.

Elspeth was delighted to entertain her old friend that evening. She hated to admit that life had become a trifle dull since removing to Rose Cottage after the relative excitement of living at the Royal York Hotel.

"Not that the cook isn't excellent, nor the prospect perfectly charming," she explained in a hushed voice while Georgiana had momentarily left the room. "I did enjoy seeing so many people and watching the sea from the window."

Musgrave nodded, adding, "I know precisely what you

mean. I never tire of watching the movement of the waves. Restful, you know."

"Exactly. And where is Lord Thornbury this evening, if I might inquire?" she concluded with a glance at the door.

"Jason went off to Peak Hill to see if there is any truth to a possible landing of smugglers this evening," Musgrave confided quietly to his boyhood friend.

"Did I hear you say smugglers?" Georgiana asked, entering the room as he uttered the fateful words.

"Well, it is doubtful they will land tonight. Even if they know the coast like the back of their hand, there is a strong wind rising and it would be difficult to make a landing where Thornbury suspects they will," Musgrave said, aware he had been indiscreet in permitting Lady Ware to hear his words. He knew Elspeth and could trust her with his life. Lady Ware had proven to be a different matter altogether.

A maid entered with a tray holding the makings of a light supper. She arranged it on a low table, then left, while the three occupants remained in strained silence.

"What would they do to him if he was found?" Georgiana queried at last, unable to eat a bite of the appetizing food.

Musgrave, unaffected by the thought of his friend facing a little danger, happily dug in, enjoying something that had more flavor than hotel fare. "Shoot him, perhaps. Knock him in the head, most likely."

"Gracious!" Georgiana said, looking more worried than might have been expected, giving her stated feelings about his lordship.

Bel entered the room, quite ignored Lord Musgrave, and jumped up to curl about in Elspeth's lap. The three stared at the cat with amazement.

"Ought I be insulted that I am ignored?" Lord Musgrave said with humor.

"I wonder why he doesn't attack you," Georgiana mused.

"Perhaps he does not see Bennett as a threat to you, Georgiana," Elspeth said, using her friend's boyhood name.

"Is that possible?" Georgiana said. "Curious and rather fascinating theory at any rate. Excuse me, please, I just recalled something I must do."

Leaving the cat with the pair, all three oblivious to her departure, Georgiana swiftly went to her room to change into a black gown left over from her mourning that had somehow managed to come along in the trunk.

Leaving the house by the back entrance, she managed to put a sidesaddle on her mare, then ride from the small, neat stables without those in the house the wiser.

She had perused a map of the local area sufficiently to know where Lord Thornbury's property was located. In addition John Coachman had provided information on roads in the area, should she be wishing to ride out with Elspeth instead of a groom, as she occasionally did.

She made for the Esplanade, then turned west along Peak Hill road. It rose steeply, twisting and turning until she reached the top. There was nothing to see from here, scrub and scraggly trees preventing her from a view of the sea. But, she did identity Jason's horse in the darkness, tied to a modest tree off in the deeper shadows. She dismounted quickly, looped the reins over a low branch, then turned to access the area.

She proceeded with great caution, making her way in furtive steps, feeling for hazards with outstretched hands. Thus it was that she came on Jason. She put out a hand and encountered a body—warm and softly wrapped.

"Oh!" she gasped. She wasn't fast enough to back away from him. Instead she found her wrist grasped and she was pulled against that hard frame, her face buried in soft knitted wool.

"Umph," she sputtered, spitting out a mouthful of fuzz.

"What the devil are you doing up here, may I ask?" he demanded in a low tone, sounding more dangerous than any smuggler. "This is not the assembly rooms, my lady."

"What if those smugglers come and you get hit on the head? You will need someone to help you. Lord Musgrave is making sheep's eyes at Elspeth with the cat as guardian and is no use whatsoever."

"You were worried about me!" he said in slightly more than a whisper.

"No," she insisted. "I merely felt that as a friend—sort of—it was my Christian duty to see that you were not killed."

"So you put on a black gown, saddled your horse, and rode up here in the middle of the night? To do your Christian duty?"

"You don't have to laugh at me," she said, clearly wishing she had stayed at home. The blasted man sounded ready to burst into chortles of glee.

"I am not inclined to laugh, my lady," he said in that voice that always sent shivers through her from one end to the other.

Perhaps she had yearned for his touch; maybe that was why she had dashed off from Rose Cottage in what had to be a harebrained manner. At any rate she did not fight when he pulled her more tightly against him and fiercely kissed her until she thought she might well dissolve into a pile of melted bones.

She wrapped her arms about him, digging her fingers into the soft wool fisherman's jersey as black as her gown. Giving as good as she received, she was utterly breathless when he drew away from her.

"So, why did you flee from Kenyon Hall when there is this between us?"

Outraged that he should spoil the moment with the reminder of what had pained her so much, Georgiana tore herself from his arms, distancing herself in the black of the night before she answered. "I *heard* you talking with Lord Musgrave. You mentioned me."

Unable to bring herself to speak further regarding a tender subject, she turned and quickly stumbled her way back to her mare. Jason was directly behind her but he tripped on a rock and half-fell, rending the air blue with his words. This allowed Georgiana to reach her horse and mount, dashing down the hill at breakneck speed.

Jason gave up on the smugglers. Had they been around Georgiana had made enough noise to warn them away. He found his horse and silently and thoughtfully made his way back to the mews.

Now where did he stand? There was no mistaking the passion in her kiss. She cared enough about him to see he was kept safe, although he shuddered to think of what might have happened should the smugglers have chanced upon her. Little fool!

He tried to recall his conversation with Musgrave the night of the ball at Kenyon Hall. What had he said? Whatever the words had been, they had sent Georgiana dashing off into the night.

Confound his memory. Whatever he said must have involved her. But what? He couldn't remember.

Back in his room, he changed clothing and settled down with a bottle of fine brandy he had bought at The Old Ship.

Georgiana rested her head against the mare's side after removing the saddle. Was there any fool in the world more stupid than she? Mindlessly she rubbed down the horse, then put the saddle away. It was a simple matter to slip into the house by one of the many French windows. This house was about as secure as a wicker cage with no clasp.

Which thought led her back to Bel's odd behavior. Had the entire world turned upside down?

Chapter Eight

Georgiana quickly changed from her black to the gown she had worn before her utterly stupid and dangerous chase to the Peak. Collecting her shattered nerves, she hurried down to the entryway to find Lord Musgrave about to take his leave.

"Are you unwell, dear?" Elspeth asked after a sharp look at her friend.

"I feel better now, thank you," Georgiana said in a half-truth that bordered on silly. That was like saying one felt better after being hit in the head—the pain continued even though the battering ceased.

With a questioning frown, Lord Musgrave bid Elspeth good night after a promise to call for her the following day to take a drive about the countryside.

Once the door was shut behind his departing figure, Elspeth guided Georgiana to the drawing room and urged her onto a chair. "You look rather odd, if I may say so," she said mildly. "You were a long time in your room. Hanging out the window, perhaps?" She plucked a leaf from Georgiana's hair and held it before her.

"I do believe the sea air has addled my wits. When I realized that Lord Thornbury was up on Peak Hill, likely to consort with the smugglers, I completely lost my head. Would you believe I dashed up those stairs and changed into that dreadful black gown, then hared off to the Peak with God knows what excuse in the back of my brain."

"Did you find him? Or the smugglers?" Elspeth asked with breathless curiosity.

"Indeed, I found him, the utterly awful man. He is a cad, a bounder, a . . . a . . . rake!"

"No!" This was followed by a properly horrified silence before Elspeth asked, "What did he do?"

"He accused me of worrying about him and then when I said it was no more than my Christian duty to see he was not killed, he laughed at me."

"It does seem a bit strange, if I may say so. Your behavior, that is." Elspeth compressed her lips as though to keep from smiling.

"Of course it is strange. I said my wits had gone begging! I am quite as mad as a March hare!"

"And then?" Elspeth prompted gently. "After he laughed?"

"And then," Georgiana said with a sigh, "the dratted man kissed me. I had run into him full tilt, you see, so I was rather close to him, and it must have seemed to him that I was asking for something other than the time of day."

"Oh, Georgiana," Elspeth said, covering her face with her hands and peeping over them at her friend as her shoulders shook in silent laughter.

"Had he been a gentleman, he would not have taken advantage of me," Georgiana insisted. "It is not the first time he has been so bold. I think I neglected to tell you that he kissed me while in the conservatory at Kenyon Hall as well. That was shortly before I learned the kiss was in aid of seducing me."

"Do you suppose he yet continues his intent?" Elspeth asked, becoming serious.

"You mean, does he still desire to seduce me by fair means or foul? Oh, I cannot accept that to be true. I mean, the wretched man scarcely looked at me while attending the assembly. I hardly believe that is the behavior of a man who wants me in his bed. And he was utterly furious after Bel attacked him, which ought to have scotched any remaining desire. Which, by the by, brings me to the curious behavior of that cat. It is not long since he literally tore the clothing from Lord Thornbury's front and yet this evening he quite ignored Lord Musgrave. Most curious. Pity that cats cannot talk. I would dearly love to know what his opinion of Lord Thornbury is in so many words."

"I believe Bel has constituted himself your protector. Perhaps he senses that predatory desire within his lordship in your regard. One predatory male recognizing another, so to speak."

"Gracious!" Georgiana said, sinking back against her chair while contemplating this notion. "I can believe I need a glass of sherry. Join me?" She rose from her chair to pour some wine into pretty crystal glasses, handing one to Elspeth before resuming her seat. There she sat, deeply in thought, slowly sipping the excellent sherry.

"Any conclusions?" Elspeth queried.

"None with regard to the cat. However, as far as Lord Thornbury is concerned 'tis best to simply avoid the man. I truly feel dreadful about the damage Bel did to his clothing. Do you think the local tailor can begin to match the superb fabric and cut of the ruined waistcoat?"

"The mantuamaker has exquisite fabrics. If she does, the tailor likely does as well."

"You think the material is French? Smuggled?" Georgiana asked.

"If you look around this town, there is a great deal of evidence that quite a bit of goods come in via the smugglers. It is a poor community otherwise, with a number of lacemakers employed to create delicate lace for the London market via Honiton. Fishing is really the primary industry. Even with the influx of visitors and resultant building of seaside cottages, life for the locals is not easy. At least this sherry is legal, having been traded with Spain for our fish. I fear the profit from fishing does not spread to the entire town, hence the irresistible lure for smuggling."

"Goodness, where did you learn all this?"

"I chat with the mantuamaker, the baker, and any other shopkeeper I happen on. My modest garb proclaims me as one of them. I fear when my grand wardrobe is complete, they will not speak to me again—other than to say yea or nay."

"I shall make a point to purchase some of the lace and see what else I may do in my own small way." Georgiana set her empty glass on the nearest table, then rose, yawning. "Come, let us go to bed, for I would forget what an idiot I have been for just a little while."

"Surely his lordship will be too polite to remark on it?"

Georgiana said dryly, "The dratted man will think of some way to discompose me, you may be sure."

Jason leaned back in his chair, lifting his glass of brandy to admire the rich color in the gentle light of the two candles burning in his sitting room. The contents of the bottle on the table had sunk considerably. He turned his head as Musgrave entered the room, locking the door behind him.

"Pleasant evening?" Jason's voice had not the least slur.

"Interesting one, in any event. How about you? Learn anything about the smuggling?"

Jason shook his head, gestured to the half-empty bottle on the table, and said, "Join me?"

Pouring a glass for himself, Musgrave eased himself into the companion to the chair Jason lounged in and waited.

"Devil of a time this evening." Jason stared at the bottom of his glass.

"How so?"

"Wildest thing imaginable happened. You won't believe me." Jason put his feet up on a wooden chair conveniently near and leaned back to further contemplate his brandy.

"Well, let me decide that. What *did* occur while you prowled the grounds of Peak Hill?"

"Lady Ware came to find me."

The following silence was finally broken with Musgrave's denial. "You're right. I do *not* believe you, old man."

"I can scarce believe it myself," Jason mused. He plucked at the woolly black fisherman's jersey he still wore and said, "I was all in black so hard to see, especially as I had doused my light, when this creature came hurtling at me full tilt. I caught it, and *it* turned out to be her ladyship. You see before you an unrepentant cad, Musgrave."

"How so?" the amused Musgrave inquired.

"I kissed her again—I had done so at the conservatory, in case I forgot to mention that detail—and I must say, the lady is most gifted in that respect." Jason grinned in memory.

"Indeed. And how does her ladyship feel about this, er, encounter?"

"Utterly furious. I had the effrontery to ask her what had

happened at Kenyon Hall. She said rather cryptically that she had heard me talking to you—about her. Ever since I returned here I have been racking my brain to remember what we talked about. Do you have any clue?"

Musgrave pondered that fateful night and shook his head. "We were both a trifle on the go, hardly in a condition to recall a casual conversation."

"Precisely."

"One wonders what prompted her to come haring up to the Peak in the dead of night," Musgrave mused soberly.

"Said it was her Christian duty to prevent my being killed." Jason sniffed in derision. "If there was a smuggler within a mile of the place, he was soon gone, believe me. Sound carries well, in spite of the closeness of the sea."

"Still, had one or more of them happened on you, I could now be arranging your funeral."

Jason paused in the act of bringing his glass to his mouth to stare at his friend. "You think so?"

"It is possible. The stakes are high and the smugglers as a rule are not squeamish men. Although I understand they are generally more humane in *these* parts. Rather than murder they simply burn you in effigy, parading the likeness about town first. The entire population participates, which indicates the involvement of more than one or two."

"They play tricks on the preventatives around here, so I have heard. It's a nasty business."

"What about Lady Ware?"

"I had bloody well mend my fences there, I suppose—if I can evade that blasted cat of hers. I see you are unscathed. Tell me how you managed that feat."

"Bel curled up on Elspeth's lap and ignored me. Should I feel insulted as being unworthy of attack?" He grinned at Jason, then polished off the last drop of his brandy. "Elspeth believes Bel fancies himself Lady Ware's protector and intends to guard her from—shall we say, predators?"

"And the cat sees me as a predator?"

"If the shoe fits . . ." Musgrave rose from his chair, stretched, then ambled toward his room. "I am taking Elspeth for a drive tomorrow following her fitting at the mantuamaker's. That might be an opportune time for you to make amends with Lady Ware."

"Devil a bit if I can figure out what to say on that score. I merely took advantage of something literally thrown at me. And, Musgrave, she did not slap my face. In fact, I would swear the lady enjoyed it excessively."

"Which would distress her a great deal," Musgrave said, pausing at his door. "A true lady is not supposed to enjoy that sort of thing, is she?"

"Blast!"

Come morning the most amazing thing was that Jason did not suffer any ills from his consumption of brandy the night before. In fact, his head seemed remarkably clear. Must be the sea air, he concluded charitably.

And then recollection of his confrontation with Lady Ware returned and he reached for his cup of coffee with a shaking hand.

"Toast?" Musgrave inquired.

"I had better fortify myself with the entire table, I should think—eggs, steak, toast, marmalade, the lot. I rather envy you going off on a pleasant drive with an old family friend. She *is* still just an old family friend, I take it?"

"At present she is companion to Lady Ware, her father having made numerous unwise investments, sending the family to the wall. She is on her own now, papa having had the grace to go aloft, soon followed by a worried mother. Elspeth was the youngest. The others are married and saddled with families. Elspeth was always the smartest of the lot so she became a governess until she chanced to work for the lecherous Lord Ware. Lady Ware rescued her most generously, providing her with a home and lovely clothing. Elspeth is most appreciative."

"What happens if Lady Ware marries? A natural event with a beautiful woman," Jason said, consuming his meal in dedicated concentration.

"Lady Ware insists she has no intention of marrying again. Once was more than enough, in her estimation. Must say, having seen the previous holder of that title, I can understand why she might feel so inclined."

"I know," Jason murmured. "Well, then I imagine your Elspeth is set for life. Do you plan to gift her with a collection of caps as suitable for an old maid?"

"Caps? To cover that glorious blond hair? Why, that would be a sacrilege. She has the hair of an angel." Musgrave gave his friend an affronted look and rose from the table.

"Unless she marries she will be an old maid, doomed to wear little white caps and sit listening to other women talk about their children and husbands. That, my friend, is a fact of our society. Or else she must find a position such as she just left—with its inherent dangers."

"She deserves better than such fate."

Jason shrugged. "Perhaps. Such things happen. I think the beautiful Lady Ware ought to be warming a man's bed but she would scarce agree with me."

Musgrave glared at his friend, then stalked from the room, closing the door behind him with exaggerated care.

Upon finishing his breakfast, Jason met with Martin to discuss the state of his damaged wardrobe, deciding to try the local tailor with the hope he could use the lining of the ruined waistcoat as a pattern. The breeches had already been mended. The boot was something else.

"I shall try my best, milord. I have a few tricks up my sleeve that may work. May I suggest you keep a distance from that vile cat?"

"You may, but I fear I am doomed to ignore it. I see Lady Ware later this morning."

"Oh, dear."

His words echoed in Jason's head as he clattered down the rear stairs and out to the mews where he found his horse saddled and waiting for him.

The ride along the beach was pleasant, the air fresh and the wind nicely brisk. No evidence could be seen on the horizon that any bad weather was coming. A few puffy clouds enlivened the sky. People were out and about their business. When he passed Wallis's Library, he thought he saw Lady Ware inside but he was not about to meet her in public. It would not serve his purpose and certainly not hers. He shuddered to think what she might say should he attempt to talk to her there!

All was serene up on Peak Hill. He rode past the place where he had encountered Georgiana. She had broken off the branch where her reins had been looped, and he slid off to examine it more closely.

Holding the branch, he sauntered along toward Peak Hill road, hearing a cart squeaking its way along the narrow track. A man of indeterminate years walked alongside the pony that pulled the load of cut wood and turf. Jason thought a moment, then recalled that a fellow named Mutter had rights to do this. Earned a living this way, so it was said, selling the fuel to the townspeople. Jason had no reason to doubt that, but he would watch the chap just the same.

He mounted his horse, riding off to inspect his house, all the while wondering what in the world he could say to Georgiana, Dowager Marchioness of Ware. Such an absurd appelation—dowager. Anyone less like the usual elderly matron, he couldn't imagine.

How different this inspection tour had turned out to be from what he'd anticipated—embroiled in possible smuggling, involved with the unpredictable Lady Ware, and fending off attacks by that miserable beast on his limited wardrobe. Had he known what to expect, he would not have ventured forth without at the very least another trunk of clothes.

Georgiana returned to the cottage after selecting another book to replace the one she had decided she did not like. A pause to purchase some lace at the Shipton shop and a look-in at the Sidmouth church had completed her morning's errands.

She could hear someone pounding nails not far away. There was a good deal of construction going on, which was good for the local business, if rather noisy.

Dropping her parcels on the hall table, she wandered out to greet Bel, scooping his enormous body into her arms with an effort. "I declare, you become fatter and I shall cease cuddling you, my friend," she cautioned while she scratched the cat beneath his chin.

A flock of the prettiest birds chose to settle in a nearby tree and Georgiana, rather than risk having Bel make them his dinner, elected to pop the cat into the conservatory attached to the house. She had just closed the door and was enjoying the delightful view of the birds when that now too-familiar voice reached her ears again. She hoped she might not blush too deep a shade of red. It would be too, too humiliating.

"Good day, my lady. I trust you are feeling more the thing this afternoon?"

"Is it that late? I hadn't noticed. I vow, the time flits by so quickly in this charming little village."

"How are you?" the persistent man demanded, this time quite close to Georgiana's side.

"I am fine. The cat is in the conservatory, fortunately for you. Have you ordered a new waistcoat as yet?" She nervously plucked a leaf from a shrub, then dropped it when she recalled Elspeth pulling one from her hair last evening.

"Martin is seeing to it now. I instructed him to duplicate the original if possible. I understand the local tailor is likely to possess some fine fabrics." He paused, then ventured, "You made it home in one piece, I take it?"

"Indeed. The gentlemanly thing to do now would be to apologize for the kiss last evening, but you, sirrah, are no gentleman," Georgiana stated firmly.

"Fortunate for me. I've no intention for apologizing for a kiss I found exceedingly delightful. If you were as honest as you once claimed to be, you would admit the same."

She stubbornly refused to face the dratted man. She had no wish to allow him to read her thoughts, for they blazed on her face as sure as fire.

"I would rather not discuss last evening," she said primly at long last, after listening absently as Bel yowled in the conservatory.

"I would," he said, putting a hand on her shoulder to compel her to face him. "And I would know what it was I said to distress you so much that you found it necessary to flee Kenyon Hall in the dead of night. I find I cannot recall any particular conversation with Musgrave."

Anger flared up within her and she spun about to glare at him. "What a convenient memory you have, sirrah. Yet I suppose the discussion of your plans to seduce a young and innocent widow are nothing to a man of your stripe. Oh"—she pushed past him to rush toward the house—"I do not know why I cared the least what happens to you, you wretched creature! 'Tis a pity they did not find you after all." She stabbed him with her final words. "To think I *trusted* you!"

Jason stood rooted, listening to the birds, the yowling cat, the pounding coming from the next property, all the while absorbing that the reason Georgiana had decamped in the middle of the night was that she feared his advances. She had not the fortitude to tell him "no." She must have feared she would be forced, ravished. Had he given her that impression?

Much disturbed, he thought back to what Musgrave had said earlier—that they had been a trifle on the go—bosky. That didn't excuse him, but perhaps it explained his loosened tongue. It also might explain why he ignored her innocent response to him, the other little signs he overlooked because he was convinced she welcomed his advances.

Blast. She had trusted him. *That* cut deepest of all. He realized he had lost something precious, something he very much wished to retain. Turning around, he headed for where he had left his horse and within minutes was riding away.

From within the house Georgiana watched him leave. To his credit he had looked thunderstruck when she accused him of considering seduction a mere trifle. But hadn't that been his attitude? Maybe another, more experienced woman could shrug it off. Georgiana found it impossible to ignore for she worried about her reputation. It must remain unblemished. She couldn't bear to have her pompous stepson toss that in her face.

Feeling restless, she decided to try out the bathing machines since the weather was so fine. It would be good to wage battle with the waves, quite as though she vanquished his lordship.

The walk to the beach was blessedly short. She had changed to an old muslin gown and once at the shore, her towel securely in hand, she sought out the most friendly of the dippers. The wooden, two-wheeled hut was drawn by a pathetic pony whose master urged it to back into the sea so a lady might enter the water without being viewed.

Georgiana might not agree with the notion that bathing in seawater cured every ill from stomach disorders on, but she felt wondrously cleansed with her dip in the waves.

"Here, now, deary, just let the waters hold ye up. 'Tis salty, they are—ye'll float."

Georgiana tried that and when she began to sink, she wondered if perhaps she was heavier than ought be. Then she recalled her swim in her girlhood pond and paddled happily about under the watchful and approving eye of the dipper.

This went on until she began to feel decidedly chilled and turned to leave the water. Her wool flannel dress was wet and unpleasant, clinging to her form. When she complained, the woman had a ready reply.

"There's many ladies what swims in the nude, if ye do not mind. 'Tis less emcumb'ring, I think. Nothing amiss with it in my es-tee-mation. Good for the skin."

Shocked just a little at first, Georgiana could see where it would be a very nice thing to swim about without the dreadfully heavy flannel weighing her down. Perhaps—if she grew brave enough—she might even dare to try it.

All would have been fine had she not chanced to look off to the west. Since she had gone to the bathing machine that was the farthest away from the circulating library and thus the most people, she had thought herself relatively alone. No one had been about when she entered the sea.

There was now. Wouldn't you know that the sole observer to her departure from the water, with the thin flannel plastered to her body like a second skin, was Lord Thornbury? He was seated in his gig and gazed out to sea—she hoped.

Quickly slipping into the wooden interior of the wheeled contraption that had rolled her out to this depth, Georgiana hastily changed back to her muslin, first rubbing her skin with the towel, but not drying as well as she ought in her rush. The result was that when the pony came to a stop well up on the bank and she went down the steps to the ground, the muslin clung to her almost as well as had the flannel.

Refusing to give his lordship the satisfaction that she had recognized him or that his presence disconcerted her, Georgiana toweled her damp hair, then folded the large length of linen. She marched up to the Esplanade, then crossed to continue her way home.

"My lady, I insist upon giving you assistance. Permit me to escort you to your house."

There was no question in his voice. He was warning her that he fully intended to see her into his gig without delay whether she liked it or not.

"I am quite fine, thank you."

"That I can fully see, my lady," he replied, amusement creeping into his voice.

Georgiana looked down at her gown, dismayed to see that it still clung to her, outlining her limbs in a shocking manner. What it looked like from behind did not bear thinking. She looked up at him then. He did not smile, but there was a light in his eyes that was most suspicious.

"I suppose I had better accept your most gracious offer." She glared at him, hoping his horse ran away with him before she had to put a foot in the gig.

He held out a hand, leaning over in order to do so. Georgiana accepted his help, sitting as far as possible from him—which given the narrowness of the seat was not much.

She had a sneaking suspicion that her bosom was showed too much in the damp muslin. She'd not worn stays, thinking it was silly to put them on when she would have to take them off minutes later. The mortification of it all was simply more than any woman should be required to endure.

"You enjoyed your dip in the water?" he inquired with commendable restraint.

"I did," she replied curtly.

Silence took over for the remainder of the drive, each one evidently trying to think of something to say and failing.

When they reached Rose Cottage, Georgiana, now a trifle drier—climbed down from the gig without accepting his aid. She braved a look at him and quietly declared, "I must thank you for your consideration—particularly after what was said earlier today." She looked away, unsure how to proceed.

"We need to sleep on our differences, ma'am. Perhaps tomorrow something will come to us?"

"Indeed," she replied stiffly, then hurried into the house as fast as was seemly.

Jason watched her dignified retreat. How she had hated to be taken up by him in the gig. He could almost feel her anger, frustration, her annoyance that she had been placed in such a position.

But, he reflected as he turned the gig about and returned to the Esplanade and his original destination, she certainly had a splendid figure. Long-limbed, full-bosomed, with a dainty waist just right for holding—Lady Ware was a delectable armful. And, to make matters the worse, she was about as far removed from him as a woman might become, and all because of a ridiculous misunderstanding. Not but what he found her attractive. He admitted he wanted her as much as he had ever wanted a woman in his life. Would she ever accept that he never could have ravished her? That she might have trusted him to be a gentleman?

It wasn't a matter of luring her to bed, either. The battles they had were far more stimulating than any lovemaking he'd known.

What to do? He caught sight of the man named Mutter leaving a public house on a side road and wondered what need for wood and peat they might have. Surely they would prefer coal? Or was that too costly? Then he sat straighter, thinking that while wood and peat did cost less, something else might be concealed underneath them.

He put the luscious Georgiana out of his mind while he decided to follow the trail left by the man named Mutter.

Chapter Nine

Georgiana gathered Bel in her arms and left the house to be on her own for a bit. Perkins was safely busy with Elspeth's new garments, while Elspeth herself had left with Lord Musgrave for the mantuamaker's to have final fittings on a new ball gown—a simple affair of blue jaconet. How kind of him to offer her a drive in his newly rented gig.

Ignoring the pounding that persisted at the property nearby, Georgiana sought the solitude of a pretty little stone bench she'd found in the garden. With the peacocks keeping a sharp eye out for Bel, she need have no worry on their score. They would shriek the place down should the cat come near them—or anyone trespass on the property for that matter. What excellent watchdogs, er, birds, they proved to be.

Threading her fingers through Bel's thick fur, Georgiana pondered what had happened the day before. What a topsy-turvy day it had been, too. How angry she had been with Lord Thornbury, the wretched cad. To think he could kiss her *so* then offer no apology was the outside of enough. To make matters even worse he had not remembered saying the words that had stung her so deeply.

Did he then flit about the countryside, seducing widows with such abandon that he couldn't recall which widow he'd occasioned to discuss and when? He claimed he had enjoyed her kiss and challenged her to deny the same for herself. Well, she might have enjoyed it had not the memory of what had happened previously suddenly come to mind. Nonetheless, he ought not have kissed her.

What cut her more deeply than anything else was that she had trusted him implicitly. He had been the perfect gentleman, her shining knight, the antithesis of all her horrid relatives and those groping old men who had plagued her life following her marriage and Lord Ware's sudden death. That had been the worst of it all.

The touch of a gentle breeze on her face caused her to realize that tears dampened her skin. Furious that she could cry over such a man, she dashed them away, then buried her face in Bel's thick coat.

"Such a coil," she murmured. What did that dratted man have to do but rescue her from the embarrassment of being seen in her dampened muslin gown. While driving her back to Rose Cottage he had made no truly suggestive remark, other than he could fully see that she was quite fine. Which, upon reflection, was quite enough.

The breeze caught at a rose bush close by where she perched and tossed the fragrant blossom in the air, as though it nodded in agreement. The sight of the pink rose carried her memory back to Lord Thornbury and the roses in his aunt's garden, then to Lord Thornbury and the minuet-dancing glow-worms, and finally to Lord Thornbury and the tranquil ride in the little boat along the shore of the pretty ornamental lake. She sighed woefully.

Her trust of him had been the linking thread all through these lovely events. *That* was what had truly sent her in the impetuous dash from Kenyon Hall. To think that the one man she had come to trust could betray her trust had crushed her beyond belief.

And this realization brought her to an uncomfortable truth of her own. She—who had never known what love was—had tumbled into love with this odious creature, this cad, this seducer of innocent widows!

Innocent widows? What man would believe that she was an innocent widow? The very words were seemingly contradictory. And yet she was utterly ignorant of what passed between a husband and wife, other than the husband made some claim on his wife while in bed. That had been apparent when Lord Ware accosted her in her bedroom, demanding she yield to his wishes. No one had seen fit to enlighten her before her wedding, and those who sought to assist afterward had personal demonstrations in mind.

Yet she knew that with Lord Thornbury her "duty" would be different from what it would have been with Lord Ware. And what else but love would have compelled her to dash through the darkened night to the top of Peak Hill to save his wretched hide? It was all beyond belief.

The sound of a carriage in the lane not far away brought her head around to see who it might be. No one she knew, she thought with relief, as it continued past the house.

She rose, permitting Bel to explore the garden while she inspected various roses. *Rosa Gallica simplea*—a single white and pink, *Rosa Sulfura*—a rich sulfur yellow, *Rosa bifura offincinalis*—a cup-shaped delicate pink of rare fragrance, all with neatly labeled tags. The owner of this garden did well indeed. And his lovely garden served for a few moments to take her mind off her troubles.

But what of Lord Thornbury? He had been on Peak Hill last evening, perhaps to consort with those evil smugglers. Never mind that Elspeth said their efforts improved the lot of the local citizens. Thornbury could be aiding and abetting a crime! And he claimed to be a gentleman? Bah.

But what could she as a public-spirited person do? She had little inclination to personally intervene. See what her initial efforts had brought her! Crushed in the arms of that scoundrel and kissed nearly senseless, that's what!

Nursing her feeling of ill-usage, she wandered back to the house, determined that she would take a walk in the village center to see if there was some small manner in which she might assist the local citizens to better their lot.

Jason entered The Old Ship on his own as Musgrave was pleasantly occupied in squiring Elspeth Pettibone first to her dressmaker, then a drive about the countryside. It never ceased to amaze Jason that no matter what time of day he entered the tavern there were men in quiet conversations, hoisting a pint of home-brewed. No brandy for them. That liquid was undoubtedly shipped away from Sidmouth to London or some point in between.

There were other wines smuggled in as well as the brandy—claret and burgundy, for example, those wines so beloved by the gentlemen in London and elsewhere. Devil a bit, he'd be torn in his actions between relishing a supply of the wine he enjoyed and stamping out a reprehensible enterprise.

He nursed a pint of surprisingly good ale while surveying his fellow occupants. Then the chap he knew as Mutter entered the place and Jason became more alert. Here was a man who had daily occasion to frequent Peak Hill. He made short trips about the village, pausing with his small loads of wood and peat. Seemed quite innocent, but that quality could be most deceiving. Witness Lady Ware. She looked as innocent as a newborn babe, yet he questioned what his eyes saw and senses told him.

Mutter casually strolled toward one particular group, calling for a pint. His preference being known, a mug of ale was quickly brought to him.

And then a conference of sorts was held. At least that was what Jason suspected it was. Nods, a few quiet words were exchanged, a handshake was given, then all settled back to make casual conversation about the weather and likelihood of the next fishing expedition catching a full load.

Feeling as though he had witnessed a scene of import, Jason nevertheless knew frustration. He had not the least idea of when a cargo would be off-loaded, nor where it might land. It meant that if he chose to pursue this course he would of necessity be required to spend a considerable amount of time following these fishermen about their business.

Shaking his head in disgust, he finished his ale, then left the tavern at the same time as several of the burly fishermen. Their rustic garb gave off ample evidence that they spent long hours in proximity with fish.

The others turned in the direction of the beach where the fishing boats were drawn up for the day. He headed in the opposite direction, determined to see something of the village.

The first person he saw was Lady Ware, who stared at him with something akin to alarm on her face.

"Lady Ware, I see you are indulging in a bit of shopping."

"Yes, well," she said hastily, "I departed my home so precipitously that I find I left a number of items behind. I thought to purchase what I needed here." She gestured to the neat row of shops behind her. "Those were fishermen that left with you from The Old Ship, were they not?" she inquired, suspicion in her voice.

"They were," he began, then realized it was better not to reveal his intent—for he really wasn't all that positive what he intended to do.

"I see."

"I doubt you do, but allow me to offer my escort and parcel-carrying ability, my lady," he said with his most suave manner that had never failed him in the past.

"Oh." She looked frantically about her, and seeing no help from any other quarter other than an odd look or two from three genteel ladies who stayed at the Royal York, she agreed. "Very well. Although I cannot see why you would want to assist me. I am not," she hissed, eyes narrowed disdainfully, "available for seduction."

She obviously had not intended to say those words for she blushed a deep pink and looked anywhere but at him.

"Please believe me that the situation was not as you plainly presume, ma'am." He collected her parcels, making sure she would not walk off and leave him holding her purchases.

She gazed past him, along the street to where the fishermen had paused to chat with several others of their occupation and then glanced at Jason again. "That is often the case, I suppose."

What the devil she meant by those words was beyond Jason's reckoning. "Where do you go next, my lady?"

"The lace shop is where I had intended to go," she said doubtfully, as though she suspected he'd not wish to enter that feminine establishment.

"I think we should join those three ladies and partake of the tea at the Royal York Hotel. Confess, does that not appeal to you? With Miss Pettibone off on a jaunt in the countryside, you must be all alone this afternoon. Surely you could spare a lonely gentleman your company?"

Jason could not believe what he had just done. He had literally begged her to be with him. He, who had women seek him out, sometimes in a most brazen manner, was reduced to beseeching this beautiful black-haired witch to take tea with him. How fortunate none of his friends would ever know such a thing had occurred.

"It does sound appealing. Bel is not the most agreeable company for luncheon. He tends to eat anything that has fish or meat in it. The cook who came with the house does very nicely with dainty meat sandwiches that Bel is certain are made just for him."

"Which means you must be famished," Jason said with satisfaction. He would obtain his wish.

"Well . . ."

He settled the matter by guiding her along the street in the direction of the Royal York, having found some years ago that there were times when a gentleman simply had to take charge of things.

The proprietor was transported to see the elegant Earl of Thornbury and beautiful Dowager Marchioness of Ware enter the hotel to partake of tea. They were ushered to a table that overlooked the sea. Around them ladies dressed in charming afternoon gowns sipped tea and watched the newcomers with avid eyes.

"How fortunate I am that the mantuamaker near where I live is so clever at interpreting the designs of *La Belle Assemblée* and the *Ladies Monthly Museum*. I vow that every thread of this gown has been examined," Georgiana murmured, forgetting for the moment that she was most annoyed with this man.

Tea was brought and Georgiana poured, almost sloshing the brew when a delighted squeal reached her ears from just behind her.

"Lord Thornbury, how utterly marvelous. A little bird told me that you had come to Sidmouth this summer. We thought it would be great fun to join you. You must be bored to death in such a quiet place."

Affronted by this nasty little barb, one that had obviously included her, Georgiana turned to give the newcomers a frosty look from beneath the brim of her simple but becoming cottage bonnet trimmed with pink roses that matched the pink of her muslin gown.

His lordship rose from the table looking as remote as Georgiana had ever seen him.

"Georgiana, Dowager Marchioness of Ware, may I present Miss Brompton, Lord and Lady Yeldham, and Mr. James Rood." He smoothly gestured to each in turn. "Lady Ware is spending the summer in Sidmouth."

Georgiana nodded as regally as she had seen older women do when presented with inferiors. That these people were members of the *ton* was evident in the flurries of whispered conversation that immediately sped through the room. But Georgiana bore an old and respectable title—never mind it was acquired through a brief marriage. She outranked the lot of them, she suspected. The gentlemen looked a trifle uncomfortable, as though they didn't relish crossing words or swords with Jason, Earl of Thornbury.

"What prompted you to hare off to this remote village, dear Thornbury?" Miss Brompton cooed. She artfully batted her lashes at him and smiled in a familiar manner, tapping his arm playfully with her beautifully gloved hand.

Lady Yeldham wore a fatuous expression on her face when she gazed at his lordship as well, boding ill for her husband.

"I own property here and came at the insistence of my agent to oversee needed improvements. I had met Lady Ware at my Aunt Kenyon's house party not long ago and was agreeably surprised to find her established here when I arrived."

Miss Brompton gave Georgiana a doubtful look, as though wondering how much he said was true. "How nice, for you both," she purred. "Tell me, Lady Ware, is there anything to do here?"

"It depends on what you enjoy. There is Wallis's Circulating Library and the Wednesday assembly at the London Hotel. Tea is served here at the Royal York every afternoon. There are pleasant walks and drives, excellent bathing, and pretty shops with all manner of enticing things to buy. I believe there is a splendid billiard table to be found at the Shed by the library just down the street from here." Georgiana tossed a questioning look at Lord Thornbury for confirmation of this bit of knowledge regarding male interests.

"Lady Ware is correct. Life is not dull here."

"I look forward to the next assembly to see if it meets the standard of those in Brighton. Usually affairs in these provincial places are so insipid," Miss Brompton opined in her high fluting voice that carried beautifully throughout the room.

Georgiana caught a glimpse of the expressions on the faces of several of the other women seated in the tearoom and barely suppressed a smile. Miss Brompton might impress Lord Thornbury with her air of *tonnish* ennui, but she had annoyed the women in this room. That might prove to be a bit of poor judgment on her part.

"Well, we had best settle into our rooms," Mr. Rood ventured to say, earning glares from Miss Brompton and Lady Yeldham. However, Lord Yeldham agreed and the four left to find their rooms above.

"I believe I shall remove to my house tomorrow," Lord Thornbury said musingly. "I'd not thought to encounter anyone from Town."

Georgiana knew from her limited exposure to society that Town spoken of in that manner meant London. "It will surely be more pleasant for you to have more space and there is nothing better than your own table."

"Indeed. Is that why you repaired to Rose Cottage?"

"Of course. Why else would I leave the comforts of the Royal York?"

Lord Thornbury gave her a doubtful look and Georgiana felt as though she had scored a point in their continuing battle.

They left the tearoom shortly afterward. Georgiana recaptured her parcels and insisted upon walking home by herself. "I wish to inspect the Shipton lace shop and perhaps find some other, more personal items as well."

Jason bowed to her desires—what else could he do? He walked with her out of the hotel, feeling that matters had altered with the arrival of the acquaintances from London. There was nothing he might do about that, but he could move to his own house.

When she had turned the corner and was lost to view, Jason strode around to the mews to request his horse be saddled. Once ready, he mounted and was off to the other end of the village.

While the smell of paint was still fresh, the house was tolerable. All else was in readiness. He requested his agent supply him with a cook and other needed servants.

"I intend to move in myself for a time. This is as good a place as any from which to investigate if there is any skullduggery going on hereabouts."

The agent quickly agreed and took himself off to comply with his lordship's pleasantly worded requests.

Jason strolled about his house on the hill. From the front windows he could see the wave-splashed beach and the Esplanade. He could also make out most of the house that Georgiana rented. He frowned in thought. She enjoyed playing the pianoforte, yet he did not recall seeing an instrument in the drawing room and suspected there was none in the house. He would investigate to see if such a thing might be rented. Surely he would not have to send to London for such an item?

It turned out upon inquiry that a pianoforte might be leased for the summer from an establishment in Exeter. Word would be sent immediately with the order should Lord Thornbury desire. Lord Thornbury did.

For Georgiana several pleasant days followed the tea at the Royal York Hotel. The ladies who heretofore had ignored her presence now sought her out for polite conversation, and invitations to Rose Cottage, it seemed, became quite desirable, for when she issued such they were quickly accepted.

She was agreeably occupied with entertaining four of the Royal York ladies when the dray arrived with a splendid pianoforte. Confused, she denied knowledge of the instrument or its order.

"Lord Thornbury ordered it, ma'am," the younger man insisted. "That's all we knowed. Here 'tis."

They deposited the fine pianoforte in the drawing room, then departed, leaving Georgiana midway between confusion and fury.

"Do you play, Lady Ware?" Mrs. Swinford inquired.

"I do, although not very well. How kind of his lordship to recall that I played while visiting his aunt's home. Lady Kenyon is such a dear person," Georgiana said with more enthusiasm than she'd shown heretofore.

This tidbit of information from the reticent Lady Ware pleased her audience greatly. Knowledgeable looks were exchanged, for one and all knew of the fashionable Lady Kenyon.

"You may wish to have a party with such a handsome instrument to entertain. Those people newly arrived from London have been busy looking down their noses at what Sidmouth has to offer. One wonders why they did not seek to go to Brighton instead," Mrs. Arbuthnot declared.

Georgiana knew as well as they did that it was because Lord Thornbury was not in Brighton. She smiled a trifle and took a deep breath. She owed these ladies, widows like herself, for championing her as it were. "I insist upon giving a little party here come Saturday evening. That shan't interfere with the coming Wednesday assembly."

Coos of delight issued from each of the four and they settled around her to suggest people who would make agreeable additions to their numbers.

"Of course you will ask Lord Thornbury in appreciation for his gesture," Mrs. Swinford declared, exchanging looks with the other women. They all turned to stare at the splendid pianoforte that occupied a pride of place in the room.

"I expect it would not do to exclude his friends from London," Georgiana said with reluctance.

"No, indeed," Mrs. Swinford said after another one of those rounds of exchanged looks.

Georgiana wished she knew what those looks meant, or for that matter, what these dear ladies intended. That they were on her side was small comfort.

Shortly after, they all left, Mrs. Swinford carrying the invitations addressed to those who resided at the Royal York to be given the proprietor to dispense.

Georgiana stood in the middle of the French door that led to the garden for a time before succumbing to the urge to try out the pianoforte. Such a splendid instrument deserved someone more talented than she was, but it had been sent for her use and use it, she would.

Working her way through a Haydn piece she knew well, she

again tried the Mozart sonata she had played while at Lady Kenyon's. She fared no better here than there.

"Still having a spot of bother with that one part, eh?" Lord Thornbury said, stepping into the drawing room through the open French doors.

Her fingers crashed a discordant chord. "You!"

"As of tomorrow I shall occupy my house on the hill. Oddly enough, the music drifts up my way and I shall enjoy listening to you practice."

"You ought not have done this. You must realize how this will look once word spreads about. A gentleman simply does not order a pianoforte for the use of a stranger. It implies a closeness of acquaintance." She rose from the dainty bench to confront him.

"But we are scarcely strangers, are we? And you must admit to a certain amount of closeness, would you not, dear Lady Ware?" That deep purr was in his voice, the one that reminded her of Bel when he was well pleased with his life.

His lordship took a step toward her, that peculiar light in his eyes again, the one that had made her knees weak last time. Now, she knew full well what would happen should she not keep her distance from him.

"Georgiana, I do not wish to be a stranger to you."

"I am well aware of what you wish, Lord Thornbury."

"You might call me Jason. I give you leave to do so."

"I do not—it might cause gossip were someone to hear."

He glanced at the little writing desk where he saw his name inscribed on a cream sheet. He walked over and picked it up with a glance at Georgiana to more or less obtain her permission. Realizing he would know sooner or later, she nodded.

"A party this coming Saturday and I am invited," he said after reading the slip. "How charming, dear lady." He looked at the sheets below his and exclaimed, "What's this, invitations to Miss Brompton, the Yeldhams, and Mr. Rood?"

"They are your friends, and I thought you would wish them here."

"I would not say they are friends, more like acquaintances. But they are acceptable people and you will cope with them admirably. It will be good for you to entertain. I fear you have been too removed from society these past years."

"Considering I was not given a Season nor did I enter society following my marriage it is little wonder, is it?"

"All the more reason to test the waters."

"I would rather go swimming, frankly," Georgiana said impulsively.

Lord Thornbury burst into laughter, his handsome head tilting back to expose the strong column of his neck above his intricately tied cravat.

"And what is so amusing, pray tell?" Elspeth said upon entering the room in the company of Lord Musgrave.

"You, dear lady, have allowed the vultures of Sidmouth to descend upon the unprotected Lady Ware. She has been browbeaten into giving a party come Saturday next."

At Elspeth's stricken expression Georgiana hastened to deny this assertion. "That is not true. Several of those nice ladies we met before came for tea. The pianoforte was delivered while they were here. Naturally one of them suggested it would be a happy occasion for a party. I agreed."

"I would wager it did not go precisely that way," Lord Thornbury murmured for Georgiana's ears alone.

"I will thank you to keep your thoughts to yourself."

"Yes, I ought to make a practice of that."

Georgiana threw him a swift look, trying to figure out what was meant by that aside.

The two gentlemen left shortly after that and Elspeth drew Georgiana into the garden while interrogating her.

"I feared I ought not leave you again. A fine companion I am. I shall be drummed from the companion society, I fear," she said in mock severity.

"I am so pleased to see you enjoy a bit of time with your old friend. I would not have you sacrifice that merely to sit at my side."

"Lord Thornbury did not upset you, did he?"

Georgiana knew what was implied in those words and she quickly replied, "No, other than to present me a piano for my use while we stay in Sidmouth. The dratted man! How can I be furious with someone who does such things?"

"It is a problem, I can see that," Elspeth said reflectively.

Georgiana picked a full-blown rose, sniffed it appreciatively, then twirled the blossom in her fingers. "I shall invite Miss Brompton, the Yeldhams, and Mr. Rood as well. I wonder if they will come." She turned to look at Elspeth. "What do you think?"

"I think you were a fool to ask them, but I can understand why you did. They will come and doubtless spoil the party or at the very least cause a scene," Elspeth said in her frank manner.

"I trust not!" Georgiana cried, dismayed at the prospect of a scene at a party she hostessed.

"We shall see. But first, before we decide on menus and the like, we must decide upon what to wear. We do not wish to look like country bumpkins. Those *tonnish* sort have enough to sneer at now without any other things, like our gowns." Elspeth turned, intent upon regaining the cottage.

"Lord Thornbury will have a lot to answer for, if I do not miss my guess," Georgiana grumbled as she followed Elspeth back into the cottage.

"Indeed, my dear, but think of the prestige you will have. You will have one of the premier catches of the London scene at your little party, a gentleman a great many ladies of the *ton* pant after, if Bennett is to be believed. When you do go to London, your name will already be known as one who intrigued Lord Thornbury. That is no small accomplishment, my dear."

"Really," Georgiana exclaimed dryly. "Charming. And what manner of man will seek me out then, pray tell?"

"Someone who wants to capture you for his own, knowing you will accept nothing less than marriage."

Georgiana knew that Elspeth meant well. She might even be correct in her assessment. What Elspeth did not and would not know was that Georgiana had already given her heart to another, a gentleman who did not want it in the least and certainly would never offer marriage.

Chapter Ten

"All invitations sent out have been accepted," Georgiana said to her companion, tapping the crisp cards of acceptance against one hand. "I should admit to dreadful vanity did I not know they were prompted by curiosity and boredom, not to mention a desire to assess these London paragons. 'Tis not every day that one possessing the elegance of Miss Brompton comes to Sidmouth."

"How fortunate for the residents, in that event," Elspeth said dryly. "I cannot imagine why she remains here when it is obvious to anyone with eyes that Lord Thornbury has little interest in her."

"Do you think so?" Georgiana said with care. "I thought he was most civil at the Royal York. You were driving with Lord Musgrave and so could not see, but Lord Thornbury was all that was gracious to the four of them. Although I must admit that Miss Brompton did not endear herself to the occupants of the tearoom by her condemnation of Sidmouth as a dreary provincial place. One must know, if one has selected a spot in which to enjoy a respite or a change of climate, it does not sit well to have a fashionable woman decry it."

"Indeed. Rather off-putting I should think. I should not wonder but what our Royal York ladies take her words in ill fashion."

The two women exchanged looks but said nothing more on that score.

By Wednesday the menu for the coming party had been settled, not without a number of changes based on suggestions from Lord Musgrave.

"Been to a goodly number of these parties, you know.

Learned what is done and what is not, what people like and what is dreadful. Lobster patties and crab cakes are well liked, for example. Did you know"—and he gave the pianoforte a dubious glance—"that Miss Brompton plays rather well? She is quite in demand when in London and elsewhere. I should imagine most young women would dread comparison with perfection such as hers. Not but what her manners might do with a bit of improvement, mind you." With those words he bestowed a warm look on the most proper and considerate Miss Pettibone who always behaved just as she ought.

Georgiana blessed Lord Musgrave for his revelation. "Since this party is in honor of the instrument—more or less—it is only fitting that it be played with respect. Certainly my poor skills will not match such excellence."

"But you play with charm and grace and a wonderful feeling, dear Georgiana," Elspeth interposed. "Skill is all well and good, but it needs passion to enrich it. Does Miss Brompton have such passion, Bennett?"

He gave her an amused look, a slow smile crossing his kind face. "She would think passion misplaced at the pianoforte, my dear Elspeth. I feel certain that she would apply it elsewhere, if at all. There were a few gentlemen in London who dubbed Miss Brompton the Ice Maiden."

"Oh," both ladies said in unison with an understanding look shared between them.

When it came time to leave for the assembly, Lord Musgrave drove up to the house in his gig to escort Elspeth. She was upset that the gig held no more than two people.

"I shan't leave you to be by yourself, Georgiana. It is unthinkable for you to go alone. We should have summoned John Coachman."

"But I did," Georgiana countered. "Why do we not all go together? Then should the wind rise or something equally dire occur, we will have a covered carriage."

Lord Musgrave immediately declared this to be an excellent idea. They were about to enter the carriage when Lord Thornbury drove smartly into the carriageway, coming to a halt next to the coach.

"What a worry, I feared you might be gone. Of all the nights for Martin to have problems!" His lordship did not offer further explanations, but tossed the reins of his rented gig to his groom and joined the others by the coach.

"I suspected you would have the sensibility to order your coach and beg to join you." He smiled at Georgiana.

In spite of her contrary feelings regarding this man, there were too many interested spectators for her to be other than gracious. Georgiana assured him he was welcome to join them, then motioned Elspeth into the carriage, following on her heels.

Jason took his place opposite Georgiana and studied her averted face. She was barely tolerating him, and that was a blow to his sense of well-being. Had he sunk so low in her estimation that even after the pianoforte she held him in contempt? He was worse off than he had expected. Well, it couldn't be helped. He wouldn't pull back now.

"I had a purpose in joining you this evening. I trust you will not think ill of me if I confess I would like Miss Brompton—and the others from London—to acquire the notion that there is an interest between Lady Ware and myself."

"That is rather presumptuous," Georgiana exclaimed before the others could respond to the ramshackle proposal.

"Indeed, sir. It would place Georgiana in a dreadful position," Elspeth rushed to add. "We may be provincial here, but word from Sidmouth does reach the rest of the world. How else did those Londoners know *you* are here?"

Lord Thornbury raised his brows, the smile fading from his face. "I beg your pardon. I had no idea the thought of depressing that woman's regard would be so repulsive. I sought help from those I deemed friends. Forget I mentioned it."

"It was impulsive," Lord Musgrave said. "Not like you to be impulsive, Jason. You usually think a thing through first."

"Chalk it up to addled wits," Lord Thornbury murmured.

"You have encountered problems at your house, my lord?" Georgiana inquired with a slight thawing in her manner.

"The cook either offers the food half-cooked or charred. I vow I shall return to the Royal York for my meals," his lordship complained.

"Why do you think I am so often at Lady Ware's table?" Lord Musgrave said with a chuckle.

"That is true," Georgiana admitted. "Fie on you, my lord. I thought it was our company you valued."

That stimulating topic was dropped when the carriage pulled to a halt before the London Hotel, where the assemblies were held. The street was busy with people walking from the Royal York and carriages letting off passengers bound for the ball.

Georgiana and Elspeth hurried inside, then up the stairs to the rooms. Once their wraps had been set aside, they entered the main room to be greeted by the Royal York ladies, as they called those older widows who had taken Georgiana to their collective hearts.

"My, you do look lovely in blue, Lady Ware," Mrs. Arbuthnot declared fervently. "Brings out the blue in your eyes."

"And you, Miss Pettibone, are most pleasing in that shade of pale green. What is it called?" Mrs. Swinford inquired, drawing Elspeth along with her to where the other women were gathered.

"Willow green, ma'am," Elspeth replied, casting a puzzled look back at Georgiana.

"It seems your companion has acquired sudden popularity," Lord Thornbury murmured into Georgiana's tender ear. "Not but what she deserves it; she is a lovely young woman. Far too nice to be a governess."

"Did your friend tell you of her background, then?" Georgiana said, ignoring the pang that contracted her heart at his praise of her dearest Elspeth.

"He did. He also informed me of your gracious generosity toward her. It does you great credit, you know. For a woman, especially one as beautiful as you, to offer such consideration to another pretty woman is unusual. I am impressed."

Georgiana was taken aback at these words from one who had caused her such grief and heartache. Could it be that he repented of his desire to seduce her? Might he now see that she was not a woman to accept such attentions? That he had totally misread her character at Kenyon Hall?

When he led her into the first dance, she was still preoccupied with this new image of Lord Thornbury. She unthinkingly smiled at him, accepting his hand in the pattern of the dance with genuine pleasure. That he showed her more of those little courtesies she had come to appreciate while at Kenyon Hall was not noticed at first. When she did, Georgiana wanted to give him the benefit of the doubt and credit him with the change of character he seemed to deserve.

"You are enjoying the dance?" he asked when they chanced to be side by side.

"Indeed, sir. This favorably compares to the assembly at Cheltenham, even if it is a bit smaller. I have no great background of such affairs, but I find it most pleasing."

"The group from London has stirred interest. I vow there is a larger number present this evening." He looked around the crowded room with a practiced eye, gauging the count to a nicety.

Georgiana chuckled. "No one would wish to miss anything of possible interest, my lord. Having spent most of my life in a small community, I well know how the least little thing must be discussed at great lengths the following day. To have missed the occasion is not to be borne. The Royal York widows desire food for tea, if you follow my meaning."

The pattern separated them for some time, but when they came together again, he said, "And what will be the topic of conversation tomorrow?"

"Why, Miss Brompton's magnificent gown." Georgiana cast another look at the creation worn by the elegant young woman. Of heavy rich silk in a luscious plum color and trimmed with exquisite blonde lace and ribands, it fairly screamed a premier London mantuamaker, one of French background to be sure. Her evening hat of matching plum silk was ornamented with puce plumes and a splendid gold tassel. Lady Yeldham came a close second in brilliance with a gown of antique moiré in deep bottle green, much tucked and ornamented with clusters of pink silk roses.

In her simple blue gown of glacé silk with modest tucking and a single white silk rose at her bosom, Georgiana felt her original pleasure in her appearance fade. That is, until she caught Lord Thornbury's admiring gaze.

"They are overblown roses in comparison to your fresh budding beauty, my lady. Any gentleman of discernment will tell you that."

Indeed, it seemed that while Miss Brompton did not lack for partners, she was not besieged as was Georgiana. The gentlemen thronged about her in a delightfully satisfying way. At one point she found her gaze entangled with Lord Thornbury's and she gave him a very private and amused look, certain he would share her entertainment in the situation.

Miss Brompton sought out Georgiana between dances, pausing on her way to the refreshment tables.

"I must thank you for your kind invitation to your little party this coming Saturday. I suppose Lord Thornbury will be there as well? You appear to be good friends." There was a definite note of inquiry in her words that Georgiana was not about to satisfy.

"He has been invited as has his friend, Lord Musgrave."

"Oh, yes, the baron," Miss Brompton said, quite dismissing the fine gentleman who came from a wealthy and respectable family.

"I have found him excellent company, as has his old family friend, Miss Pettibone."

Miss Pettibone obviously did not rate comment in the least, which angered Georgiana. She had met snobs like Miss Brompton, but none so lovely in face or patronizing in attitude.

"It should be vastly amusing. You intend to come to London next Season, Lady Ware?" Apparently the beauty had heard that Georgiana was considering such a possibility.

"Lady Kenyon has invited me to reside with her as long as I wish," admitted Georgiana, knowing better now the high position her ladyship held in society.

"Lady Kenyon?" Miss Brompton said in faint accents. This information seemed to render the lady speechless, for no additional queries followed. She nodded slightly and turned to her companion, requesting Lady Yeldham join her at the punch bowl.

When Lord Thornbury presented himself for his second

dance, Georgiana was in greater charity with him than previously.

"It would seem I owe your aunt a great deal for taking me up, as it were. Miss Brompton was most impressed that her ladyship has invited me to reside with her next Season."

"And shall you?" Jason wondered if he ought to tell Georgiana that he ran tame in his aunt's house, much preferring it to his own domicile.

"I consider it more seriously as time goes on. After all the entertainments in Sidmouth, I fear life in the country may seem too mild, dull by comparison."

"You do not fear your stepson, then? When Musgrave and I met him I could see he might not be to your liking." Jason had never revealed to her his conversation with Ware and wondered if he ought to warn her what a dangerous man Lord Ware might prove to be.

"True, sir. However Bel is a most adequate guard. Ware detests that cat."

"Were I Bel, I would be careful what I ate."

"You do not think he would harm Bel!" Georgiana cried in distress, although softly so no one might overhear her words.

Lord Thornbury bent his head so she might hear him better. "It depends on whether or not he can hire the right sort of maids, does it not?"

Georgiana looked at his lordship with complete understanding in her eyes and a very aware expression on her face. Then she smiled at his lordship—one of those startling, disarming, and quite brilliant smiles that had so captivated him while at Kenyon Hall. He had not expected to see one again.

"I thank you for the warning, my lord. Bel means a great deal to me and I would not take kindly to anyone harming him."

Jason wondered if it was possible to make waistcoats in fabric that didn't shred quite so easily.

Across the room this exchange was carefully noted by the beautiful Miss Brompton and her friend Lady Yeldham. They exchanged angry looks with raised brows. Their feelings were not improved when they overheard two of the Royal York widows speaking nearby.

"Such a fine gentleman, Lord Thornbury, and so captivated by Lady Ware. I believe they will make a match of it. She is the dearest girl. He seems worthy of her, do you not agree?" Mrs. Swinford said in a voice calculated to carry just so far.

"Indeed, Mrs. Swinford," Mrs. Arbuthnot replied in the same manner. "Such charm and beauty, not to mention her excellent jointure and inheritance, make her a most desirable and eligible bride."

"I wonder when the wedding will be?" Mrs. Swinford replied with evident interest.

"Judging by his lordship's ardent attention, it will not be overly long," Mrs. Arbuthnot said gleefully.

Miss Brompton swished angrily out the door and down the stairs to her waiting carriage, the Yeldhams and Mr. Rood hurrying to follow her.

It was late when the carriage brought Georgiana and her party back to Rose Cottage. She invited the gentlemen to join them for a glass of sherry, not having port or brandy in the house.

Musgrave began to voice his intention to return to his friend's house even as Jason took him by the elbow to push him toward the door.

"We are loath to return to our bachelor establishment. I believe what I need is someone to guide me in the selection of help. I have the most confounded luck when it comes to servants. How do you fare, my lady?" he inquired of Georgiana.

"I suppose there is no established agency here as there would be in a larger town. Either you seek help through your agent from a place like Exeter or Cheltenham, or you go to London. I was fortunate that my servants came with the house—except for Perkins and John Coachman."

"I shall investigate the possibilities." He wandered over to inspect the contents of her tray of bottles and decanters set out by the housekeeper.

"You had better leave word to have a number of bottles of wine dropped off for you," he commented, then caught her look of dismay. "Even the parson has his brandy left at his doorstep during the night. Besides, you would not wish the party from London to have another reason to look down their noses at our little society here."

She frowned, then nodded. "I expect you have the right of it, but it distresses me a great deal. The housekeeper knows how this is done?"

"Do not give it another thought. I shall be happy to tend to it on your behalf."

"Oh, yes, The Old Ship. I expect you leave word there?" She bent her head to study her hands so missed his start of surprise at her words.

Not about to commit himself, he shrugged and said, "I told you not to worry, dear lady. Now, I would hear a tune—the theme and first two variations of that Mozart sonata if you please."

Georgiana gave him a speaking look, but seated herself at the pianoforte to commence playing the music he had seemed to enjoy before. When she finished she turned to face him, awaiting the comment sure to come.

"Still have a spot of trouble with that one part, I see. Best not play with Miss Brompton here. She has no charity in her soul and does not appreciate passion in music."

Georgiana shrugged. She would rather be deemed to have charity in her soul and passion in her music than be considered a beauty of the first water, not to mention a snob, and never an Ice Maiden.

"Well, who cares a fig for Miss Brompton? As far as I can tell she is nothing more than a mushroom," Elspeth declared in a rush of support for her friend.

"I believe"—Georgiana spoke before the men could champion Miss Brompton—"she comes from a wealthy old family who may not have a title, but assuredly have position. Mrs. Swinford was kind enough to provide details."

Elspeth was suitably impressed, more or less.

Thus it was when Saturday evening arrived and Georgiana greeted her guests, it was with the knowledge that she had an ample supply of beverages and a charitable heart toward Miss Brompton. She had also learned, but not repeated, that Miss

Brompton had enjoyed three Seasons in London and had not taken. Perhaps the poor dear was becoming a trifle desperate?

Mr. Rood was a soft-spoken man, his sandy hair tumbling over his brow in controlled disarray, while the silent Lord Yeldham looked as though he suffered from dyspepsia. He escorted his wife with the resigned air of a man who knows he will be miserable come what may.

Miss Brompton was glittering in an exceedingly low-cut mauve gown covered with a sequined gauze overskirt and wore a feathered and sequined ornament in her hair. She fluttered her fan about as though directing the ensemble of guests to her own particular tune.

At her side, Lady Yeldham bloomed mildly in a pale orange gown of shagreen bedecked with masses of bows from which sprang sprays of tiny white blossoms. Georgiana suspected they were intended to represent orange blossoms.

Meeting her guests, Georgiana felt assured that her own gown of delicate Bishop's blue in gossamer satin might not have the grandeur of Miss Brompton's, but she deemed it far more suitable to a small party given at a seaside resort. And she had to admit that the admiring gaze offered by Lord Thornbury did much to boost her confidence.

Elspeth hurried to join her between arrivals, having successfully set the Royal York widows to chatting with any and all who were in the drawing room.

In her pretty Indian muslin gown of peach trimmed with Bruges lace Elspeth looked lovelier than usual. Her cheeks were becomingly flushed and she leaned over to confide, "This brings back so many memories of my girlhood when Mama entertained. I had forgotten so much."

"Then we shall entertain more so you may recall happier times," Georgiana said as Lord Thornbury strode up to the door. He was all elegance, having donned the deep velvet coat he had worn while at Kenyon Hall over a pristine white waistcoat and his black breeches. His black patent shoes and hose were the very latest in style.

Lord Musgrave, having come over earlier to be of assistance to the women, stared at his friend when he met him in the hall.

"Recall that. Wonder if Lady Ware will. 'Tis what you wore the night she decamped from your aunt's house."

"I had forgotten. Pray she is not blessed with that sort of memory." Jason turned to look back to where Georgiana greeted another arrival. He had not observed any change in her attitude, but she was becoming more skilled at concealing what was in her mind.

"La, my lord"—Miss Brompton simpered as she drifted up to join the two men—"such elegance for a simple country party." She waited for the usual compliments on her attire. When none were forthcoming, her eyes acquired a dangerous glitter.

Belatedly, but too late to be of great help in the matter, Jason said in a most perfunctory manner, "May I say you look charming this evening, Miss Brompton? Lady Yeldham as well. Veritable butterflies in this small paradise."

The dangerous light in her eyes faded some, but Jason determined the damage had been done. If she took it out on him, all was well. She had better not try Georgiana or she would find herself beyond the pale in this tight little circle. It was a good thing that Bel was confined to the conservatory for the evening. The cat would not have liked Miss Brompton at all.

The evening went well, considering it was Georgiana's first attempt at a party of this scale. She was enormously thankful for Elspeth's support and advice.

Then it came time for Miss Brompton to be asked to play.

"The party is in honor of the fine pianoforte Lord Thornbury caused to be brought here from Exeter for my use," Georgiana explained, which truly did not set well with the spoiled beauty. "Since my own skills are modest, I would deem it a pleasure if you would entertain us with a selection."

Miss Brompton inclined her head a trifle, then grandly swept to the instrument, seated herself, and proceeded to play—quite perfectly—the very same Mozart sonata that Georgiana had attempted to play and frequently mangled. With Miss Brompton the skill and technique were professional. Had the lady desired, she might have given concerts.

Georgiana gave Lord Thornbury a dark look, wondering if he had by chance or design revealed the very sonata that she tried to play, then acquitted him of this ignoble deed. He was not so fond of Miss Brompton that he would encourage her to make her hostess angry or uncomfortable.

Upon her conclusion came all the applause even a person like Miss Brompton might wish. She graciously consented to play a second selection, this time a piece by Clementi that Georgiana had never attempted.

"See what a bit of practice will accomplish?" Lord Thornbury observed quietly to Georgiana, leaning over the back of her chair under the benevolent gaze of the Royal York ladies.

"But can she sketch a rose?" Georgiana asked sweetly in a near whisper. She bestowed a knowing smile on his lordship, then sat back to enjoy the music and the knowledge that Lord Thornbury leaned against her chair and did not hover by the pianoforte. Mr. Rood did that quite nicely.

Following Miss Brompton's superior playing, the guests promptly rose to mingle and chat, not requesting a third selection. Georgiana took note of the musician's flushed and annoyed face, but she was not about to compel her guests to listen when they clearly wished to do otherwise, merely to satisfy the vanity of a lady in her third Season.

Elspeth assisted by encouraging the company to drift in the direction of the dining room where a splendid supper was set forth, the cook having outdone herself for her admired Lady Ware.

"I say, if you were serious in welcoming us at meals, I vow we will camp on your doorstep," Lord Thornbury said after filling his plate a second time.

"I cannot say you appear to have suffered since your removal to your house on the hill. Peak House is it called?" Georgiana said with a laugh. "However, I believe we might take pity on you if your cook is truly as bad as you say."

"She is." He chanced to look over and took note he and Georgiana were being acutely observed by Miss Brompton and her friend Lady Yeldham. "In addition to not being able to draw anything at all, I doubt Miss Brompton would be so kind as to invite poor bachelors to share her fare. It is a most noble deed you perform, Georgiana. Quite in keeping with your character, I must say." His eyes twinkled with mischief, or something akin to it.

Georgiana could not help but blush at these words from the man who drove her out of her mind at times. She had not missed the color of his coat. If it was not the same one, it was identical to the one he had worn at Kenyon Hall.

"Now, my lady," Lord Thornbury said engagingly, "you must not neglect your guests. I shall help. Perhaps I can persuade the ladies from the Royal York to indulge in second helpings as well?"

Georgiana could not help but laugh at this, for he was behaving like a naughty boy. "Very well, do. I shall demand an accounting later, I assure you."

"*Later?* I am yours to command, my lady." He touched her lightly on her shoulder, a touch that must appear disturbingly familiar to those who watched.

Unaware of what others might think, Georgiana spun around to stare into the darkness beyond the candlelit dining room, unable to believe she had uttered those words in jest or otherwise. Had she actually said she would see him later—for an accounting, no less? The very word had haunted her. Of course it had been uttered in raillery, but still . . . Before she could assimilate the complications, Miss Brompton appeared at her side.

"Lady Ware, may I offer my felicitations? You appear to have well and truly captured Lord Thornbury. I do hope you will be able to hold him once you reach London."

Georgiana stared at her elegant guest, aghast at her words. So Lord Thornbury had achieved his objective after all. How dreadfully shabby of him.

Chapter Eleven

"What has you looking so blue-deviled this morning?" Elspeth queried as she studied her friend while seated at the breakfast table. "You ought to be on top of the world after that lovely party last evening. Everyone seemed to have a marvelous time."

"Yes, I thought so. The Royal York ladies were truly delightful, were they not?" Georgiana replied politely, not meeting Elspeth's gaze.

"So what is the problem—unless it is something you do not wish to discuss." Elspeth rose from the table to pour herself another cup of tea, then returned to her seat, sipping the steaming brew while watching her friend. "A more woebegone face I have yet to see."

"It is nothing I wish to talk about just now. Perhaps later." Georgiana pushed a bit of egg around her plate, then finally finished the remainder of her tea before excusing herself from the table to stroll in the garden with Bel.

It still bothered her—what had been said last night. And done. Had he remembered his use of the word *later* or was it merely happenstance? And what about the impression he had given Miss Brompton? Had that been deliberate? Or had it all been an accident?

She had let her defenses down, had begun to trust him again. And what happened? He betrayed her—the handsome, charming, thoughtful, debonair . . . rogue. Scoundrel. Cad. The man was utterly incorrigible. He had suggested they dupe Miss Brompton and after it was decided—by the rest of them—that it would not be the thing to do, he had managed it anyway by the merest touch of his hand and a lingering look.

Hers to command, indeed. Well, she would see about that. He would have to prove himself worthy of her trust before she gave it again. And somehow, she thought, sinking down on her favorite stone bench, she doubted he would be constant.

"Fool. Simpleton," she berated herself.

The sound of a cart squeaking along the drive caught her attention and brought her to her feet once again. A nondescript man clad in faded gray clothes walked at the side of his donkey, pulling a cart piled with wood and peat. She watched him amble around to the back of the house, where she supposed the housekeeper would tell him what was needed. Odd, with all the coal to be had, that locals would prefer wood and the smoke-producing peat. Perhaps it was cheaper.

She turned to Bel, who had bristled up, his fur standing every which way, looking twice his size and most ferocious. Gathering the cat in her arms to prevent his attack on a hapless delivery person, she waited for the man to depart.

"Now there is a picture," a gentleman said in his lazy familiar way. "Am I safe? Or must I send to London for another supply of waistcoats? My tailor will probably send Bel a shipment of kippers in gratitude."

"Lord Thornbury," Georgiana said, slowly turning about to give him a deliberately cool look. She clung securely to Bel, who wiggled in a desire to attack his lordship. While she might be angry with the man, she did not wish to see more damage to his clothing or person.

"I gather I did something to displease you," he said after a glimpse of her face.

"You did." She decided on the instant that she would attack him in her own way. "We distinctly said that it would be unseemly to give Miss Brompton the idea that there was something between you and me. And yet before she left, Miss Brompton so kindly congratulated me on well and truly capturing Lord Thornbury. You! How do you account for this, sirrah?"

"I protest. I am innocent as accused. If Miss Brompton made that assumption it was the working of her own fevered brain, not something I said to her." He walked toward Georgiana, step by step drawing closer to where she stood.

"Perhaps it was not something you said but did that brought her to this conclusion?" Georgiana said wildly.

"Did you consider that it might have been something that *you* said or did that gave her this charming and quite untruthful impression?"

"No," Georgiana said, backing away from the slowly advancing man. In this present mood he struck her as being rather dangerous. Of course he would not do her violence, but he had other means of most effective punishment at his disposal that could utterly undo her.

"You did not flirt with me intentionally—your eyes lighting up with delight as I returned your banter? Turn to me a dozen times with little questions that only someone intimately acquainted might answer? Laugh up at me when I leaned over your chair? Beg me to assist you with the widows in the hearing of several persons?"

"I did no such thing!" she denied, completely aghast at his words.

"But you did, my dear."

"That is so much nonsense and I am not your dear!" Georgiana protested, trying to retain a semblance of sanity. He drew closer and she backed into a particularly thorny rosebush, preventing further retreat.

With a swiftness that took both Georgiana and Bel by surprise, he covered the final distance with one long step and pulled her and the cat into his arms.

"Rather a wicked armful, but I must talk with you and I dare not let that animal free," his lordship said, picking up his captives and striding through one of the French doors to the drawing room. Here he sat down on a sofa, dropping Georgiana and Bel alongside him.

"Well, of all the high-handed people in this world, you must take the prize." Georgiana gave him an affronted glare, while from the protection of Georgiana's arms Bel sat eyeing Jason's waistcoat through narrowed eyes.

"I probably take a prize, all right. I hardly doubt it is for being high-handed, however. More like prize idiot. I do not know why I find you enticing, madam, but I do. Heaven knows there are an abundance of other women in this world, but I find myself attracted to you whether I wish it or not."

"Lord Thornbury, you do me great honor with your, er, interest, but I truly do not desire you—in any way. And if you think to seduce me with your words, do think again. You are scarcely loverlike! My mistake was that I did not confront you long ago and tell you to your face that I was not available for dalliance. There will be no 'later,' Lord Thornbury. Not now. Not ever."

He studied her for a moment, then looked away. She had no idea what went on in his mind, for his face was that smooth mask she had seen him wear while at Kenyon Hall when he entertained Selina Woodburn.

She held Bel snugly in her arms, then slipped from his lordship's light clasp. "I shan't permit Bel to destroy that lovely waistcoat, no matter how I feel. You may rest easy on that score."

"You do not know how comforting that is, dear lady," he said, rising to hover over her.

Refusing to back away from him, Georgiana sought words. "I believe it best if you leave, sirrah."

"No, I shan't depart like a whipped puppy with my tail between my legs." Instead he placed a brief, tantalizing kiss on her very surprised lips. "That is far more satisfactory, I believe." His eyes now gleamed with a wicked light that made her utterly furious.

"I once said you were a cad, and that confirms it," Georgiana cried. "Elspeth?" She looked at the door as though to summon up her companion who never seemed to be around when she was truly needed.

"I saw her talking with Musgrave on the other side of the house. I doubt she can hear you."

"Did you plan this . . . attack?" Georgiana demanded.

"Plan something so spontaneous? You give me more credit than I am due, dear Lady Ware."

"Can you not see I wish you gone?" she cried in total frustration.

"You promised me breakfast," he calmly replied, strolling off to the dining room where food was still to be found.

"I do not believe this. It must be a nightmare. No, a day-mare, for the sun shines," Georgiana said in bemusement, following in his lordship's wake.

The maid entered and upon seeing him, scurried out to return moments later with a pot of tea. Disappearing once again, she hurried back with a steaming egg and bacon pie.

Lord Thornbury sniffed appreciatively. Seating himself at the table, he gave Georgiana a reproachful look. "If the Royal York ladies could hear you this morning, they might be disillusioned. They seem to hold you in high esteem." He served himself and began to eat.

Georgiana dropped Bel to the floor. His lordship growled at the cat, who promptly ran from the room and out to the garden. Georgiana also fled, followed by masculine laughter.

The man was insane.

She examined nothing in particular, merely stared off at greenery until she heard soft footfalls behind her. Turning, she found Elspeth approaching.

"My dear, are you well? I thought you would be entertaining your guest."

"I was wrong. The entire world has gone mad," Georgiana said with a hint of bitterness. She massaged her crooked little finger that ached this morning.

"Do you deny that you invited two gentlemen to take potluck with us? Bennett and Lord Thornbury are most grateful, for the cook burned everything this morning and they were starving by the time they presented themselves at our door."

"I trust he fired the cook," Georgiana said, not budging a foot nor looking the least repentant at her neglect.

"Of course he did," Elspeth said gently as one might reassure a recalcitrant child.

"The man is demented, you know. He claims he did nothing to give Miss Brompton the impression that there is something between him and me. Would you credit that he insisted *I* am the one at fault? He claimed that I flirted with him, welcomed him at my side, all manner of nonsensical things. It isn't true!" She studied Elspeth's face a moment, then added hesitantly, "Is it?"

"Well," Elspeth temporized. "He was here, there, and everywhere, quite as though he was the host, you know. It would not be impossible for a woman to jump to conclusions such as Miss Brompton reached."

"I treated him as a friend, nothing more. And he had transgressed that standing this morning. He kissed me and growled at Bel."

Elspeth compressed her lips, trying to look severe and failing miserably.

"It is not amusing," Georgiana insisted before giving way to tears.

"Oh, my dear girl. Do come inside for tea. A missive came for you from the Royal York. Most likely a pretty thank-you from one of your guests. It will cheer you immensely, I am sure."

Georgiana permitted herself to be led into the house while frantically dabbing at her eyes to erase all sign of tears. She did *not* want that dratted man to think he had reduced her to this state. Even if he had.

Once seated in the drawing room she listened to the pleasant sound of male conversation and laughter, thinking to herself that both men had unusually nice voices. Then she recalled what manner of man one of them was.

Bel crept into the room from the garden, looking about with wary eyes. Georgiana scooped him into her arms.

"Poor darling, that nasty man frightened you out of your wits," Georgiana said, soothing the beast in her lap with gentle hands.

"Here is your letter," Elspeth said gaily as she entered the room, pausing to look at the cowering Bel with an astonished expression. She said nothing, merely handing over the creamy stiff paper available for guests of the Royal York Hotel.

Abandoning Bel, Georgiana broke the seal, unfolded the paper, and began to read.

"What is the matter?" Elspeth cried, clearly alarmed at Georgiana's reaction.

"We are invited to dinner Monday evening at the Royal York," Georgiana said, striving to remain calm.

"But that is lovely. Nothing surely to take amiss."

"The invitation comes from Miss Brompton and the Yeldhams. I gather Mr. Rood is still around, much like a lapdog. He is not a part of the invitation issuers, however."

"Oh, my." Elspeth sank down on the nearest chair to contemplate this development.

It was at this point that the men entered the room, both looking replete and content.

"Oh, did you receive a summons to dine as well?" Lord Thornbury inquired, sauntering across the room. He lounged against the fireplace mantel, looking far too at home. "Ours arrived just before we left the house."

"I see."

"You had best attend," Elspeth said hesitantly.

"You are invited as well, so I would not be required to go alone," Georgiana retorted.

"You have us, you know," Musgrave inserted. "We would not dream of leaving you unprotected."

"Particularly since your cat has been found vulnerable," Lord Thornbury added. He turned to his friend to explain. "I discovered the cat is nothing more than a furry bully. He was set for an attack and I growled at him. Sent him off to the garden with a flea in his ear."

"What a taradiddle," Georgiana declared.

"I think you are in the suds now, Jason, old fellow."

"Why? Because I put the cat in his place?"

"About the invitation," Elspeth began.

"We shall go. You could wear your new lavender silk. I may return to my blacks," Georgiana predicted glumly, giving Lord Thornbury a narrow look that strongly resembled Bel's just before he attacked.

"Now, now. This is a perfect time to put a stop to any business you wish. Had you considered that?" he said.

Georgiana thought for a moment, then brightened. "The very thing. Kind of you to suggest it, my lord. I shall accept the lovely invitation. And I believe I shall wear that new silver tissue that arrived before we left."

Encouraging Bel to go out the French doors, which the cat did with more haste than grace, Georgiana found a quill pen and paper in the small writing desk. Ignoring the gentlemen, she promptly sat down to write her note of acceptance. "It is always polite to be prompt in replies."

After she had sealed it with red wax and was about to call for her groom, Lord Thornbury sauntered to the desk and held out his hand.

"Musgrave and I are going that direction. I should be happy to execute this small commission for you." He slipped the paper from her hand while she watched in dumb surprise.

"But—" she began, to counter his presumption.

"Your profuse thanks are not necessary, my lady. After that excellent breakfast it is the least I could do. You must think of a few more tasks for us. Oh—I almost forgot," he said, pausing at the doorway, missive in hand, "I intend to order some extra food be delivered here. We refuse to impose on your hospitality without doing some small thing in return. We shall see you before dinner."

With those words he disappeared down the hall and out the front door. After a look at Elspeth, Musgrave followed.

"That man will drive me mad. One of these days you may be carting me off to Bedlam," Georgiana prophesied.

"Come, we had best have Perkins take a look at our gowns. I do not recall the silver tissue. Have I seen it?"

The more normal topic of gowns and gloves, evening hats and slippers restored Georgiana's feeling of normalcy as nothing else might have.

After a quiet lunch at which the gentlemen did not appear—thank goodness—the two women strolled down to the Esplanade and Wallis's Circulating Library.

"It is amazing all the things one may find in the library besides Minerva Novels and periodicals and, of course, ordinary books," Elspeth said while inspecting the interior of the spacious shop.

"Indeed, there is everything from elegant French-style soaps to fancy teas."

"I could spend hours in here, just browsing," Elspeth confided.

"I suppose some women do," Georgiana replied with an eye on the ladies of the Royal York who now reposed on the wooden benches out in front beneath the shelter of the porch. "Gossiping appears to be quite in favor."

"Well, as to that, how else does one learn what is going on in a place?" Elspeth said with a smile.

"I believe you would enjoy a comfortable coze," Georgiana challenged.

"I would," Elspeth replied and wearing a happy smile headed in the direction of Mrs. Arbuthnot.

"Dear Lady Ware," Mrs. Swinford said when Georgiana left the interior of the library carrying the latest Minerva Novel in her arms—she felt that the heroine of one of these silly books might have a more rational view of life than she did at the moment. "Such a splendid time we had last evening."

"I am so pleased you enjoyed it—" Georgiana began but was ruthlessly cut off by the lady.

"Miss Brompton played with such elegance. What a pity she has not found a gentleman to appreciate her talent. Mr. Rood informed me that he is tone deaf and has no sense of rhythm in the least. Poor man, he is not for her!"

"I see," Georgiana said, feeling as though the floor had just moved. "And whom might you suggest?"

"Not Lord Thornbury, that is certain. Someone will turn up eventually." Mrs. Swinford spoke with such certainty that Georgiana fully expected a man to come around the corner any moment wearing a label that designated him to be the property of Miss Clare Brompton.

Georgiana expected Miss Brompton would be most comforted by the news, should she hear of it.

"You are coming to the Royal York Monday evening, are you not? I understand that Miss Brompton thought it would be nice to have a dinner party to enliven our lives. We are invited as well."

"We shall be gay to dissipation, shall we not?" Mrs. Arbuthnot demanded cheerfully.

"Indeed." Georgiana wondered what they served for breakfast at the Royal York these days. The ladies sounded as though they had been at the wine bottle.

It was some while later that she managed to pry Elspeth

away from an intriguing conversation about everyone who was presently visiting Sidmouth.

"Did you know that Major Giles has arrived in town? Mrs. Arbuthnot said he is an old beau of Mrs. Swinford's. What fun," Elspeth said with a chuckle.

"I should think she would be past all that," Georgiana said without much consideration for her words.

"I should hope we would never be past all that," Elspeth protested. "It would mean the death of all hope, of all expectation of love."

"Mercy," Georgiana whispered, then entered the house to head for her room until dinner. She wondered if a nasty fairy had decided to take over her life. It seemed that no matter what she did, nothing went right.

Monday evening the gentlemen arrived promptly at six of the clock. Dressed to the nines and looking far better than any man had a right to look, Lord Thornbury examined the silver tissue gown with a connoisseur's eye.

"Your little mantuamaker does very well with silver tissue." As a tribute it left much to be desired.

"You are too kind, my lord," Georgiana said with mock humility.

They drove to the Royal York in the coach. Georgiana listened with half an ear to Elspeth and the men conversing. For the most part she gazed out of the window, taking note that odd-looking man in drag gray was about again.

"How peculiar. That fellow who delivered the wood to the house is just turning up Fore Street. Going to The Old Ship, most likely. He's no cart of wood now."

Lord Thornbury and Musgrave exchanged looks, but made no response to her remark.

Miss Brompton greeted them with gracious charm in the private dining room available for patrons of the Royal York.

"Lord Thornbury," she purred, setting Georgiana's back up, "you are to sit next to Lady Ware. And of course Miss Pettibone will be with Lord Musgrave."

Even as she absorbed the information, Georgiana noted that Miss Brompton had been compelled to take notice of Elspeth and Bennett. But Georgiana did not welcome partnering Lord Thornbury, not in the least.

The gathering milled about for a time, then all were summoned to the table by the ringing of a crystal bell. Georgiana glared at her place card, set so cozily next to his lordship's.

"Best not to say anything, you know," Jason said, looking down over Georgiana's shoulder to note this position offered a splendid view. "To call attention to the seating arrangements would not be the thing."

"I am well aware of that, sirrah," she countered softly.

"It seems that we are destined to spend the evening side by side, sharing the excellent food offered by the Royal York."

"Do you never think of anything but food?" Georgiana asked crossly before thinking how her words might be interpreted.

He gave her what could only be deemed an assessing and appreciative look, one that she was sure made her blush.

"You are a wicked man," she whispered.

"I am innocent. Did not utter a word," he replied in an undertone, then said something to the lady at his other side.

Having said more than she ought, Georgiana subsided into silence. Fortunately Lord Thornbury took it upon himself to be charming to one and all. He chatted with the woman at his other side, then turned to Georgiana when the next remove was brought in.

"Oysters in cream sauce, lobster patties, and fish soup. Ah. If you compel us to go elsewhere we could always return here," he said with a mournful note in his voice. "But Musgrave is determined to fix the attentions of Miss Pettibone. Or were you aware things had progressed to that point?"

"She is a wonderful person. He could find no finer wife no matter how long he searched."

"So, you are not against the institution of marriage," he said in a conversational manner.

"Not in the least. If it pleases both parties, I believe it a most agreeable circumstance." She glanced down the table to where Major Giles, retired, now chatted happily with Mrs. Swinford and smiled. "It seems that age makes no difference."

"But you are not a great age, my dear."

"What has that to do with anything? If Elspeth agrees to marry your friend I shall hunt for another companion. I feel certain there must be other charming ladies who would welcome an opportunity to"—Georgiana searched her mind for something unexpected—"travel in Europe."

"There is a war on, in the event you had failed to notice," he said wryly.

"Well, we can begin in Sweden, then progress to Russia and back to Denmark, then south to Italy. I read it is possible to avoid the army of Napoleon if desired. After all," she pointed out reasonably, "his men cannot be everywhere."

He gave her a considering look, as though he doubted the sincerity of her words or her sanity, possibly both.

"I thought you intended to help me catch the smugglers."

Arrested in the act of taking a bite of mushroom fricassee, Georgiana turned to give him a speculative look. "Do you mean that?"

"You appeared quite interested in the matter some days ago."

She blushed and stared at her plate for a moment, recalling her precipitate midnight dash to Peak Hill and all that followed. "You thought I was worried about *you* at the time," she reminded, "not smugglers."

"Well, it is a mere transfer of interest. Something to occupy an odd hour or two."

"You cannot be serious," she replied, bending her head close to him so there was no danger they might be overheard.

He leaned toward her, saying, "I am most serious, my lady."

Georgiana gave him a quick look, uncertain as to the tone in his words, the possible implication. Or was she imagining things again?

Life had been so simple—and blessedly dull—before she had gone to Kenyon Hall on what was supposed to have been a modest reintroduction to society. What had gone wrong? It was the man at her side. The moment he had entered her life all had been topsy-turvy.

Now it seemed impossible to avoid the dratted man. She could not take refuge in lace shops and looking at silk and muslin underthings forever, could she?

"I would find that an interesting challenge," she said at last under the cover of other table conversation. She would have sworn that he muttered something like "It takes one to know one," but *that* did not make the least sense.

Jason forked a bite of excellent roast lamb into his mouth and chewed while wondering what next to do with the lady of his intentions. She was driving him quietly mad. What a pity he couldn't growl at her and bring her to heel as he'd done with Bel. This woman had to be the most contrary female in the world.

She also had good reason to be wary of him, he must not forget that. It had gradually come to him what it was he had said that night during the ball at Kenyon. He'd been intent upon seducing her, misreading her reactions, having his senses scrambled by their intoxicating kiss. If he'd had an ounce of functioning brains he'd have picked up on her innocence, her lack of understanding when he had murmured that he would see her later.

Evidently she had tumbled to his meaning somehow. Could she have overheard a conversation between Musgrave and him? Now, *that* was vague, but he suspected he had mentioned the beautiful widow and his intent to his friend. She'd not have fled otherwise.

They sat companionably close at the dinner table. The Royal York ladies looked delighted at the sight. Pity they had it all wrong. Georgiana was as far from being in his bed—legally, of course—as possible. He dare not bring up the topic for fear she would let Bel attack before he could growl at the beast.

Life without her did not bear thinking about. He must continue as he had determined. He would have to move in on her, sneak up on her like she was a shy partridge. Meals were a beginning. He bent toward Georgiana and began.

"I must thank you again for your consideration regarding the meals, my lady. All teasing aside, I am greatly in your debt. How that woman could claim to be a cook is beyond us. 'Tis a wonder we were not poisoned!"

"Mercy, I had no idea it was that bad," she replied, looking adorably concerned. That was it. Keep her worried about his safety.

"Between the cook and the smugglers, life has taken an interesting turn of late."

"You do not think they will try to murder you in your bed!" she whispered after first casting a glance about to see if anyone might overhear her.

"I can only hope they forget about me," he said humbly.

"Perhaps you ought to return to the haven offered by the Royal York?" she ventured, her brow pleating in a precious little frown he longed to kiss away.

"No. I would lure them into the house. I have no wish for my land to be used in such a manner."

"But how will you prevent it unless you remain here? The moment you are gone, they will do just as they please again."

Jason looked at Georgiana with greater respect. He had not anticipated her to be so clever.

"It is all the more reason to nab them now. We must discuss it when we have greater privacy. Tomorrow over breakfast?"

He didn't miss her suspicious look at him, quite as though she wondered if he was serious. He would have to do something to stir the pot a trifle. And he couldn't tell Musgrave, for that fellow would spill the budget to Elspeth Pettibone in a trice. No, this he would do alone.

Once he figured out what to do.

Chapter Twelve

Life was no simple matter, Georgiana decided the following day. She had made it utterly plain to Lord Thornbury that he need have no expectations of seducing her—or doing anything else to her for that matter—and yet he haunted her doorstep—or table, to be more precise.

She paused in the hallway, listening to the counterpoint of voices—Elspeth's sweet soprano contrasted with Lord Musgrave's pleasant tenor and Lord Thornbury's rich baritone. Had circumstances been otherwise, she might have welcomed the gentlemen. As it was, she fretted about a number of things over which she seemed to have little or no control.

For a gentleman supposedly astute as Lord Thornbury was reputed to be, he was extraordinarily dense when it came to his repeated dining at Rose Cottage. Surely he must see how it would appear to others—a gentleman of his reputation frequenting the home of a widow, especially one who already had a history of creating gossip, no matter how innocent she may have been. However he simply did not take no for an answer.

He must have been spoiled as a lad. Unlike their prince, who, it was said, had been raised with a heavy hand and frequent canings, Jason Ainsley, now Lord Thornbury, must have been reared by an indulgent parent or nanny and allowed to go on as he pleased. Eton was not a gentle place, so she had been informed by an elder brother, nor was Oxford particularly without pitfalls. Yet Lord Thornbury seemed to have sailed through them all unscathed, particularly in his understanding of what was proper in this instance.

The rain that had fallen during the night had ceased, and the clouds now reluctantly parted. Perhaps, she thought with great hope, she might escape these people and do something on her own. Elspeth still had not taken to the idea of the bathing machines. With the rainstorms gone and the sun shining again, the water ought to be lovely. It might wash away some of the cobwebs in Georgiana's brain.

She paused at the door to the dining room, looking beyond to the pretty garden that bloomed for their benefit. With the French doors open, it was as good as sitting in the midst of the flowers. And it brought memories of that lovely day at Kenyon Hall that she had spent with Lord Thornbury. Had he been sincere in his encomiums? Or had his compliments been made with the view to bedding her?

"Tea, Georgiana?" Elspeth said, rising to fetch the teapot. "This is a fresh pot."

"Your cook does uncommonly well with scones," Lord Thornbury said, one of those lazy smiles on his face, his eyes shadowed just enough so she couldn't tell their expression.

"And jam," offered Lord Musgrave. "Excellent preserves—made locally, I believe." He gestured to the crystal jar of rich red preserves that sat before him.

Rather than make a fuss, Georgiana accepted a cup of tea from Elspeth, a scone from the plate handed her by Lord Thornbury, and a spoon of preserves from the jar nudged in her direction by Lord Musgrave.

"Did you find Bel?" Elspeth inquired, for the cat had gone missing before breakfast.

"Indeed, I did. Poor beast was in my bedroom, half buried in the pillows. Did you growl at him when you came this morning, my lord?" she said to Lord Thornbury in a half-scolding manner.

With an amused look at the others who sat around the table, his lordship nodded. "I confess I did. I'm particularly fond of this waistcoat and had no wish to see it shredded. I cannot be assured that the fabric could be duplicated, you see."

"How mortifying to think that great beast of a cat is terrified of you, of all people," Georgiana shot back before thinking of how it might sound.

"I beg your pardon, ma'am," his lordship said with a smile. "I am no ogre nor am I a dandy. I simply like my waistcoat.

Surely you must have something you treasure? A shawl, perhaps? You owned a lovely shawl I chanced to admire while at Kenyon."

He had draped that shawl over her shoulders with such tender regard—or had that been a sham as well? Georgiana fired a mistrustful look his direction, then blandly replied, "I do enjoy that shawl. I suppose there is something I would not care to have ruined, but such material things can usually be replaced." It was only trust placed in a person one admired that could be greatly damaged, not to be easily repaired.

Dismissing him in a rather careless manner, she turned to Elspeth with a warm smile. "What are your plans for the day, my dear?"

Elspeth blinked, obviously surprised at this turn of conversation. "I had thought to go shopping with you, perhaps stop at the Circulating Library. I fancy the Royal York widows will be there in prime fettle. They are such dear souls; I quite enjoy their company."

"Perhaps we could invite them to share tea with us this afternoon. They must long for a change from the Royal York, no matter how elegant it might be," Georgiana said, darting a glance at Lord Thornbury. "I fancy you gentlemen will be out and about all day, doing whatever it is that gentlemen enjoy doing."

Jason exchanged a look with Musgrave, then said, "We had thought about riding over to East Budleigh, perhaps chatting with the vicar there."

"Admirable," Georgiana exclaimed with more enthusiasm than she had shown heretofore. "An excellent day for a ride. The sun is shining and the world is fresh and clean."

Not long after, the men found themselves being ushered from the house while being commended for their plan to visit the vicar in East Budleigh.

"That was rather hasty, Georgiana," Elspeth reproved when they had disappeared from sight.

"Those men are spending far too much time here. I'd not wish the gossips to wag their tongues over the matter."

"Possibly," Elspeth admitted. "Although Mrs. Arbuthnot expressed sympathy that Lord Thornbury had such dreadful luck with his cook and declared you quite a heroine for taking pity of the gentlemen."

Georgiana was about to snap back that the men could jolly well take their meals at the Royal York but didn't. How could she? It was plain that Elspeth nursed a *tendré* for Lord Musgrave and Georgiana would not selfishly throw a spoke in that particular wheel just to possibly save her own reputation. She had weathered storms of gossip before; she could do so again.

In a remarkably short time they were set for the morning. After convincing Elspeth that it was perfectly permissible for her to enjoy a comfortable coze with the widows at the Library while Georgiana took a dip in the water, the two set off on foot for the Esplanade. They both carried pink parasols and Georgiana brought a large linen towel with her in addition to her reticule. Elspeth had an improving book she intended to return in exchange for a more interesting novel like the one Georgiana had found previously—a Minerva Novel.

Of the dozen or so bathing machines that lined the beach, Georgiana chose the one at the far western end, away from the Library and the greatest amount of activity. Children frolicked in the shallow waves, for the sea was more calm than usual. Their squeals of delight mingled with shouts of youthful laughter. Fond mamas and nannies watched from beneath colorful parasols.

The same bather greeted Georgiana with her cheerful expression much the same. "Fine day," she said.

Georgiana paused to offer the pony a carrot, which the poor beast promptly snatched. Giving an apologetic look at the bather's husband who drove the pony back and forth all day, she walked around to the door.

"It is indeed," Georgiana replied while climbing up the steps to the wooden hut on wheels. The woman's husband urged the pony to move backward and they were soon deep into the water. Looking at the drab short-sleeved, high-necked gown with a dubious gaze, Georgiana said, "I believe I should like to swim in the nude today. That flannel drags one down far too much." It was also unpleasantly scratchy and offended her senses.

"I shall protect you, my leddy." And so she did—very well, too.

Georgiana placed her clothing on the high shelf, then wrapped the linen towel about her slim form. Once down the steps, she plunged beneath the water, handing the towel to the old woman.

It was utterly lovely, paddling about with the silken flow of the water over her skin. Instead of the heavy folds of flannel entangling her legs and dragging her down, she felt free and moved through the water with the ease of a fish, she thought, smiling broadly.

"The men doesn't swim with flannels on, my leddy," the bather said. "They be as God made 'em when they goes into the water." This image was firmly ignored by the young dowager, whose rise in color could not be wholly attributed to the sun.

It was a delightful time and she willingly paid extra to remain in the water longer than usual.

"My leddy knows Lord Thornbury?" the bather asked when Georgiana finally decided that she would turn into a salted prune if she didn't leave the sea.

"Indeed, I do," Georgiana said, startled at this query.

"He be nosing about where he oughtn't," the bather said in what could only be considered a cautioning tone.

Alarmed, Georgiana said, "I doubt he means harm to anyone. He inspects his property, I believe."

"Tell 'im if he knows what be good fer 'im to leave well enough alone." The old woman gave Georgiana a narrow-eyed, sober look from beneath the small-brimmed hat she wore. Even with her drab garments clinging to her and that funny little hat atop the scarf she had tied beneath her chin, she had a certain dignity, which made her warning all the more real.

Hugging the wet linen towel about her, Georgiana murmured, "I shall do that, ma'am." She scampered up the steps and disappeared into the bathing machine, exchanging the wet linen for a dry towel. This time there had been no one to view her as she left the water. She intended to scrub herself completely dry before leaving the wooden shelter for the relatively dry beach. There would be no repetition of the damp muslin gown whether Lord Thornbury was around to rescue her or not.

The bather wrung the water from Georgiana's towel, then offered to send it to Rose Cottage later with her son.

Georgiana paid for her use of the bathing machine, thinking that in a small town it was impossible for one to remain unknown. It impressed her with the importance of being exceedingly careful about her actions.

She unfurled her parasol and strolled along the Esplanade until she reached the Circulating Library and Elspeth's happy greeting.

"My, you look refreshed. Perhaps I ought to join you next time?"

"The seawater is very good for the skin," Mrs. Arbuthnot declared.

"Major Giles claims it does wonders for the digestion as well. Although whether one is to drink it or bathe in it to achieve this I am not certain," Mrs. Swinford said in stately accents.

"Should you ladies like to join us for tea at Rose Cottage?" Georgiana inquired after a time. "The day is so pleasant that we may have the doors open to the garden to enjoy the flowers and the birds."

"The birds remain even though you have a cat?" Mrs. Arbuthnot exclaimed in amazement.

"I fear Bel is a trifle fat to be successful at catching a quick-flitting bird. However, he redeemed himself by presenting a plump mouse at the door this morning."

"Yes," Elspeth murmured, "Lord Musgrave was most amused when he came to use the door knocker and espied the gift of a mouse awaiting us."

The fat was in the fire now for sure, Georgiana thought with anxiety. She need not have feared, for Mrs. Swinford beamed a look at her.

"How good of you to be so generous, and so I told Miss Brompton when she commented on your hospitality yesterday. Miss Brompton, I said, Lady Ware is graciously feeding two fine gentlemen who had the misfortune to inherit a bad cook.

'Tis but for a brief time, until his lordship can find a decent cook of his own. In the meanwhile he is able to enjoy pleasant company at Rose Cottage, which, as you must know, is one of the loveliest houses in Sidmouth."

"Dear me," Georgiana said after exchanging a glance with Elspeth. "How very kind of you to champion our humble efforts, ma'am. That is all the more reason for you to take tea with us. Please, ladies?"

Had they intended to resist an invitation to take tea with the Dowager Marchioness of Ware such resolve would have melted at Georgiana's sweet insistence. Since they'd had every notion of imbibing tea with the young dowager from the moment the idea was presented, their acceptance was a foregone conclusion.

"How very lovely, my lady," Mrs. Swinford said with a gracious nod. "It is so nice to see younger people who know how to behave properly. I do believe Miss Brompton borders on being vulgar." This last remark was made in a near whisper, but those close could hear well enough.

Georgiana spared a crumb of pity for Miss Brompton. To be declared vulgar by a woman such as Mrs. Swinford could well spell doom for any future prospects that Miss Brompton might cherish. There was nothing worse than being labeled vulgar as far as Society was concerned.

The small group strolled along the lane that led to Rose Cottage, admiring the gardens on display and the new cottages in the process of being erected. They speculated on future occupants, appreciated the pretty thatched roofs and elegant Gothic windows of what Mrs. Swinford called the Cottage Orné style. The lady appeared to be well informed, her source revealed when she mentioned having visited Strawberry Hill when Horace Walpole had been alive.

"The inside of Strawberry Hill, my dear ladies, is a mixture of the finest sort of damask, wallpaper, painted and gilded Gothic tracery filled with glittering mirror glass you could imagine. It is all very well, but I'd not wish to live in it. The house is rather a peculiar melding of an abbey, a castle, and manor house, which Mr. Walpole liked to call Modern Gothic. A trifle overwhelming in that large a dose."

"I read *The Castle of Otranto*," Georgiana said. "Perhaps when writing he received inspiration for the book from his home? The tale was excessively fantastic. But then, the bed in my room at Rose Cottage is quite out of the common way. Perhaps you might like to see it?"

This suggestion was met with distinct pleasure by all the ladies from the Royal York.

The excellent cook at Rose Cottage took great pride in offering a dainty selection of apple puffs, little iced cakes, Naples biscuits, and raspberry tarts for the ladies' enjoyment along with an immense pot of the finest bohea tea.

Suspecting that these delicacies had originally been intended for Lord Thornbury—for he had quite captured the heart of the cook with his high praise—Georgiana begged the women to partake of everything offered. Knowing the cook, all the sweets would soon be replaced.

Following suitable conversation at the conclusion of the elegant tea Mrs. Swinford declared she would adore to view Lady Ware's unusual bedroom, if her ladyship still wished to show it.

Since the house was rented Georgiana thought the owner would not mind his room put on display. She certainly was not averse to inviting these charming ladies to share the splendid sight to be had.

Chattering like so many magpies, they flocked up the stairs and along the hall to the room Perkins had immediately claimed for her mistress.

The largest of the bedrooms in Rose Cottage, it boasted an enormous bed with four posts, each post elegantly draped in blue damask edged with gold fringe. The skirt and the hanging around the upper frame was similarly draped in blue, lined with soft gold damask, and had lashings of gold fringe, as well as what seemed to be Grecian designs in gold thread at every corner and centered on the upper hanging. It was an awesome structure, indeed.

"My," Lady Peachey declared in a respectful way, "it certainly is out of the common way, to be sure."

"Indeed, it is." Georgiana smiled at the tiny wife of the

baronet, who usually said very little if anything at all when around the more talkative ladies.

Allowing the women to wander about the room as they pleased, exclaiming over the intricacies of the bed, admiring the sword-legged chairs, and praising the intricate wardrobe decorated with elaborate inlay designs, Georgiana walked to the window to stare out to the sea. She had an excellent view from up here. She could also see Lord Thornbury's house from this room.

Quite involuntarily she glanced up the hill to catch sight of two figures—probably Lords Thornbury and Musgrave returned from East Budleigh—walking along the front veranda of the house. It really was a pretty place from what she could see of it. Although it did not have the same degree of Gothic look as did Rose Cottage, not having a thatched roof or the French windows—at least none visible from here.

But it was a lovely house, rather large for a single man, possessing fine Gothic windows and what appeared to be a nice conservatory at one end. It would be interesting to see the inside. She could quite understand Mrs. Swinford's delight in viewing unusual homes. Perhaps Elspeth and she could take a tour of such places. She had heard many did. People came to Ware Court every now and again to inspect the fine paintings and the rose gardens.

Of course this was predicated upon Elspeth remaining with her and not agreeing to wed Lord Musgrave. The latter was becoming the more likely course from the way matters went at present.

Eventually the women had seen enough. After peeks into the other rooms on the floor, they straggled back to the drawing room. Before long they were gone.

The silence following their departure was almost deafening—but not unwelcome. Elspeth agreed. Each took the book she had selected from the library and found a quiet spot to read.

Georgiana curled up on the sofa in the drawing room, having tugged it over by the window for better light. Soon she was deeply engrossed in the adventures of a silly young girl called Leonora and a suspicious fellow named Rodrigo. They seemed determined to murder a woman named Matilda who stood in the way of their future happiness. Georgiana was relieved when it was discovered this was not necessary. Murder seemed a rather drastic way to arrange one's future life. There was a ghostly presence that persisted in interfering, and he was at it again when an interruption caught her by surprise.

"Improving your mind, I take it?" There was a distinctly wry note in the baritone voice.

She jumped about in alarm, her novel tumbling to the floor. "That was unkind, my lord. I have a taste for mental pleasures of considerable variety, including silly novels. Yet I do not think good sense is wanting in my conversation." She gave Lord Thornbury a look that clearly revealed her opinion of people who sneak up on others to frighten them half to death when they are reading a book that had all manner of eerie ghosts and strange happenings.

"I believe those people of superior birth ought to improve their mental capabilities when able. Reading of any sort is to be commended," he said in what appeared to be an attempt to mollify her.

"Then you are unlike my father, who deems a book of sermons the most respectable reading material to be found. Perhaps a few of what he terms the 'best authors,' such as Maria Edgeworth and Hannah Moore, might also be included."

"You have never said much about your father. What is he like? I confess I was surprised you elected to remain at the dower house rather than return to your family." Giving her a curious look, Lord Thornbury settled on one of the saber-legged chairs that decorated the room.

"I believe I mentioned my father sold me to Lord Ware at the direction of my uncle," she replied, bristling at the very memory of that humiliating experience. "Papa made it quite plain to me when my late husband expired so soon after my marriage that I was not to return home. Whatever his reason, I was only too pleased to obey him in this instance. I have grown to enjoy my independence."

"I see," he said, rubbing his jaw in reflection. "Cannot say I blame you all that much. Parents can be the very devil. Oh, Musgrave is chatting with Miss Pettibone in the garden. A quiet afternoon with a book is just the thing for you two after all the parties lately."

"Scarcely that, my lord. The ladies from the Royal York were here earlier. Did you forget we intended to invite them? Lady Peachey actually spoke an entire sentence. We all took tea and an assortment of sweets, then went up to view the uncommon bed in the room where I sleep. 'Tis an impressive sight." Too late she realized that was a topic best left unmentioned.

To his credit Lord Thornbury gave no inkling that what she had said was in any way amiss. "Wild dissipation, indeed," he murmured.

"And how was the jaunt to East Budleigh? I trust you found the vicar in good health?"

"He certainly was. I charmed the fellow into showing us the secret passages that lead from the parish room in the rectory underground to the church. We strongly suspect the good vicar indulges in a spot of smuggling from time to time. He's fond of tobacco and no more inclined to pay the exorbitant duty than a good many others."

"The vicar? Smuggling? Whatever would Papa say to that!"

"Regardless, I know that you'd never reveal that privileged bit of information."

She nodded, then thought a few moments before deciding she had best reveal her own knowledge from the bather.

"I must tell you that I received a bit of information this morning that pertains to you," Georgiana said, trying to calculate his mood. "I went to that last bathing machine at the west end of the beach for my morning plunge. Just before I left the bather cautioned me that his lordship—meaning you—was altogether too nosy, poking about the area and making certain people uncomfortable. Her words of warning certainly chilled my heart."

"Ah, there you go again, worrying about me," his lordship said with a smile.

"This does not deserve to be laughed away, indeed, if it *can* be dismissed. Your friends would take it greatly amiss were anything to happen to you." Georgiana edged along the sofa, placing her hands on it and gazing earnestly at his foolish lordship. It did not bear thinking as to what might be done to him if he were found prowling about when a run was to be made.

"I am pleased if you include yourself in that grouping. One must always be gratified to have friends who care about one's poor self."

"My dear sir," she exclaimed, "you ought not take the matter of your safety so lightly. I beg of you to overlook these smugglers. If, as you claim, everyone in the town is involved in the smuggling, it scarcely behooves you to risk your life to report them."

"Why, even you benefit from the smugglers."

"You mean the French silks and Belgian laces?"

"Perhaps, but I saw Mutter delivering his wood here the other day. Along with the wood comes brandy, or tobacco, possibly Hollands gin."

"I do not drink brandy or gin, much less smoke tobacco," she said indignantly.

"The brandy is for us and Cook enjoys a tot of gin from time to time. The tobacco is left at my house, not yours. At present."

Georgiana ignored that last bit, concentrating on what else he had said. *She* directly benefited from a smuggler's efforts? That odd little man with his cart full of wood and peat was a smuggler? Come to think on it, she had wondered if anything else might be in that cart. But her own house?

"Promise me that you will be careful," she insisted at long last.

"I will do what I feel is necessary, no more." He leaned back in the chair, watching her with an enigmatic expression that revealed nothing of his thoughts.

With that ambiguous reply she had to be satisfied. It would be beyond her ability to push further.

Turning her attention to a more general topic, she said, "The Royal York ladies were quite delighted with the interior of Rose Cottage. Mrs. Swinford in particular is most knowledgeable. Of course, she has been to Strawberry Hill—while Walpole was in residence, yet."

"Mrs. Swinford is to be congratulated, I gather."

"Naturally. Your house appears charming. I can just see it from my room."

Admirably taking her hint, he gallantly said, "Would you and Miss Pettibone like to view it someday, perhaps?"

"Tomorrow?"

"So soon? I have not found a proper housekeeper as yet."

"Speak to mine. I feel certain that she knows a number of capable women who would do nicely in the position."

"I shall. And you may come to tour the house the day after I find a housekeeper."

With that promise Georgiana had to be content.

"Good day, Lord Thornbury," Elspeth said as she and Musgrave entered the house, both looking a trifle self-conscious. "Bennett says you had a most interesting trip to East Budleigh."

"Musgrave says too much at times," Lord Thornbury replied but with good grace and a smile.

Georgiana turned to Musgrave and said, "I received a caution regarding his lordship this morning when I went bathing. The bather said that his lordship should keep his nose out of what doesn't concern him if he knows what is good for him."

"Georgiana," Elspeth exclaimed, "you said not a word!"

Musgrave exchanged a look with his friend and then turned to Georgiana. "We shall be careful. I doubt if Jason wishes to anger any of the locals. He simply wants to know the extent of what goes on here."

"I know, the taxes are dreadful. Is there nothing that can be done to make things more bearable?"

Jason cleared his throat and said, "At present there must be some one thousand five hundred revenue laws on the books to deal with trade our good government wants to regulate and tax. Everyone from the wife of one of the members of the Cinque ports, to mere travelers abroad, to our smugglers flout the revenue laws. There is little respect for the extravagant duties on goods that in some cases are deemed necessary."

"Like Hollands gin, French brandy, and Belgian lace?" Georgiana asked sweetly.

"Salt and tea as well," his lordship shot back. "Did I neglect to mention that tea is also in Mutter's cart?"

"Good grief!" Georgiana said, sinking back on the sofa in bemusement. She was well and truly compromised.

Chapter Thirteen

"I still cannot accept that the vicar at East Budleigh could be involved in smuggling," Georgiana murmured to Elspeth as they came down for dinner later.

"You doubt their word?" Elspeth said with a slight frown, quite as though it was impossible to imagine anyone not believing their lordships' information. "It is odd they would have two secret passages from the rectory to the church, is it not? After all, Georgiana, they are human and have the same failings as the rest of us."

Georgiana paused at the bottom of the stairs to consider this statement, then said, "I suppose I ask a great deal, but I would have a clergyman I can respect above all other men." She had heard of the fox-hunting clergy who rushed through a service so to dash off to their sport. That did not mean she had to approve of such behavior. She expected a clergyman to be someone she might look to as an example of what was good and right.

"Then I fear you are doomed to disappointment if you expect perfection in men." Elspeth placed an arm about Georgiana's shoulder to give her a comforting squeeze.

"Perfection in men? Put that way I must agree with you. I expect too much."

The two women shared a look of amusement as they entered the drawing room to find their guests.

"How pleasant to see smiling faces," Lord Musgrave said, going at once to Elspeth's side. Her pretty pink gown reflected her pink cheeks, enhanced her blue eyes.

"At least we may feel we have not worn out our welcome when greeted with a smile." Lord Thornbury leaned against the fireplace mantel, his favorite place in the room, and contemplated Georgiana's appearance.

She had changed into a lovely evening dress of rich lilac crepe, vandyked around the petticoat. Short sleeves were similarly vandyked and the bodice cut straight across from shoulder to shoulder, very low indeed for a dinner at home. It hung perfectly straight in the front but the back had an enticing fullness that bordered on a demi-train. It was an example of what he admired in the widow, her quiet understated elegance.

Toying with her fan, she approached him with a quizzical look on her face. "Do you join us for church in the morning if you breakfast here?"

"Trying to save my soul, my lady?" He raised a brow in ironic acknowledgment of his reputation.

"That is not a joking matter. I give fair warning—should you eat with us, you will go to church with us. I'll not have you corrupted by that vicar in East Budleigh."

"I doubt if he could have any influence, madam. He is either too far removed, or we are too far gone."

"Wicked, wicked man," she reproved lightly. "Did you speak with our cook? Has she recommended anyone to you?"

"Her cousin from Ottery St. Mary arrives sometime tomorrow. I gather I am luring her away from a nice position, but the mistress is as cross as crabs and the master is but a knight. An earl commands more respect within the servant echelons," was his dry conclusion.

"I daresay you are correct." She studied him, as though wishing to say more, yet remained silent.

"Have you ventured to any of the picturesque areas in this region? I thought, weather permitting, we might enjoy a picnic tomorrow after church." He watched the changing expression on her face become one of anticipation.

"It sounds delightful. Where would you suggest?"

"There is an area called the Byes just north of the town. The river runs through it and it is a very pretty place with grassy banks and many trees for shade."

"I shall have Cook prepare a picnic and we may depart directly after church if that is your desire."

"Charmed, my lady."

She turned then to share the proposed outing with Miss Pettibone and Musgrave, who enthusiastically endorsed it.

Jason firmed his mouth, thinking that his desires had taken a good many twists and turns in the past weeks. When he was able to think straight, he wanted nothing more than to woo and win this beautiful woman at his side. His bad luck was to have put his foot wrong while at Kenyon. He doubted she believed half of what he said—certainly nothing he said in regard to her. There were dubious, suspicious, disbelieving looks cast his direction all too often. What would it take to convince her that his intent had undergone a major change of direction since learning to know her? He was stumped. but the more time they spent together, the better chance he had.

Going to church with her was, upon reflection, an excellent notion. If he could occupy as many moments of her day as possible, she might become so accustomed to his company that she could not bear to be without it. When dinner was announced he offered his arm to her with a Machiavellian smile.

While at the table he recalled something he had overheard earlier while at The Old Ship. As near as he could figure out, there was to be a smuggling run on Tuesday evening. He had tried to think of a way to help the poor devils who earned a mere seven shillings each time they assisted the fearless men who brought the cargo from France—or wherever it originated. Finally he'd thought of something that might help.

"I have enjoyed your hospitality greatly these past days, Lady Ware. I feel it is only right that I repay it in some small manner." He bestowed a warm smile on his benefactress. "Since you have found me a cook vouched for by your own, I shall give a small dinner party Tuesday evening—you and Miss Pettibone, Mrs. Swinford and Major Giles, and Musgrave of course. I thought to include the local preventative officer and his wife, the Ridleys. Poor souls scarcely are invited anywhere—or so I have been told. Nasty business, to be a preventative officer."

"How thoughtful of you, my lord," Georgiana replied pleasantly. "I accept your kind invitation. If there is anything I might do to assist—since you are not too familiar with your cook as yet—you have but to ask."

There was a general discussion of the prospect of a dinner at Peak Hill house, and possibly inviting Mrs. Arbuthnot with a friend of Major Giles for her partner.

They sat over their dessert for about twenty minutes, savoring the little iced cakes that Cook did so well.

"I must say," Georgiana said before leaving the table and the men to their port, "life in Sidmouth is far more exciting than at the dower house. Dinners, picnics, the assemblies. Mrs. Swinford declares they will have a card party at the Royal York for us tomorrow. I had not the heart to tell her that I am a poor card player."

Along with Musgrave, Jason had risen when the ladies elected to head for the drawing room. Now he gave his hostess a bow and said, "I shall deem it a privilege to tutor you in cards, my lady. Another small way of thanking you for your generous hospitality."

"I have yet to compensate you for your damaged waistcoat, sir. Perhaps we are even?" She paused by the door, a curious expression in her eyes.

"Hardly, ma'am. Kindness such as you have given two poor bachelors is beyond price."

"Doing it a trifle too brown, sir," Georgiana murmured as she left the dining room.

"You do not doubt his sincerity, surely?" Elspeth whispered so her voice would not carry.

"You pointed out that we are not to trust men. I foolishly lowered my guard while at Kenyon Hall and see where it *almost* put me—in Lord Thornbury's arms and bed."

Elspeth nodded, her expression one of sympathy—whether for Georgiana or his lordship, it couldn't be said.

At the table Musgrave studied the rich port in his glass a moment, then said, "What are you up to now? Giving a dinner party at a bachelor establishment? On Tuesday next?"

"There is to be a run that night. While I will not inform on the men, neither will I help them directly. However, by inviting the preventative officer and his wife I shall effectively remove him from his post. He can hardly hunt for smugglers whilst at my table. And he'd not think to associate me with that crew."

"What about his assistant?"

"I suspect Mutter has in mind to deliver a bottle of fine brandy to him that evening. Mind you, I did not suggest it. He overheard me telling one of the shopkeepers that I intended this little feast. Later, while pausing at The Old Ship, I chanced to hear that he intended a generous gift of brandy to the gentleman."

"That is aiding and abetting, I believe. I might do it, but you?" Musgrave gave Jason a questioning look.

"Smuggling will exist whether we wish it or no until we can persuade the government to more realistic duties on goods coming into the country. Once there is no profit in smuggling, it will cease to exist." Jason fiddled with the stem of his wine-glass while meeting the frank gaze of his friend.

"Huskisson rose in the House of Commons to wave a bandanna handkerchief around—you know they are heavily taxed and everyone owns at least one of those colorful squares—and was greeted with roars of laughter when he pointed out the same. Even in Parliament it is a joke. He pushes for free trade. Perhaps he will accomplish a lessening of the duties given time."

"Precisely. But that does not help the poor devils who work here and now. Hence the dinner party." Jason finished his port and rose from the table.

Musgrave followed suit. "Tomorrow we have church followed by a picnic. You spend a good deal of time with Lady Ware. Dare I hope it is in aid of my courtship? Or do you have another motive?"

"I do, but it is long, hard slogging and all uphill. It has taught me a lesson—be very careful what scheme you embark upon, for it may rebound right in your face." Jason gave his friend a rueful look, then headed toward the drawing room and a pleasant evening with the woman he admired above all others.

Sunday morning breakfast proved to be a lively affair with a sideboard set with chocolate, tea, and coffee, along with plum cake, pound cake, hot rolls and fresh butter and raspberry jam. The aroma of coffee and chocolate mingled with the scent of hot rolls proved quite irresistible.

Georgiana was downstairs first, and saw to it that everything was ready—her reticule and prayer book set out for the morning service—and that the picnic was in readiness. Cook had gone; one of the maids served and cleared.

"Good, you are early," she said when Lord Thornbury and Musgrave appeared in the door to the dining room where she was already helping herself to a hot roll and jam.

"This is a special day. Best to start off on the right foot. Miss Pettibone not joining us?"

"Miss Pettibone is right behind you, my lord. May I admit to being starved?" She slipped past them to pour a cup of hot chocolate and take a plate of plum cake to her place.

The men debated on the merits of plum versus pound cake and coffee over chocolate. Once all were seated at the table the conversation was lively and Georgiana began to think it truly would be a good day.

John Coachman drove the group to church. There were a good many curious stares when the party left the coach to enter the pretty stone building.

When they had found a pew, Georgiana whispered to Elspeth, "We could have walked for all the distance it is, but I'd not deprive them the sight of an earl, a baron, and a dowager marchioness arriving all at once in a fine carriage." The twinkle in her eyes revealed her amusement at the notion that anyone should be impressed with them. But having lived in a small community most of her life, she well knew how the shopkeepers and local people loved to speculate on the lives of the gentry, not to mention peers.

It was difficult to concentrate on the sermon this morning with Lord Thornbury at her side. She thought it nice to see him at church and wondered when he'd last attended. Perhaps if nothing else came of this stay in Sidmouth she would have the reforming of Lord Thornbury.

Following worship service they were greeted by the vicar with genial enthusiasm. Mrs. Swinford bustled up to greet them as well.

"My lord, I was delighted to receive your kind invitation to dinner on Tuesday. Major Giles and I are both pleased to accept. And in answer to your question regarding a gentleman friend of the major's for Mrs. Arbuthnot, that is all settled if you please. His name is Major Sir John Netherwood, now retired. A very pleasant person, as you will discover."

"Very good of you to take all this trouble, Mrs. Swinford. We shall look forward to Tuesday with great enthusiasm." The earl bowed low over the lady's hand, a courtly gesture bound to impress and please.

Mrs. Swinford blushed like a schoolgirl and said lightly, "How you do go on, my lord." Turning to Georgiana she added, "I shall talk with you later regarding that card party." She smiled, then walked toward the Esplanade with the escort offered by Major Giles.

"She is an amazing person," Georgiana said while the four strolled back to Rose Cottage. The carriage had been fine to arrive in, but they could dispense with it afterward. The day was far too nice to require the shelter of a coach.

"Most charming," Lord Thornbury agreed.

"I have enjoyed the people met here so far," she ventured to offer.

"I trust that also includes those you knew beforehand?"

"There are many pleasant people in the world, are there not? Your aunt is one of the finer ones," she replied evasively.

"Indeed." Well, Jason thought, I should have known better than to test my luck like that. It had been asking a great deal to hope she might admit to liking me.

The hamper was ready to go in the back of the curricle Jason had rented for the day. Placed where his groom would have sat, had he been there, the hamper had a lordly look about it, for it was a splendid size.

Musgrave and Miss Pettibone went in his gig, following not too closely behind Jason to avoid the dust.

Jason cut down to the Esplanade, then drove smartly along to where he turned north just before the river. Before long, he urged the horse across the Mill Ford, then north again until they were on the road leading out of town to the Byes.

The river was lower this time of year, allowing the stones to glimmer through the shallow water that rippled gently over them. Georgiana gave the scene an appreciative look before the carriage climbed up the opposite slope.

Her vow to maintain a cool distance from the earl was a bit difficult in the snug confines of the curricle. And yet, was it necessary to be aloof? He'd not once tried to seduce her since they came to Sidmouth. Other than a few teasing remarks, he had been most civil. And he had certainly been a pleasant dinner guest, in spite of her sometimes harsh treatment of him. She really ought to be nicer to him. It seemed as though he was trying hard to overcome his initial mistake.

"It seems as though your little dinner party will be most agreeable," she said at last for some conversation.

"I could use a bit of help with the menu," he said ruefully. "I am not accustomed to this sort of thing. Usually I leave my chef to present a menu to me which I then approve, and then it is for a bachelor dinner."

"And that is so different?" Georgiana said, surprise obvious in her voice.

"Fewer sweets and heartier foods. The thing is"—and Jason hoped he sounded convincing at this—"I have not the least notion of what this cook can do. It's not the same as my chef at home."

"That is true," she agreed. "I did offer to help."

"I rather hoped you would. Now"—he began tooling easily along the road to the Byes—"what would you suggest for a first course?"

"Oh, me. Allow me time to think on this. Perhaps a white soup followed by plaice. Dressed lamb is nice. Chickens are easily available, with a fricassee of turnips as a side dish. What about buttered prawns—fresh from the sea? Peas, macaroni, sole with wine and mushrooms, and broccoli served hot," she concluded with a rush.

"Excellent—for a first course. What about the second?"

"Goodness, I shall have to try to recall some of the meals I have enjoyed recently. Well, pheasant à la braise, if you can find them, a ragout of celery, forcemeat balls, and wine-roasted gammon. Apple pie is always well received and our cook could help with that. Candied apricots are nice, perhaps a trifle, with a bit of ice cream if the cook is able to prepare it."

"You are making me hungry. Dessert?"

"For a gentleman's dinner I should think nuts and raisins on the table followed by tea and negus with raspberry cordial, my cook's apple puffs, little iced cakes, perhaps some ratafia cakes as well—all on the sideboard. That way those who wish a variety can have it. I have noticed that at times older gentlemen do like sweets."

"*They* do not worry about their manly figure," Jason said with a laugh. "Do you think those dishes would be beyond the new cook?"

"I shall send mine over to help if needs be and of course you will want extra help in the kitchen. Do not worry about a thing."

Jason suppressed a smile at her housewifely manner. He had yet to observe a woman who did not like to plan dinners, organize parties. It was but another point in his strategy to truly win Lady Ware for his own.

At last they reached a scenic area through which the river ran in a gentle path to the sea. Splendid shade trees were clustered here and there with grass that obliging sheep had nibbled close to the ground. Thanks to Jason's forethought, any reminder of the animals' presence had been removed before the picnic. He wanted nothing to mar this day.

The cook apparently believed they were in danger of starvation, going so far from the village and her table. In addition to an excellent cold chicken, there was cold gammon, several sorts of rolls, fruits, and cheeses. Jason had made certain that bottles containing claret, hock, lemonade, and negus were also tucked inside. Indeed, as far as he was concerned, it was a very nice feast.

Georgiana had brought her drawing book along as well as her little pencil case but left it in the curricle. It was a last resort in the event she needed a distraction.

Jason and Musgrave spread rugs on the bank for the ladies. It was a bit different from a good many picnics Jason had attended where servants served the guests at linen-covered tables and every possible convenience that might be found at an interior dining table was to be had in the fresh air and dappled sunlight beneath well-branched trees.

They settled down to enjoy the alfresco meal. The cheeses were fresh and outstanding in flavor, the chicken perfectly done, and the gammon most excellent when paired with a fresh roll. Jason could not recall when he had enjoyed anything so much as this simple pleasure. Perhaps it was who you were with rather than what you did that mattered most.

"Splendid," Musgrave murmured at last after polishing off his third chunk of cheese and bread. "I shall either require a stroll or a nap." He looked to Elspeth, who turned a pretty pink.

"I venture to say a walk would be very good, indeed. What about you, Georgiana? Lord Thornbury?" Elspeth said demurely.

"I believe a pleasant rest spent listening to the gurgle of the river passing by would be soothing to the digestion," Jason said with a mock solemnity, leaning back against a convenient tree trunk.

"I may try my hand at drawing those pretty little flowers near the water's edge," Georgiana replied, wondering why the earl preferred to be here rather than with the others. Suspicions rose, only to be tamped down again. He had been most agreeable and not the least rakish in his behavior as of late.

Once Elspeth neatly packed the hamper with the remains, she set off with Lord Musgrave to amble along the riverbank. They would be in full view, so Georgiana could see no difficulty with propriety.

A fly buzzed low over the river, which contributed its own little rippling melody; birds sang in the leafy branches of the trees in seeming counterpoint. She sat quietly for a few moments, waiting to see if his lordship brought up a topic, or if he dozed off to sleep—in spite of his protestations to the contrary.

"Do you intend to take in the card party at the Royal York tomorrow evening?" the earl inquired, startling her from her thoughts.

"I had forgotten it was then. As I said, I am an indifferent player. Not but what it was lovely of them to think of such entertainment. I vow, it seems as though there is something to attend every evening of the week. The card party, your dinner, the assembly on Wednesday—we shall look forward to a quiet evening at home at this rate."

"Wait until you go to London. At times there are two or three parties you wish to attend per evening. Then you must make your way through a crush of people coming and going."

"It's as well that women no longer wear those broad panniers anymore, in that case," she said with amusement.

"I promised to tutor you in cards. There is a deck in the hamper. Shall I find it? The sooner we commence, the better." He rose to his feet, awaiting her decision.

"How thoughtful of you." Georgiana watched him walk back to the hamper and return with a new deck of cards. Then he began to query her regarding the games she knew.

"Loo is acceptable," he said. "Whist is popular and always helpful to know. Suppose we concentrate on those two?"

The rudiments were gone over carefully in each case. To Georgiana's chagrin she proved to have no head for numbers or remembering what had been played, much less the avid interest in winning that seemed to be essential.

"Come now, try again."

It was a phrase she was to hear over and anon that afternoon and the next day as well. It spoke well for Lord Thornbury's patience that he didn't toss the cards aside or explode in annoyance at her lack of skill.

They discussed the intricacies of whist all the way back to Rose Cottage. If Georgiana thought the picnic was to be in any way a romantic interlude, she had been soon disabused of that notion. His lordship proved a hard taskmaster. She never did capture the wildflowers in pencil on her drawing tablet.

Sunday evening turned out to be extraordinarily quiet. Elspeth and Georgiana had Bel as company and the remainders of the picnic for supper, Cook having traveled to Ottery St. Mary to assist her cousin with her removal.

"It is very quiet," Elspeth said for perhaps the fourth time, sipping a cup of tea. She had made a full pot and Georgiana helped herself to the warm fragrant brew, thankful to have something with which to occupy her time.

"I suppose it would be easy to accustom oneself to having a gentleman about the house—for a contrasting voice if for no other reason," Georgiana said, looking at her friend over the top of her teacup.

They had an early night, both reflecting on the pleasant day at the Byes by the river.

"Although," Georgiana said when she later paused at the top

of the stairs, "no matter how much patience Lord Thornbury has I doubt he shall turn me into a card player."

Elspeth chuckled and drifted off to her room with her head full of nonsense, judging from her silly expression.

Monday proved to be rather busy. Elspeth and Perkins supervised the laundry, particularly the gowns and linens.

Mrs. Swinford came in the morning to beg Lady Ware to attend the card party even if she was not an accomplished player. Why, she could partner Lady Peachey, who was likely the worst player in the world. They could spend their time chatting, if they so pleased.

Georgiana explained about Lord Thornbury's attempts to tutor her in card playing and how it had not gone well.

"A most amiable gentleman, to be sure," Mrs. Swinford said. "But promise me you will come?"

Georgiana agreed, hoping she might not seem too dim.

Electing to stroll with Mrs. Swinford as far as the Esplanade and the Circulating Library, Georgiana left Elspeth contemplating two of her new gowns in an effort to make up her mind which to wear.

Bidding the older woman good-bye, Georgiana was about to enter the library when she saw Lord Thornbury in conversation with a truly disreputable man. They were farther along the Esplanade at the corner of the Marine Baths. There was no mistaking the matter, for she had become well acquainted with his lordship's distinctive bearing. As far as she knew, not a gentleman in town could wear a coat and hat with precisely that distinction.

He had not promised never to deal with the smugglers again. He had merely said that he would do what was necessary, no more. Precisely what did he deem necessary with that scruffy character?

Then, annoyed with herself for being so curious about someone whose business was none of her own, she hurried into the Circulating Library and the company of several other women she enjoyed—as well as the elegant Miss Brompton.

"How pleasant to see you again," Miss Brompton said in her

elevated manner and a fluting voice that could be heard clearly throughout the library.

"Good day, Miss Brompton. You are looking very well, I must say," Georgiana softly responded.

"I vow the sea air is most restoring. And I use Gowland's lotion to keep the freckles away." She gave Georgiana a scrutinizing look as though hunting for elusive spots.

"How fortunate that I have never had freckles," Georgiana said while edging toward the shelves that housed the novels she enjoyed.

"You intend to remain in Sidmouth for the entire summer?" Everyone in the library paused to turn and stare at the two engaged in conversation, for Georgiana's replies were scarcely heard in contrast to Miss Brompton, who might have been vying in a contest for strength of her vocal abilities.

Georgiana wondered what was behind this questioning. "I may," she temporized. Since it was none of Miss Brompton's business precisely how long Georgiana intended to stay at the seaside, her impertinent query didn't rate a detailed reply.

"I understand that Lord Thornbury is to be off before long. He said he had need of some papers or some such thing. Do you know which day he leaves? He is much in your company, if I make no mistake."

Georgiana felt a surge of anger sweep up within her. This odious woman was trying to create trouble where none existed. She thought a moment before turning to face Miss Brompton and her sinister smile.

"I have no idea what plans his lordship may have. We are several of us to dine at Peak Hill house tomorrow, and he mentioned being at the assembly come Wednesday. But beyond that, I venture to say you would have to ask him yourself." Since not even Miss Brompton possessed that much effrontery, it was safe to say that his lordship could come and go as he pleased.

But Georgiana wondered about his departure. He'd not mentioned it to her and to have Miss Brompton know of it was disturbing. Did he deliberately keep Georgiana in the dark? And if so, why?

Chapter Fourteen

"It was truly most peculiar," Georgiana confided to Elspeth later over a cup of tea in the garden.

"I should think so. Yet surely you cannot believe all that woman says, can you? I believe she is one of those whose tongue is a sword which she never permits to rust." Elspeth fed a contented Bel a bit of beef smuggled from the kitchen. She gave Georgiana a questioning look, recalling the original behavior of the society darling.

"Did she not sound so convincing, I would dismiss it as a mere attempt to tease me. Still, I do not trust her and shall wait to see what we learn from Lord Thornbury. He has given no indication that he intends to leave Sidmouth just yet. How odd," she reflected. "There was a time when I would have fled his presence, or at the very least denied him access to mine. Perhaps I am improving, offering him a chance to redeem himself, as it were."

"Indeed," Elspeth murmured. "How pleased I am that you had a change of heart. I have enjoyed renewing my friendship with Bennett Musgrave."

"Is there any chance that friendship might bloom to something more enduring?" Georgiana set her cup down, then gave her friend a searching look.

Elspeth blushed and shook her head. "Not unless his mama has altered her feelings a good deal. In the past she set great store by wealth in a prospective bride for her son. I should think she would be even more adamant now he has succeeded to the title. A baron is more eligible than a mere honorable, as you well know."

"I am sorry to hear that, for I know you hold him in great

esteem. Perhaps something may come about. He might prefer a lady he knows and cherishes even if she is poor to a woman of wealth who is a stranger and he cannot like in the least."

"And pigs might fly," Elspeth said succinctly, giving Bel the last of the purloined beef, then brushing off her hands. She plucked a rose blossom from the nearest bush and buried her suspiciously damp face in the bloom.

The two women sat in silence for a time. Georgiana watched Bel stalk a butterfly through the maze of blooming plants. High in the leafy boughs of the trees birds trilled their songs, seeming to dare the overly plump cat to venture into their realm.

Georgiana eventually rose from her chair to wander close by along the garden path, pausing to break off a deep pink rose. Holding it to her nose to inhale the rich fragrance, she thought how difficult it was to be a widow. She was expected to behave with all the modesty of a young girl, without the comfort of feigning ignorance. In her case it was doubly difficult, for she knew nothing to pretend. She was truly as ignorant in regards to matters of marriage as the greenest girl, yet who believed her?

"Do you know," Georgiana said, returning to the matter at hand, "I do not understand what the earl was doing in conversation with *such* a scruffy character." She returned to her chair and perched on it to gaze earnestly at her friend. "I saw them quite plainly when I was about to enter Wallis's. I paused, confused by what I saw, unable to believe such a fine gentleman would have the slightest thing to do with a base creature. He was most disreputable. And yet, I believe I have seen him about once before."

"Not the man who brings our firewood? Mutter, I think his name is?" Elspeth cleared her expression of her pensive thoughts, meeting Georgiana's troubled eyes.

"Not him. This was a taller, more muscled man. He had shaggy side-whiskers and wore one of those colorful bandannas about his neck. But what caught my eye and alarmed me most was that the man looked to have not a shred of mercy in him. He was hard as nails and twice as inflexible looking. There are dreadful stories about things that happen to people who tangle with smugglers—like murder or torture. I doubt this man would be easy to deal with in any sort of bargain. And that upset me greatly, for I fear that the earl has entered into some manner of arrangement with the man. What it might be worries me."

"You do not think the earl would resort to smuggling, do you? I've not heard a word as to his being in need of funds," Elspeth said quietly.

"As to that," Georgiana responded in kind, "I heard that Lord Norfolk of Arundel Castle claimed salvage rights to a great many casks of wine that came ashore near his property—to the consternation of the revenue officials. They wanted him to pay duty, which he refused. You do not have to be poor to be caught up in smuggling."

"We will attend the earl's dinner tomorrow night. Perhaps we may learn more of this at that time?"

"Perhaps." Georgiana thought otherwise. In her experience men told you only what they thought you ought to know and no more. Considering that women were deemed to have inferior brains, this wasn't much. Her own mother had never given voice to an opinion of her own, always echoing her husband in every way.

"If he considered turning informer, they might take it strongly amiss," Georgiana continued. "I would not wish to see him tortured or murdered. For all his faults, he is a fascinating man."

Elspeth half-smiled, then gathered Bel into her lap. He had abandoned chasing the butterfly and even now contemplated a tall tree that had a warbler singing in its upper branches.

"What did you decide to wear to the card party at the Royal York this evening?" Georgiana relinquished the matter of the dangerous earl to a topic more enjoyable.

"My peach sarcenet, I believe. And you?" Elspeth inquired with the genuine interest she always gave to the attire of her friend.

"I have a pretty violet India mull I've not worn while here. I shall wear that—and hope that it will detract from my woeful card playing. Dear Mrs. Swinford said I might partner Lady Peachey, for she is a very bad player. I should think it might be better were I to play with someone who is better, in order to redeem me."

"Excellent notion, madam," said that familiar baritone voice. "I heartily approve."

"Lord Thornbury! And how long have you been here?" Georgiana asked in alarm, wondering if he had heard her speculation regarding his acquaintance with the scruffy-looking man. She hastily rose and made a neat curtsy, as did Elspeth.

"My, my. Is that a contrite expression I see? Naughty conversation from my lady? It must be a secret. I shan't tease you on it." He strolled up to where they had relaxed on the finely wrought iron chairs set to either side of a small glass-topped table. Teapot and teacups held pride of place here, along with a plate of biscuits that he eyed wistfully.

"Actually, I was telling Elspeth that Miss Brompton said she understood you were to leave us soon. She wished to know if I knew your departure date." Georgiana plunged into forbidden territory with the fortitude of one who dares most anything. She watched his expression with an intent gaze.

"Silly woman," he responded.

Georgiana noted at once that he neither denied he planned to leave Sidmouth nor informed them of the length of his stay. Very closemouthed, he was, and why?

"I cannot imagine why she should think you might confide your plans to me. I chanced to mention your dinner on the morrow and your promise to attend the assembly on Wednesday. She is a very persistent woman," Georgiana concluded pensively.

"May I join you?" He eyed Bel with a wary expression.

"I think you already have," Georgiana observed. "Elspeth, would you be so kind as to request another pot of tea? More biscuits, as well."

"Of course." Elspeth sped to the house to make arrangements for more tea and biscuits with appropriate china.

Lord Thornbury took the chair that Elspeth had vacated, giving Georgiana a look that made her long to squirm. "Is there anything amiss, sir?"

"I thought we were close enough friends that you would know that were I to leave Sidmouth, I would never do so without telling you of my intent." His gaze was direct and open. She bent to scoop up the cat to prevent any attack on the earl. It was an effective way of stalling for time.

"As to that" she said, feeling as though she were sinking beneath the waves, "I would never wish to be thought so imprudent as to broadcast my feelings to the world. And you must admit, telling anything to Miss Brompton is one way to have all the world and his wife hear of it."

"She does have a way with her words, not to mention her excellent command of her voice." His tone was ironic.

"Indeed," Georgiana said with a cautious smile.

"Well, are you prepared for another lesson in card playing?" He pulled a deck of cards from the depths of his coat pocket, placing them on the table before him.

"Elspeth will come with tea," Georgiana said evasively.

"Never say you are a coward!"

She firmed her mouth and said, "Never. Deal, my lord."

So, with the pervading scent of roses drifting about them, the pair sat in a most romantic setting among the flowers and shrubbery, beneath trees that swayed in a gentle wind and dainty white clouds that floated overhead to concentrate on the finer points of loo.

"The idea in loo is to win as many tricks as possible," he reminded. "Once you decide on the amount you wager, you must put five times this amount into a pool. If you wager the princely sum of ten pence, you put in fifty."

"I can readily grasp that," Georgiana said with a hint of irritation.

"Ace is high. The jack of clubs is known as Pam and is the highest trump, beating all other cards, and can be played at any time you wish." He continued to explain what seemed to her the impossible rules of the game; then when Elspeth approached with tea he concluded, "Since it is a game for at least three, Miss Pettibone will have the goodness to join us, I feel certain. Miss Pettibone?"

"Of course I shall play with you, although I am not very good at it," Elspeth said as she rejoined them.

Georgiana paid attention as she had never before, determined not to look the idiot before the patient gentleman across from her. Surely if a man can play when nearly foxed, she could play when sober!

After several rounds she felt as though the concept of the game was at last becoming clear to her and she actually won a round. Then she was dealt five cards of the same suit and tried not to look smug. Placing them down, she declared a flush. "I believe that is my round."

"*I* do believe you have caught on to the game at last. I vow, you may become a terror," his lordship said with a smile.

"What about whist?" Elspeth asked hesitantly. "Must she learn that as well? Could she not focus her attention on one game for now?"

"That is possible," he said, collecting the cards, then accepting a cup of tea from Elspeth while he considered the matter. "I shall grant Lady Ware that request—if she will allow me the privilege of teaching her the game of whist at a later time," he concluded, giving her a challenging look.

"I scarce doubt it a privilege, sir." But Georgiana was pleased, for it meant that he intended to be in Sidmouth for longer than Wednesday. What a turnaround for her—to be desiring the attention of a man she not so long ago deemed a cad and a scoundrel. It could not be said of her that she was fixed in her notions!

The three continued to chat—about the weather, the coming card party, and Lord Thornbury's dinner the next evening. Apparently Cook's cousin from Ottery St. Mary was up to snuff and pleased to have an assist from her cousin with the dinner.

"You still plan a menu such as we discussed? Your new cook is not horrified at your request?" Georgiana ventured.

"No problem from that quarter."

"Captain Ridley and his wife are to be of the party for certain?" He had seemed hesitant on this point and she was curious to know if the young couple would feel at ease in such rarefied company.

"His wife is the daughter of a knight and so should not feel uncomfortable. Seems she had a splendid come-out, only to disappoint her parents in marrying this young chap. I think they may be pleasantly surprised, for he has the look of an ambitious man." Lord Thornbury leaned back in his chair, a biscuit in one hand, his teacup in the other. He looked so thoroughly at ease it was impossible to consider he might consort with smugglers. He was too much the gentleman, never mind that Lord Norfolk of Arundel had battened on to some casks of wine. That was not quite the same thing.

"Indeed. An ambitious man may accomplish much, particularly were he to have patronage from a highly placed gentleman." She gave the earl another curious look, wondering if that was his intent. Frequently an aspiring young man hoped to rise in the world through the patronage of a man of wealth or position. It was done every day.

"You have been reading Maria Edgeworth. I have no doubt that it is possible to allow patronage to go to one's head, but somehow Ridley strikes me as a sensible man."

"You have read her book, *Patronage*? How did you find it?" She was surprised that the earl would condescend to read a novel, for most men of her limited acquaintance proclaimed them foolish nonsense.

"She is a trifle rambling—taking paragraphs to express that which could be said in a few words, but her plot is excellent, her characters interesting."

"If a bit moralizing," Elspeth offered. "She is much like Mary Brunton. Her characters are either unbelievably good or incredibly self-serving. I prefer to read Miss Austen, for her characters seem more like real people."

Musgrave rounded the corner of the house to join them in the garden, to the evident delight of Elspeth, who glowed a delightful pink on his presence.

"Matters settled?" Lord Thornbury inquired quietly.

With a look at Elspeth, Musgrave said, "You are to have all the wines you wish by tomorrow afternoon. I paused at the local"—and he cleared his throat—"wine merchant to make arrangements for delivery."

"What would an excellent dinner be without proper wines?" Jason tilted his head to give Georgiana a thoughtful look, then extended his hand. "Come, walk with me. It is time I returned to my affairs. Do I dare trust that cat to behave or shall I growl at him?"

"And have him cower under the bed for the next hour?

Merely frown at him and he will be good," she said with a laugh, rising to join him on the path that led to the house. She glanced back to see Elspeth in earnest conversation with Musgrave and gave a sigh of regret.

"You are displeased?"

"Only with a pompous old woman who would rather have her son marry to gratify his position rather than his heart. I fear she holds the purse strings and he must do as she demands. Such is often the case, you know."

"Do not despair, my dear. Musgrave has his own plans of which his domineering mother knows nothing, nor will she until he accomplishes all he intends."

With that Georgiana was content, at least for the moment. She saw his lordship to his gig, then observed his skill as a driver when he tipped his hat while skimming down the avenue at a goodly clip.

Elspeth quietly joined her when Musgrave took his leave. They both watched him follow Lord Thornbury down the avenue that led to the Esplanade and anywhere else they intended to go—Peak Hill house or The Old Ship tavern.

Georgiana turned to Elspeth after the men disappeared beyond a cluster of trees. "We still do not know how long he remains, or if he plans to leave soon. He is the most vexing man alive!"

When the ladies entered the Royal York that evening they found Mrs. Swinford awaiting them with Major Giles at her side. Not far away Mrs. Arbuthnot chatted with a gentleman soon introduced as Major Sir John Nettlewood—who requested a simple Sir John now that he was retired.

Georgiana thought he would be very excellent company at the card party as well as the dinner for he possessed a genial smile and a ready wit—both welcome assets in a single gentleman.

The earl and Musgrave arrived, bringing in with them a hint of a rising breeze. A gust of wind tugged at the ladies' skirts and caused draperies to gently sway.

"Wind rising?" Sir John queried with a knowledgeable glance at the window.

"Pity any boats out if that is the case. Poor devils'll have a bitter time of it then," Major Giles added before Mrs. Swinford swept him off to a table of cards with Mrs. Arbuthnot and Sir John in tow behind them.

Georgiana studied the earl with appreciative eyes, for he was all elegance this evening from his dark corbeau velvet coat to the biscuit pantaloons. His waistcoat appeared to be like the one that Bel had shredded, so apparently his valet had managed to find similar fabric. She decided that perhaps it was better not to remark on it, lest it bring back unpleasant memories of being humiliated by a cat.

"With all due respect to Mrs. Peachey, I suggest the four of us play as partners. We shall be far more tolerant of errors than others might," the earl concluded with a look at Georgiana.

This so annoyed her that she resolved to pay close attention to her cards and surprise everybody by playing well.

The earl guided her to a table, the other two trailing along some ways behind, speaking softly to one another.

"You are in first looks this evening, my lady," the earl said quietly so that no one might overhear him. "I particularly like that color on you. Most becoming. Your eyes have the color of spring violets."

Georgiana gave him a startled look, for he had not been one to pour flattery over her since they had left Kenyon Hall. Indeed, she had thought his compliments while there to be merely in aid of seduction, nothing more. It was most agreeable to hear soft words of admiration from him.

The evening passed pleasantly in conversation and loo, although Georgiana actually said little. She discovered early on that for her it was either play cards or chat; she could not do both.

"I fancy there is a supper table in the next room," the earl ventured at long last, laying down a winning hand and looking almost surprised at it.

"You have trounced us, Thornbury," his friend declared. "All my pence are gone, not that we wagered for more than chicken stakes."

"Beginners are better off playing for little. Is that not true, Georgiana?"

She looked about her with scandalized eyes and hissed, "I did not give you leave to use my Christian name, sir. What will people think?"

"Afraid of a connection with me?" the earl asked, lazily leaning back in his chair while bestowing the most daunting of looks at her. There seemed to be more behind that soft demand than would appear.

Georgiana scarcely knew where to turn. She had not envisioned a mild animadversion to bring this reaction. Unable to think of a proper rejoinder, she glared at the man she had rightly proclaimed the most vexing on earth. At last she said, "That is not it, and I believe you know it. I would be proper."

"I suggest that if we wish to partake of what promises to be a delicious supper that we go at once," Elspeth interrupted urgently. It was clear that while she didn't quite understand the tensions between the earl and Georgiana, she wanted no part of an argument.

"Indeed," Georgiana said with ill-disguised relief. Placing her cards on the table she rose from her chair, glad to be able to move about. All this concentration was enough to give her the headache.

Her ordeal was far from over, however. The earl clasped her elbow in his firm grip, escorting her with what she deemed an overly possessive attitude. What Miss Brompton might think, then blurt out, did not bear considering.

The lavish spread of foods set out by the Royal York was far better than she had expected. Indeed, the hotel had nothing for which it need apologize, in her estimation. There were shrimp fritters and dainty little meat pies. Elegant dishes suitable for a buffet supper were in abundance and she selected several without worry about indigestion.

"All is in readiness for the dinner. What color do you wear tomorrow?" the earl asked as they left the buffet table to wend their way back to their table.

"I had not decided," she said after a moment. This was true, for she had debated between the merits of her silver tissue—the very one she had worn to the ball at Kenyon Hall—and a simply cut gown of deep red lutestring that the local seamstress had finished for her after completing Elspeth's wardrobe. The gown was an excellent adaptation from a drawing in the *Lady's Magazine*. "Either silver tissue or a deep red. Why?" It was unusual for a gentleman to take such interest in a woman's choice of dress.

"Wear the red, please. I think it might look very nice against the decor of my home."

"You wish me to dress to complement the colors of your drawing room?" Georgiana had never heard of anything so self-serving. She took several angry steps away from him in the direction of their table before she realized that there were fascinated eyes watching her and what she did. She slowed her pace, smiled, and tried to appear as though she did not wish to dump the contents of her plate over that man's head. What a pity Bel had turned coward at the very sound of the earl's voice.

"You mistake my intent," he said, scowling at her. "I wish you to look your best. Why would I wish anything else?"

At that simple statement, Georgiana set her plate down on an empty table, most thankfully close by, then turned to give him a surprised look. "I misjudged you and I apologize."

"I am aware that a woman hates to clash with her surroundings, for I have heard such complaints often enough when in London."

Georgiana thought of all the society beauties he must have known and wished that her fate had been other than her uncle arranged for her. Life seemed hard at times. But then, there was no promise that Lord Thornbury would have paid her the least attention had she managed a come-out rather than marriage when she turned seventeen. He did not seem the sort to attend insipid balls for presentation of budding society beauties.

"Tell me about some of the places you enjoy going, my lord," she said after they were seated and had begun to eat.

"I gather you do not refer to White's or Brooks's, nor the other haunts gentlemen prefer in London."

"Of course not. I meant the drawing rooms, the elegance that must be found in the city."

"You will see for yourself when you come to stay with my

aunt next Season," he said, avoiding a direct reply to her question.

"Can it be that you play cards and do not notice what is around you? Fie, sir, think of all the hostesses who decorate in vain." Her eyes flashed in amusement at his discomfiture.

"I notice what is elegant and restrained and I abhor the garish and overdone. There is much of both. Best you decide for yourself." The look he gave her defied her to argue with him.

With that she had to be satisfied.

"Well, how did you do with the cards this evening?" Mrs. Swinford questioned as she hovered at their side. "I looked over every now and again only to see you in deep concentration."

The gentlemen at the table rose and bowed slightly to their hostess as politeness demanded.

"I actually won a round," Georgiana answered with a happy gleam in her eyes. "Lord Thornbury gave me lessons and I believe he is an excellent teacher."

"Indeed? Perhaps I should ask you to take on Mrs. Peachey as a pupil, sir?" Mrs. Swinford chuckled at the earl's expression of mock distress.

Miss Brompton sauntered purposefully to the table, her eyes fixed on his lordship with what Georgiana could only describe as a predatory glimmer.

The earl bowed to Miss Brompton but not, Georgiana noticed, with the degree of civility he had displayed to Mrs. Swinford or herself.

"Lord Thornbury," the proud beauty said, ignoring the others at the table, particularly Lord Musgrave, who still stood at Thornbury's side. "I understand you give a dinner."

"I do," his lordship said, surveying this presumptuous woman with distaste. "A few intimates in honor of the good preventative officer and his wife."

Miss Brompton was clearly taken aback that she was not included in the circle deemed his intimates. She had brazened her way to this point, likely in the hope that he would feel compelled to invite her as well. She ought to have known better. His lordship was not one to be intimidated—whether by a *cat* of the human or furry variety.

"I see. How lovely," she said lamely. "We plan a little jaunt to Exeter tomorrow," she said with a brave smile, intimating that she would not have been able to accept an invitation had it been extended.

"I say, Miss Brompton, a trip to Exeter?" the meek Mr. Rood exclaimed. "The first I heard of it. Did you know of a trip to Exeter, Lady Yeldham? First I heard of it," he repeated in bewilderment.

"Fool," her ladyship hissed, "be silent!"

Gathering the shreds of her dignity about her as she did her Norfolk shawl, Miss Brompton nodded regally and swept from the room, murmuring something about the necessity of attaining an early start to their journey come morning.

"What think you of a berry compote?" the earl inquired thoughtfully after the entourage had left the room of intrigued card players who had vastly enjoyed the drama.

"Raspberries are a favorite of mine," Georgiana said, thinking his lordship was certainly dropping Miss Brompton into the sea. She respected him for not saying a word about the bumptious Miss Brompton.

"Raspberries, it is, then. Remind me to tell the cook in the morning, Musgrave."

The Thornbury party stayed a bit longer, desiring to please their hostess and not cause more gossip than Miss Brompton had already managed to create.

"Thank you for a pleasant evening," Georgiana said before they left, giving Mrs. Swinford a very proper curtsy, then doing the same for Mrs. Arbuthnot, for both ladies had the ordering of the card party.

"We shall see you tomorrow evening. I have heard interesting things about Peak Hill House. I long to know if they are true," Mrs. Swinford said.

Georgiana glanced at Lord Thornbury to catch sight of one of those lazy smiles lighting up his face. If that was not a gleam of mischief in his eyes she would eat her reticule—the silver mesh one that would be most indigestible.

The gentlemen returned Georgiana and Elspeth to Rose Cottage in the elegant equipage that his lordship had used to travel in from Kenyon Hall south to the coast. Once they were in the house, the women went to Georgiana's room.

"He is up to something; I know it." Georgiana sighed. "Vexing creature!"

Chapter Fifteen

Wednesday dawned bright if not clear. Numerous clouds puffed their way across a delicate blue summer sky. They were not the sort to bring rain, Georgiana thought, but they would bear watching. However, the sun shone when it could, there was little wind in the shelter of the valley, and she was feeling oddly at ease with herself.

How wicked that she should be so pleased to see the haughty Miss Brompton receive what she deserved. She—who had for so long displayed her bad manners—had reaped her rewards. How humiliating for her to learn that the highly social Miss Clare Brompton was not considered among the intimates of the elegant Lord Thornbury. He might be deemed a scoundrel by many, but he was one of the most eligible peers in the land. Wealthy, good-looking, and possessing the most devilish sense of humor in the world, he attracted women the way roses drew bees. Except for Georgiana. She had run from him, denied him, had a cat who attacked him. In short she was the opposite of every other female he knew. It did not stand to reason that he would be the least inclined to such a contrary woman. Perhaps the reason he sought her company is that he believed himself safe from any charms she might own.

That was not a very pleasing thought.

"There you are," Elspeth cried, hurrying out into the garden with a little parcel in hand. "This arrived for you just moments ago."

Georgiana rose from the chair where she had been contemplating what had occurred the day before to accept a small package. "What do you suppose it could be?"

"You might try opening it," Elspeth suggested dryly.

Nestled inside the little white cardboard box was a strange flower the likes of which Georgiana had never seen before. The snowy petals were velvety soft and the fragrance was such it would likely perfume an entire room. She looked to Elspeth, but she seemed to have no notion of the flower's identity either.

"What an amazing flower. There is a pretty white velvet riband attached to it."

"Perhaps the card will tell you something?"

"'Tis from Lord Thornbury. He sends his compliments along with this gardenia."

"I have never heard of such a thing. It must be rare, indeed."

"There is a conservatory adjacent to Peak Hill House. Do you suppose it grows there? Well, I shall wear it with pride. I must say, I never know what to expect from that man," Georgiana concluded.

"Is he still the most vexing man alive?" Elspeth teased.

"I shan't change my mind on that score," Georgiana declared stoutly. But her face softened when she looked at the flower again. Such a magnificent tribute. How well it would look against the deep red of her lutestring gown.

Cook left a light collation on the sideboard for their nuncheon. She was busy assisting for the grand dinner, the likes of which Sidmouth did not see all that often. Although, with the construction that went apace throughout the valley, that looked to be changing before long.

"I hope Sidmouth will not become like Brighton," Georgiana mused to Elspeth over a cup of tea and a cheese sandwich. She ate lightly with no desire to spoil her evening meal. "Because of the Prince Regent that little village has become crowded and far too busy."

"We have an assembly here, you know. And certainly there is an interesting assortment of people visiting."

"Miss Brompton and her friends are off to Exeter today. I hope they do not encounter rain." Georgiana glanced at the sky again, a slight frown on her brow.

"They may have to overnight if the weather turns disagreeable."

"I wouldn't miss her," Georgiana admitted with a grin. "Is your gown ready for this evening?"

Elspeth nodded, then said, "I must confess that I feel a trifle out of place considering the social status of the other guests."

"That is utter nonsense and I refuse to listen to such. Come, let us go to the Royal York and call on Mrs. Swinford and her friend Mrs. Arbuthnot to thank them for the lovely card party."

"I do believe you enjoyed it in spite of your apprehension about playing loo." Elspeth rose from the garden chair to go into the house to collect her reticule and her parasol.

Georgiana followed bearing the delicate bloom intended for wear this evening. It was so lovely she scarcely dared to breathe on it. The earl, she admitted, did have his less vexing moments.

Mrs. Swinford was most gratified to have the beautiful Dowager Duchess of Ware come to call on her, especially since she had not seen hide nor hair of the elegant Miss Brompton.

"Dear Lady Ware," Mrs. Arbuthnot declared, "you quite captured the heart of Sir John last evening. He spoke of nothing else but your charms this morning."

Georgiana gave the lady an astounded look, then smiled. "I must remember to be kind to the gentleman this evening. I vow I do not have that many admirers that I can afford to dismiss one."

"And what do you wear?" Mrs. Swinford dared to inquire, having gained the impression that Lady Ware was not at all high in the instep—as Miss Brompton was.

"The local mantuamaker created a lovely gown of dark red lutestring for me. It is very simple in line with the merest scattering of embellishment along the neckline—which I confess is a trifle lower than I usually wear."

"And you, Miss Pettibone? I trust you will wear something to set off that lovely blond hair and those fine gray eyes." The shrewd eyes darted between the girls.

"Gracious, such kind words, Mrs. Swinford. I wear my peach sarcenet. I think you have seen it before at the last assembly."

"Excellent choice. I think it so foolish of women to wear a gown once, then think it cannot be seen again."

"I admit that Perkins has altered the neckline. After she saw Lady Ware's gown, she determined to make mine more dashing."

"Mrs. Arbuthnot wears rose tissue over a white petticoat, and I shall wear a gown of what my mantuamaker calls Spanish fly. What a silly name for a color that is merely dark green. But I like it well," Mrs. Swinford admitted.

They decided to walk together to the shops to see what might be new. Mrs. Arbuthnot was intent upon buying a fan for the evening.

Upon leaving the Royal York and turning up to the High Street, Georgiana noticed that there seemed to be an air of suppressed excitement about the townspeople. It was the same sort of feeling one felt before a festive fete or a balloon ascension.

"Well, one would think our pleasure in this evening's dinner was contagious," Mrs. Swinford declared.

"You noticed it too, ma'am? Perhaps they prepare for a special market day?"

"I shall inquire," Elspeth said in her gentle voice. When they entered the lace shop she did speak to the proprietor only to learn that it was nothing in particular. The lace merchant was busy preparing a shipment of locally made lace to go to Honiton and was a bit preoccupied.

"I would like a lace fan, if you have such a thing," Georgiana said, wishing to patronize a local craftsman.

"Indeed, Lady Ware. I have a pretty little thing here you may like." He produced a slender box that held the daintiest fan Georgiana had ever seen. Mother-of-pearl sticks had pierced gilt decorations on them and the delicate lace was without a doubt the most intricate she had seen.

She purchased it at once, then sought something for Elspeth, who stubbornly refused any and all suggestions.

They went on to another shop, for Mrs. Arbuthnot had decided against lace and wanted feathers, or perhaps something painted.

It was a fan made of dainty feathers dyed a delicate peach

color that weakened Elspeth's resolve. It had steel spangles decorating the sticks and she admitted that it was the perfect touch for her peach sarcenet gown. Georgiana gleefully bought it for her, wishing there was more she might do for the woman who contributed so much to her enjoyment of life.

"I declare that what I have seen in these shops is as nice as what I've found in London, although not as great a variety, but at an excellent price," Mrs. Swinford said, having found her painted fan showing shepherdesses and lambs in impossibly green meadows.

Georgiana murmured something appropriate and looked along the street to The Old Ship tavern where men bustled in and out. The tavern was doing a good business this day.

Then she saw the earl leave the tavern, that nasty rough-looking man at his side, and she shivered, a premonition of disaster creeping over her.

"What is it?" the astute Elspeth inquired.

"Do you not see him? Lord Thornbury is down there with that scruffy-looking man again. Oh, I am worried to death," she confided softly to her friend.

"Credit him with some sense, my dear," Elspeth persuaded, clutching her parcel in nervous fingers.

"Oh, I know he has sense, whether it is good or not is something else. Remember, this is the man who once thought to seduce me!"

Since that was perhaps not the best recommendation for a gentleman, Elspeth shrugged helplessly and turned her attention to the others just leaving a shop.

The joy had lessened for Georgiana and she was impatient to return to Rose Cottage. She did not wish to see what the earl was about, for she knew she was powerless to convince him otherwise.

With a pleased exclamation Mrs. Arbuthnot left the shop where she had discovered the very thing she wanted. She had purchased an amazing little fixed fan of pretty gilded wood that had a quizzing glass at one end. "I shall have my fan and a quizzing glass all in one," she declared triumphantly.

The ladies, now that they had made their purchases, headed down High Street toward the Esplanade. There, the Royal

York women said they looked forward to seeing the other two in their finery that evening and turned east.

Georgiana and Elspeth walked west on the Esplanade, both deep in thought. At last Georgiana spoke.

"I shall refuse to think ill of him. Perhaps he is merely trying to do a good deed?"

"Of course," agreed Elspeth, but without conviction.

Bel scolded them when they entered Rose Cottage. He paced up and down the drawing room, curling about Georgiana's legs, begging to be held, acting quite unlike himself, in fact.

"What on earth can be the matter with *him*?" Georgiana said, quite exasperated with males in general.

"Come, let us set out our fans and gather up the other things we want for this evening," Elspeth appealed, seeming eager for the coming dinner.

Georgiana set aside all the strange events of the day and proceeded to prepare herself for the coming party. After a welcome bath, for she had not had an opportunity to sea bathe for days, she arrayed herself in her pretty underthings, then donned the deep red lutestring gown with Perkins's help. Almost, she could forget the odd feeling she had known while on High Street. Almost.

"Allow me to fix your hair, milady," Perkins insisted, nudging Georgiana toward the dainty dressing table and stool.

Georgiana paid little attention to the manner of arranging her ebony hair until she observed that Perkins had carefully set the white flower in among her curls, cleverly pinning it in place. Her dark hair was a perfect foil for the velvety white petals. A strand of creamy pearls at her neck and a pair of pearl ear bobs went well with both flower and gown. Georgiana was rather pleased with her appearance.

"My, do you not look a treat," Elspeth said with delight while she pulled on her gloves.

"I vow we will be the prettiest ladies in all of Sidmouth this evening," Georgiana countered, admiring the peach sarcenet with the elegant matching fan.

John Coachman drove them in the traveling coach, for Georgiana wanted nothing of an open carriage tonight. She instructed him to return later, then took her first good look at Peak Hill House.

The center portion was three floors, with a two-floor section to either side. Simple in design, it was by no means as small as it seemed from a distance. The entry was impressive, with a massive Gothic door suitable for a cottage orné.

They stood between the tall pillars, then started when the door suddenly opened and they were enthusiastically greeted by Lord Thornbury.

"Lovelier than ever, I declare," he said with an indulgent look at Georgiana.

She was trying hard to remember that she did not believe Lord Thornbury was involved in anything sinister and gave him what was most likely a quavering smile at best.

"The flower looks much nicer where it is now than it did on the plant," he murmured.

Musgrave, who stood close to them in order to greet Elspeth added, "First bloom that plant has had, so the gardener said. Most upset that Jason picked it."

Georgiana gave the earl a surprised look. She had forgotten his Christian name was Jason. Somehow it suited him. In Greek legend, Jason had been the leader of the Argonauts in their quest for the Golden Fleece. She wondered what quest this particular Jason had.

Introduced to Captain Ridley and his charming wife, Mary, Georgiana took it upon herself to make the girl feel at ease. She happened to glace at Lord Thornbury and felt a glow of warmth at his look of approval.

Sir John Nettlewood arrived with Mrs. Arbuthnot, followed closely by Mrs. Swinford and Major Giles. The military men quickly cornered preventative officer Ridley and fell into a discussion of the problems with the smugglers.

Mrs. Arbuthnot, her pretty fan with the quizzing glass in hand, and Mrs. Swinford, her painted fan much in evidence, joined Georgiana and Elspeth with Mary Ridley.

At first they admired the lovely interior of the house. Georgiana took time to look about her. The walls were painted a deep rich red, slightly darker than her gown. That was obviously why his lordship had cast a vote for her lutestring. A lovely pianoforte with exquisite inlay vied with most elegantly simple furniture of the latest design; saber legs and polished rosewood abounded. The fireplace in front of which his lordship favored as a place to lounge was carved in white marble in an unpretentious design that looked vaguely Greek. A glance across the hall revealed the dining room was painted a rich green color she knew was costly. Only those with wealth could afford the rich, deep paint tones that so pleased the eye.

"The room flatters you, Lady Ware," Mrs. Swinford decreed. "Of course that is a popular color."

"So I was told," Georgiana said, looking to Elspeth for rescue.

"Do you like living along the coast, Mrs. Ridley?" Elspeth quickly asked.

"It has been nice so far," the girl admitted.

"I seem to recall your come-out," the formidable Mrs. Swinford said to Mary Ridley. "I believe I knew your mother before she married. Daughter of Sir Henry Wittlesby, if I make no mistake."

Delighted to find someone who knew her mother, Mary Ridley bloomed, losing most of her shyness and chatting away with the greatest goodwill.

They went in to dinner in proper order. Lord Thornbury escorted Georgiana, for she outranked all the other women in spite of her age. She discovered she was to sit at his side rather than at the far end of the table and couldn't decide if that was good or not. Mrs. Swinford had graciously consented to sit at the foot of the table, taking the place of a wife or mother. Georgiana thought the older lady performed her duties admirably.

The menu was much as she had suggested to Lord Thornbury. He—or the cook—had substituted buttered carrots for the fricassee of turnips and creamed broccoli for the ragout of celery. Georgiana gave the forcemeat balls a go-by, not caring overmuch for anchovies. But she quite enjoyed the buttered prawns and the sole with wine and mushrooms. He was fortunate that her own cook had a worthy cousin in Ottery St. Mary who was willing to change positions.

"You detect the hand of your cook in the apple pie, I trust?"

Lord Thornbury said. "It was most kind of you to permit her to help her cousin. Once that woman settles in, I fancy she should not need more assistance."

"You intend to do a great deal of entertaining, then?" Georgiana asked, quickly jumping to the conclusion that he would not worry about such if he had no plan to remain for a time.

"Perhaps," he said, maddeningly vague. "How long before you return to Ware Court and the dower house?"

She gave an involuntary shudder at the mere thought of being so close to the lecherous Lord Ware, her stepson.

"The thought does not please you?" he said, watching her closely.

"The house is charming, as is my rose garden," she said evasively.

"You do not fear Lord Ware, do you?" he inquired in a soft voice that could not be heard by anyone else.

Georgiana suspected her expression gave away her apprehensions regarding the man. "Elspeth left the house under a shadow without receiving a reference from him. I would not put it past him to make some outrageous claim that she had stolen something—merely to placate a suspicious wife. I do not trust him."

"But then, I believe you have little reason to trust any man, do you?" The smooth baritone flowed over her nerves, causing ripples of alarm.

Astounded that Lord Thornbury should have realized the extent of her lack of faith in the male portion of the population, much less her reason why, Georgiana studied the food on her plate before raising her gaze to meet his.

"True. But then you have met Lord Ware. I believe you have also crossed paths with my uncle, Lord Avon. With gentlemen like these for examples"—and she longed to include Lord Thornbury in that number, for he had been the latest in the line who sought to seduce her—"perhaps I may be excused for so feeling?"

"You have been opportuned a good many times?"

Not mistaking the direction of his thoughts, Georgiana nodded agreement.

"The first year after the late Lord Ware went to his reward I found an amazing number of male relatives who were eager to take his place in my estimation. For that matter, a goodly number of my late husband's friends also sought that position. Some were very persistent." She absently rubbed a little finger that had been cruelly bent when she resisted the present Lord Ware's attentions.

Jason did not miss that little action. For the first time he observed that her finger looked to have been broken and not properly set. Surely no gentleman would have done that! Then he recalled the present Lord Ware and what an oily character he was, and decided he was just mean enough to do that very thing. Without thinking, Jason placed a comforting hand over that damaged finger, giving her a sympathetic smile.

Georgiana, detecting a curious look from Mrs. Arbuthnot quickly withdrew her hand, but gave Lord Thornbury a swift smile and a faint nod of her head in that lady's direction.

He appeared to understand, for there was no coldness of manner afterward.

How her mind did battle within her. Had she judged him too harshly? Was it understood among gentlemen that any widow was fair game for dalliance? Georgiana well knew she was not ugly: every time she chanced to gaze in her looking glass she saw bright blue eyes in a passingly fair face framed by ebony curls. Indeed, she supposed she not only ought not blame the man, but accept his unwanted attentions as a compliment!

"You must have some of this trifle, Lady Ware," encouraged Sir John at her other side. "'Tis excellent."

Georgiana nodded, accepting a small portion of the sherry-flavored sweet. "It *is* good," she admitted once she tasted it. The Naples biscuits had been softened the proper degree by the sherry and the beautifully whipped custard was as smooth as possible—making an elegant sweet, indeed.

"We are fortunate Lord Thornbury has acquired such an excellent cook," she said to Sir John, but permitting her voice to carry.

"Here, here," Major Giles declared.

The earl did not return to the subject Georgiana would rather avoid, much to her relief. A final toast was offered by Lord Musgrave at the conclusion to the meal.

"To the flower of English womanhood!" The words were general but his gaze rested upon Elspeth.

She blushed a pretty rose, but gave no other indication she felt his words to be personal. She went along with Mrs. Arbuthnot from the dining room when the ladies withdrew.

"I do believe Lord Musgrave shows a decided partiality for you, Miss Pettibone," Mrs. Arbuthnot said quietly as she walked at Elspeth's side.

"How flattering. I have known him since a child, you know. He most likely enjoys the company of one with whom he may be comfortable. I know his mother well; she has great ambitions for him."

"And for herself as well, no doubt. What a pity," the lady concluded, surmising precisely what the case might be with Lord Musgrave.

Georgiana strolled across the room to gaze from the windows out to the sea. It was a rich hue, the fading light giving it depths of color not seen by daylight. There was a ship off the coast and it seemed to her that it flashed lights toward someone on shore. The smugglers?

"Would you play for us, Lady Ware?" Lord Thornbury demanded from where he stood in the doorway.

She longed to cry an alarm, alert the preventative officer, yet found she could not. He had an able assistant who must be aware of signals far better than she. She'd not wish to embarrass him in any way.

"Of course." She gave his lordship a questioning look as she crossed to the pianoforte installed at the far end of the large drawing room, not far from the fireplace. Music was neatly placed to one side and she immediately noted that the pieces she practiced so diligently were at the top of the pile.

Selecting the Mozart sonata she had worked on so assiduously, she began to play. His lordship materialized at her side to turn pages for her, his very presence encouraging her to play her best. When she concluded, she turned to him, expectant.

"Well, you mastered that spot which gave you trouble. I compliment you, dear lady. You reveal a persistence that does you great credit."

"When I want something, I do not give up easily."

"A maxim we ought all follow," he murmured, bending over as though to peruse some of the music.

"Sirrah, there is a ship off the coast that is flashing lights—I fear signals. To smugglers, do you suppose?" She was gratified at his look of alarm.

He walked discreetly toward the windows where she had stood earlier, chatting with his guests on the way there so as not to appear too obvious. Georgiana followed.

"I see nothing," he said to her when she joined him at the window. "Are you certain there was a ship and it was actually flashing lights?"

"I know what I saw," she insisted, but quietly, not wishing to call attention to their conversation.

"Well, tomorrow I will investigate. It is too late and far too dark now." The earl gave her a dubious look.

But Georgiana wondered if she imagined the hint of relief in his voice. Or was she becoming overly suspicious?

"What do you see?" Elspeth inquired as she joined Georgiana.

"Nothing, now," Georgiana admitted.

"Then do play some more for us. Mrs. Ridley desires to hear the country dance that was performed last Wednesday."

Quite willing to play, and thankful to leave the matter of a ship that flashed lights behind her, Georgiana went again to the piano to execute a lively dance tune.

Nothing would do but Mrs. Arbuthnot and Mrs. Swinford would teach the steps to the pretty Mary Ridley, so before all knew it, a spirited dance was in progress.

Sir John most excellently partnered the graceful Mrs. Arbuthnot while Major Giles gave a surprising performance for a military man with Mrs. Swinford. Elspeth blushingly took Musgrave's hand and they scarce looked at anyone else for the duration of the dance.

"Had I known they would desire to dance, I'd have hired musicians," Lord Thornbury said from behind Georgiana.

"It is often done at parties, as you know."

"I have not so often been host, however."

"Ah, yes, those bachelor parties you give," she teased.

"They are tolerably received," he said in a lofty tone.

"Now," Mrs. Swinford said at the conclusion of a second dance, "I am reckoned to be a fair hand at the pianoforte. I shall play and you shall dance, Lady Ware."

Unable to resist the chance to partner Lord Thornbury, Georgiana rose and turned to him. It was not to be. Sir John quickly stepped forward to claim her hand which she could scarcely deny and be proper.

The animated tune gave her little time with her partner. She caught the earl watching her as she skipped through the pattern of the dance. Well, he ought to have anticipated that such a sparkling group might wish to enjoy a hop—considering a hop could take place with as few as five couples.

At the conclusion to this dance, Lord Thornbury bent over to request something of Mrs. Swinford, who nodded her agreement. Then he strode forward to take Georgiana's hand.

"My lady, I believe this dance is mine."

She merely curtsied her agreement, but knew her eyes must be lighting up with her delight and amusement. He might be the most vexing man alive, but he did know what he wanted and boldly took it.

Only—he had wanted her and not succeeded. And she felt rather smug with the knowledge. Did he yet persist in his foolish intent? Or had he given up, content to be social with nothing more?

The dance was not as lively and there were several instances when they drew face to face in the pattern, hands held high, eyes meeting with messages sent and wondered at.

There was laughter and chatter when the music concluded. Mrs. Ridley declared she had never been so diverted at learning a new dance. They formed little groups, the ladies at one end of the room near the pianoforte, the gentlemen at the other end not far from the window where Georgiana thought she had seen a ship. The window was now shuttered.

Some time later a charming supper was offered. Georgiana ate sparingly, her mind on those flashing lights. It was true that Lord Thornbury could have done nothing about them, other than mention the matter to Captain Ridley. But what disturbed Georgiana was that he hadn't seemed the least surprised that she had seen the ship. He simply said *he* didn't see one. That wasn't quite the same thing.

They left rather late in the evening. It was mild and starry out. Laughter drifted about the house as the guests entered their carriages and one by one headed down the drive to the Esplanade.

"I shall see you tomorrow, Georgiana," the earl murmured.

She quite forgot to reprimand him for being so forward. It had been far too lovely an evening for a remotely cross word to be exchanged.

Chapter Sixteen

Georgiana was putting the finishing touches on a detailed drawing of the gardenia when she heard a noise behind her. She swiveled about in the wrought-iron garden chair to see Lord Thornbury approaching with an animal in his arms. A cat! Heavens!

Carefully setting aside her drawing tablet, she rose to greet him, giving the cat a wary look. "That is not Bel." Indeed, the smoky gray animal possessed slanted green eyes that bore a haughty expression quite unlike the raffish Bel.

"Correct," he said with approval as though she were but two and ten. "This splendid creature is named Aphrodite, I was told. I gave the matter considerable thought and decided that the reason Bel was so disagreeable when a gentleman came to call is that he was jealous. I sent a groom to London to a friend of mine who breeds fancy cats. Hence Aphrodite. Perhaps now Bel will be content."

"He has been irritable and unlike himself as of late," Georgiana admitted.

"Males can be that way at times if denied their, ah, pleasures."

"Well, I cannot imagine you ever being denied anything you wanted. You have a way of obtaining your way, willy-nilly," she exclaimed while examining the truly gorgeous cat who deigned to permit Georgiana to pet her.

Lord Thornbury suffered a bout of coughing.

At that moment Bel elected to leave the house for the garden and approached the couple, fur all at end and eyes narrowed as though ready to spring into action.

Then Bel saw the beautiful cat, who merely preened herself

in Lord Thornbury's arms. His lordship set Aphrodite on the ground and stood back, waiting to see Bel's reaction. Bel sat down as though thunderstruck.

Aphrodite, true to her namesake, padded up to Bel, rubbing against him and making little purring sounds.

"I do believe she is flirting with him," Georgiana said, feeling slightly uncomfortable with this display of feline affection.

"Perhaps we should leave them alone to become better acquainted."

Georgiana gathered up her drawing pad, the gardenia, and walked with the earl into the house, leaving Bel and Aphrodite behind. She failed to see his lordship give Bel a salute and a wry smile.

"I am pleased you like the flower I sent. It was named for a chap called Garden about sixty years or so ago. The bloom is devilish touchy to cultivate, so I'm told by the fellow who tends the gardens and conservatory at Peak House."

"I have never seen anything so beautiful," she said softly, turning her gaze from the flower to the giver.

"A beautiful flower for a beautiful lady—'tis only appropriate."

"Do not tease me so," she objected with a smile that revealed she was not truly angry with him.

He stood oddly ill at ease, restlessly shifting about, quite unlike his customary polished and urbane self. Then he turned to face her, eyes intent, chewing at his lower lip in what seemed like uncertainty. When he spoke, his voice was low and earnest.

"We began well at Kenyon Hall, did we not? You enjoyed rowing in the boat, observing the glowworms in the quaint dance, our time together?" he persisted. "The roses, you found delight in them?"

She thought wistfully of the hours spent together in pleasant occupation and admitted he was right. "That is true."

"Everything went well until the night of the ball. I kissed you."

"True." Her affirmation was wary, and she withdrew a little, wondering what he intended to say. She would not lie and say she had detested that kiss, for that would be false beyond credibility. She had responded too ardently for him to accept such an untruth.

"I said something—you indicated that it repelled you—something about seduction. And then you fled in the middle of the night."

"That is true, all of it. I had been the object of too many attempts at seduction by that point. I could not endure such a thing from you, of all people."

He pounced on her words. "Why me, of all people?" he demanded.

"Because"—she took a deep breath to fortify herself—"I had thought you special. I had come to trust you. I felt betrayed, humiliated, tawdry, as though all that we had shared had no more purpose than to lure me into your bed. I simply could not face you, so I ran away. Perhaps I would have been better had I remained to disillusion you regarding my availability. I vow I did not think of fairness at that moment."

"Georgiana, you must know that I have undergone a substantial change in my regard for you." He placed his hands on her arms, pleading with his eyes that she listen to him, hear him out.

"I have thought that might be the case, yes," she admitted, studying his handsome face.

He drew closer to her, and she tilted her face up to better search his eyes. They were the same eyes she had fallen in love with while at Kenyon Hall, with the same warmth in their dark depths. A raven lock fell over his brow, rebelling as it were against his usual perfection. She would not mind being crushed in his strong arms, nor kissed again in that passionate embrace such as she had known at Kenyon Hall or atop Peak Hill that dark night.

"Georgiana, I'm sorry . . ."

A door slammed and the sound of footsteps in the hall forced Jason to step away from Georgiana. The look of frustration on his face equaled that felt by her.

"There you are," Elspeth exclaimed. "I thought you might be in the garden on such a lovely day, but only Bel and a strange cat are there." If she noticed that there was an odd tension in the room, she gave no indication of it.

Lord Musgrave had followed her into the room and by the expression on his face seemed even more conscious that something had been going on before they entered. He said nothing regarding it, however.

"Bennett and I have something we wish to share with you," Elspeth continued, her face glowing with her love for Bennett and her joy in this day. "His mother has sent her blessing on our marriage. We intend to travel to Musgrave Manor as soon as matters here may be sorted out to your satisfaction, dear Georgiana."

Taking a step in Elspeth's direction Georgiana tried to absorb what she had just been told, wrenching her mind away from the scene between her and Lord Thornbury. "But that is wonderful! I am so happy for you both. Lord Musgrave, you could not find a better wife if you searched the country twice over," Georgiana declared stoutly.

"I know that," he said calmly, but wrapped one arm about his precious girl with a most possessive air. "She is all I could wish. Mama has comfort that Elspeth is a girl we have known most of her life. Elspeth is well liked in the neighborhood, knows everybody, our ways. Mama even went so far as to declare me clever." He smiled down at his beloved at that encomium from his usually taciturn parent.

"You certainly do not need my permission to leave here—or to do anything you please, you must know that," Georgiana said in a half-scolding manner.

"I scarce know what to say," Elspeth bubbled. "I owe you so much, rescuing me, bringing me safely away from Ware Court." A worried look flashed to her face and she cried, "Georgiana, you must not return there. Stay here, where you will be safe from Lord Ware. You know what an evil man he is. Whatever things you wish from there can be sent to you."

"It is not quite that simple, my dear," Georgiana said with dismay, for she knew how her finances were arranged and how his lordship had control over the dispersal if he so chose. "But you are not to worry about a thing. I have an excellent lawyer and all will be right. What we need dwell on now are bride clothes, gifts, what you might wish in your new home. Such a delectable topic."

Seeing it was hopeless to continue his talk with Georgiana at this time, Jason took his good friend by the arm to indicate they ought to leave.

"Elspeth, I shall see you this evening." Musgrave glanced at Jason for confirmation. "We all go together?"

"Indeed. I will bring my coach as it looks to coming on rain."

"It cannot rain," Elspeth cried. "I forbid it, today of all days."

The men left and Georgiana settled Elspeth on a chair in the morning room with a pot of tea and ratafia biscuits on a nearby table. They quickly restored their nerves with comforting cups of tea, then sat back to plan.

"First of all we must order your bride clothes."

Elspeth blushed and said, "I shan't wish more than a bridal gown, perhaps a new pelisse. Bel tore the other one." She shared a look of vexation with Georgiana.

"We shall see. Why do we not investigate what fabrics the local mantuamaker has in stock?"

Delighted at the prospect, Elspeth fetched their parasols, let the cats inside, then came to Georgiana with a puzzled look. "That strange cat stays here?"

"*That* cat is Aphrodite, a gift from Lord Thornbury. He reasoned that Bel was jealous and needed a lady of his own."

"I can understand that," Elspeth said with her usual practicality of mind.

The two young women hurried down the lane and along to where the widow seamstress kept her little shop. Inside they discovered the place bustling with activity. Georgiana explained what they desired and the woman beamed a smile at them.

"Thanks to you, Lady Ware, I have so much business I must take an assistant. There is nothing that would give me more pleasure than to make your bridal clothes."

"You misunderstand. It is Miss Pettibone who is to be married to Lord Musgrave. She will be a baroness and must dress accordingly. What can you show us?"

While she tried to concentrate on the beautiful silks and muslins paraded for their benefit, Georgiana's thoughts kept returning to the scene with Jason, Lord Thornbury. What had he been about to say to her? He had been in the process of apologizing for his actions. Had he intended to say anything else? The possibilities were endless. Would he confess to the smuggling? Or would he confess to something more fascinating, more personal? Her mind reeled with the prospects.

"These fabrics are exquisite, ma'am," Elspeth said. "I have never seen anything quite like them. Have you, Georgiana?"

Tearing her thoughts from Jason, Georgiana studied the fabulous bolt of delicate cream silk, the perfect thing for a wedding dress. "I have not seen it here before, that is certain."

The seamstress winked at them and gave a little shrug that had a Gaelic touch to it. "Every now and again I have new shipments brought in, if you know what I mean."

Elspeth gave Georgiana a look that dared her to censure the poor woman in any way. The silk might be smuggled, but that woman desperately needed to provide for her fatherless children and there was no silk in all of England to compare with this.

"Elspeth shall have a gown of that as well as a day gown of the celestial blue with a matching pelisse. Do you have more of that willow green I saw here last time? She ought to have an evening gown of that with a lace overskirt. A new peach as well."

"Georgiana," Elspeth whispered frantically when the woman left the room to fetch the fabrics as well as designs, "I cannot afford so much."

"I can. It gives me great pleasure to do this for you. Think how it would upset Lord Ware if he knew." Georgiana gave her dear friend an amused look.

"Well, I shall remain at Rose Cottage until all these garments are completed. Then I believe Bennett intends to take me to his mother. I confess I find it greatly to my liking to be well-gowned with lovely clothes when I see her again. Only fancy—she approves!" An ecstatic Elspeth turned to inspect the other fabrics brought out.

Georgiana allowed her mind to wander to what the future held for her. She would need another companion, but where would she find one half so agreeable?

From the mantuamaker's the two ventured to High Street, intent upon finding several pair of slippers and jean half boots for Elspeth.

"My how busy everyone looks—drays being loaded over there, and still that air of suppressed excitement," Elspeth observed outside the shoemaker's shop.

"That, my dear innocent, is because the smugglers had a run last night," Georgiana declared with the certainty of one who has had a revelation. "While Lord Thornbury entertained the preventative, Captain Ridley, at Peak Hill House, those men brought a cargo of brandy and silks and heaven knows what else up the cliff below Peak Hill. That explains the flashes of light I saw from that ship offshore."

"Oh, dear. You feel we have been used as a cover?" the astute Elspeth inquired.

"How well you put it. Come, let us order your slippers."

Georgiana didn't know whether to be furious with his lordship or congratulate him on his cleverness. So many things that had been puzzling her for the past few days were suddenly clear. Was that what he intended to apologize for—using her and the others as a screen so that the smugglers might bring their loot ashore without detection? That did not explain why the assistant hadn't spotted the men. But darkness conceals a great deal, as she had discovered the night she careened into Lord Thornbury and he had kissed her utterly senseless. That man earned his designation of scoundrel. But, she added wistfully, he certainly knew how to kiss.

On departing the shoemaker's shop they encountered Mrs. Swinford and Mrs. Arbuthnot, who had to be regaled with the news of the engagement and coming marriage.

"I told you he had a partiality for you, my dear. And you shall be a baroness!" Mrs. Swinford declared.

Mrs. Arbuthnot insisted they all had to return to the Royal York for tea with the obvious intention of learning all possible from the bride-to-be.

From a distance, Jason watched the ladies trot on down the street toward the Esplanade. If ever a gentleman was cursed with friends it was today. He wondered what it would take to have Georgiana all to himself. He thought on the matter for some time; then a devilish gleam lit his eyes and he was off to the mews, whistling as he walked.

At the Royal York Elspeth found herself much fussed over by all the Royal York ladies. Miss Brompton, having returned from her jaunt to Exeter, entered the tearoom and eyed the festive group with jaundiced eyes.

"My dear Lady Ware, is someone having a celebration?" she asked in that fluting voice that carried so beautifully.

"You will want to wish Miss Pettibone happy, for she has become engaged to Lord Musgrave. Is it not lovely? Our dearest Elspeth to be a baroness?"

Miss Brompton looked as though the chocolate she'd consumed at breakfast disagreed with her. "Indeed. Lovely. He is quite comfortably off I suppose?" Her nose descended a notch.

"I should estimate an income of around ten thousand pounds a year give or take a few," Georgiana said, having ascertained his status some time ago when it seemed he took Elspeth in particular regard.

"Gracious," Miss Brompton said in a faint tone. "Why she will live most splendidly."

"Splendidly, indeed," Georgiana replied with relish. "Musgrave Hall is said to be a showplace with fine gardens and wondrous paintings to view. I am so pleased I shall be invited to visit her there."

Miss Brompton found that more than she could tolerate and spun about to march from the room, poor Mr. Rood trailing behind her.

The silence after her departure was broken by soft giggles from Elspeth. "Georgiana, how could you?"

"Well, I investigated, my dear girl, and every word is true. I am pleased you will live so well."

"In that case, should you need a haven once you leave Ware Court, you must come to us," Elspeth insisted.

Georgiana gave her a grateful look but said nothing more on that score, not wishing it to become a topic of discussion for the Royal York ladies.

When Lady Peachey rose to leave, the others took it as a signal that the tea was over. They straggled from the room, all promising to meet later at the assembly rooms.

"Promptly at eight of the clock," Mrs. Swinford reminded. "Do not be late, for the hours fly past far too quickly as it is."

Elspeth turned to Georgiana and said, "Eight until midnight! I vow it will be like a ball to celebrate in honor of our betrothal with so many friends attending."

"It will, indeed."

When they returned to Rose Cottage they found flowers awaiting them. Elspeth had a delicate yellow rose and Georgiana had white.

"I believe a white rose has the message that 'I am worthy of you.' Do you feel that Lord Thornbury sends yours with a particular intent?" Elspeth touched the petals of her flower, watching Georgiana with a curious expression.

"He is more than worthy of me, if you think on it. The man has an income of at least twenty thousand a year, several magnificent homes, and is as handsome as can stare. Before you entered earlier he was in the process of apologizing to me for his behavior at Kenyon Hall. *That* is what the white rose is about. As well," she murmured, "white also represents innocence."

"And you should know of that," Elspeth said, placing the roses on the table, then going to wrap her arms about Georgiana in comfort.

"I have mentioned the matter to him in a roundabout way. I have no idea if he believed what I said or not. Gentlemen can be so inscrutable."

"Whereas, you, my dear Georgiana, wear your heart on your sleeve and your face reveals far too many emotions."

"I know." Georgiana sighed with annoyance. "Let us hope that his daunting lordship does not understand what is on my mind this evening."

"You love him. What a pity there is no simple solution to that dilemma."

"Yes, well, Lord Thornbury will complete his stay in Sidmouth, then return to one of his many homes, or perhaps to London. I feel certain he will be groomsman at your wedding."

"And you shall be my only attendant as well," Elspeth declared. "Perhaps while he is standing near the altar with you not far away he will get ideas."

Georgiana laughed at that quaint notion and went up to her room to change from her walking dress to one suitable for sitting around the house until it was time to dress for dinner and the assembly.

Lord Thornbury promised to bring his carriage just before eight. She hoped it didn't rain.

Fortunately Georgiana found she was not required to say much during their light dinner. She found herself on edge, wondering when Lord Thornbury would leave Sidmouth. Oddly enough her ire regarding the smugglers had faded some, although she was certain he had been deeply involved.

Elspeth bubbled with her newfound happiness, thinking everyone was splendid and her new gown of delicate lavender the prettiest thing ever made. She even had a kind word for Aphrodite.

"Bel has settled down amazingly. I believe Lord Thornbury had the right of it."

"He informed me that male cats get testy if they are denied their pleasures. Although, to be perfectly honest, he merely said 'males,' now I think about it. I told him that I suspected he had no trouble getting his own way."

"Except with you," Elspeth reminded.

"Yes," Georgiana said with a faint smile of complacency. "He will apologize for his words and that infamous kiss and be done with it." She did not mention the kiss at Peak Hill for that had been as much her fault as his. "His business at his house is complete. I doubt there is anything to hold him here." She offered Elspeth a second helping of pigeon pie, then fell into a reverie.

Since Elspeth was in the same state, contemplating that magnificent home that would soon be hers along with the very nice man who owned it, Georgiana's silence was not noticed.

They were ready when Bennett and Lord Thornbury came to fetch them. Georgiana remarked on the elegant traveling coach in use for the brief trip to the London Hotel.

"No point in using the gig—too open," his lordship said while studying Georgiana in the soft light from the inside lamps. "The rose is most fortunate," he said. They might as well have been alone for the other pair were deep in planning the trip to Musgrave Manor.

Georgiana touched her bodice where the rose had been tucked into the neckline and pinned in place.

"Thank you, sir; roses afford many pretty memories."

"I trust that will continue to be the case."

At least that was what she thought he said, for he spoke softly, as though to himself more than to her.

When they walked up the stairs to the assembly rooms they found everyone they knew in attendance. Both Sir John and Major Giles congratulated Elspeth and Bennett Musgrave on their coming marriage. Mrs. Swinford had that knowing look on her face that said she had been certain of the attachment from the very first.

Georgiana welcomed the first dance and willingly accepted the hand of Sir John for a country dance quite as rollicking as the one last evening at Peak Hill.

She felt almost numb. She had quite decided that Lord Thornbury would be leaving at once. His smugglers had made a successful run, he had apologized to Georgiana—almost, his house looked lovely and ready to let again, and his best friend had found himself a wife. Nothing remained for his attention in Sidmouth. Nothing at all. He had even seen to Bel! Georgiana was quite decided this would be farewell.

From Sir John she found herself in Bennett's hands and from him she went to Major Giles. She glanced about the room to discover Lord Thornbury watching her with a brooding look. It did wonderful things to his eyes, making him look the most romantic man in the room. She wanted to cry.

She made the rounds of all the gentlemen attending the dance. Since there was yet no Master of Ceremonies she had no way of ascertaining whether they were truly acceptable as partners or not, but they all seemed presentable and made agreeable partners as far as she was concerned.

It was nearing midnight when Lord Thornbury claimed her hand for a dance. They faced each other in the line, Georgiana wishing to memorize every aspect of his face, the expression in those indescribably dark and beautiful eyes. He was indeed a romantic figure from the top of his stylish dark hair to his perfectly tied cravat to that elegant white marcella waistcoat and wine coat to the black breeches and black stockings that fit too well for her ease of mind to the tip of his patent shoes.

"You approve, madam?" he said when they met in the first figure of the dance.

She flashed a reproving look at his impudence. Rascal, he would say things to disconcert her. "The music is most charming. I have enjoyed the dancing, although I daresay I shall be fatigued by the time we return to Rose Cottage."

"Undoubtedly. We have yet to complete our conversation begun this afternoon."

They were parted in the pattern of the dance and she studied him, intrigued that he wished to speak further.

They continued in a stately silence until the music ended. The clock struck midnight and a sigh of regret went up around the room. The musicians began to gather their things and the ladies to hunt for their shawls and cloaks.

"I shall take Elspeth," Musgrave murmured to Jason.

"Right. I'll see you later." They exchanged a meaningful look that was lost on anyone else.

Georgiana made her way down the stairs and out to the waiting carriage with head held high. Once inside with Jason beside her she peered out into the lamplit night for Elspeth and Bennett. When the coach started off, she gave a cry of alarm.

"Not to worry," Jason said calmly. "We have a few things to settle and I will tolerate no more interruptions."

Her concern subsiding somewhat, Georgiana eased back against the cushions to watch him with wary eyes.

"We were interrupted this afternoon," he reminded.

"Yes, you were apologizing to me for something?" She half-turned to look at him, wishing she might see his face better. Then she recalled what Elspeth had said about her lack of ability to conceal her emotions and welcomed the dim light.

"I believe I said I was sorry and I am, but I was not really apologizing for any wrong. I am sorry that there have been misunderstandings. I am sorry that you were frightened away from my aunt's home. I am not sorry I kissed you, however. I treasure that kiss, as I do the one you gave me at Peak Hill. That was quite a collision."

"Wicked man," she scolded. "However you had no need to be at Peak Hill last night. With the preventative man at your home, those smugglers could come and go as they please."

"I might not actively take part in smuggling, but I'll not stand in their way, either. As I have observed, the needs of these poor devils outweigh adherence to a law that must be changed. I intend to do my best to see that it is, so there will be no need for such a dangerous trade."

She murmured something indistinct, but she was impressed with his intent.

"To return to more interesting things, there is the matter of my attempted seduction of you."

"You do speak plainly, sir," she said quietly, folding her hands primly in her lap.

"First of all, I knew little of your circumstances when I plotted the thing. I'll admit that I have had ladies seek me out in the past. I thought you might do the same. I never have had to seduce any woman, Georgiana."

"You bewitched them so they came to you?" she queried in a wisp of a voice.

"I doubt I bewitched you, did I?"

The husky warmth of his words curled about her ears, reached down to her toes and wandered about all through her until she could readily believe he bewitched women by the dozens. "I'd not say that, precisely," she whispered.

"You know me, my dearest Georgiana. I am not perfect. I'll tease you, torment you, adore you—I'll not make your life easy." He reached out to cover her hands with his, his touch sending tremors through her.

"What do you mean?" she demanded in a breathless voice that did not sound the least like her. In the soft light from the sole lamp she could barely make out his face, but he wore an intriguing smile, one that seemed almost tender.

"I have learned that things are not always what they seem. You are *not* the experienced widow on the prowl, but a modest, talented, and delightful woman who seems quite the innocent." He placed an arm about her and she had no inclination to pull away from him.

"I am the widow of a man who never touched me, who instead left me quite vulnerable—feeling I must beware of all men. Likewise you are not *quite* the rake or smuggler I thought you were, are you?" She leaned forward to better study his dear face.

"Not quite. However my desire for you has only increased. I love you most passionately, dear Georgiana. I can think of nothing but making you mine forever." He pulled her across the carriage to cradle her in his arms.

"Do I call you a scoundrel, sir?" she demanded, scarcely able to breathe at this point.

"I think not," he murmured. "Husband has a far better sound to it." He placed a kiss on her willing lips, then drew a ragged breath. "I think it best we marry, and soon."

"I believe you can teach me all I need to know about loving. I do love you, Jason—however, I suspect there is a great deal to be learned and I've no doubt you're a splendid teacher." She slid a trusting hand along the smooth fabric of his coat until she reached the back of his neck, and then his hair. He seemed most affected as she threaded her fingers through the crisp dark hair as she had longed to do.

"I can think of no more pleasant task, my precious love," he replied, drawing her closer. "I'm willing to devote as many years as necessary to the matter."

Before she could answer that delightful remark, he was kissing her again and she forgot everything in the world but Jason Ainsley, Earl of Thornbury, the passion and love of her life for now and evermore.

He surfaced long enough to murmur, "I do believe it ought to be a double wedding. *Quite* soon." And then there was little of sense to be heard in the coach as it slowly traveled the long way around to Rose Cottage.

Author's Note

There are a few words that may be unfamiliar to a new reader of Regency Romances. I trust the following will serve to unscramble some of them.

An *abigail* is a lady's personal maid.
A *downey one* is one who is shrewd, sharp, and knowing.
A *nodcock* is a simpleton.
A gentleman who is *bosky* or *foxed* is either mildly or completely drunk.
To *go aloft* is to die—as is to come to an untimely end, go west, hop off, and pop off.
The *South Sea Bubble* was a disastrous failure of a joint-stock company in 1720, bringing ruin to many.
A *Stanhope gig* was a two-wheeled gig made by a coach builder named Tilbury to the designs of the Hon. Fitzroy Stanhope. It was hung on four springs and often had a serviceable hood. The driving seat was designed as a rib-backed chair.
The *mantuamaker* created the gowns, pelisses, and other wearing apparel for milady. Fabrics such as *gros de Naples*—a corded Italian silk similar to Irish poplin—could be found in her well-stocked shop. One edging was called *vandyked.* It was a dentate border, either in lace or material, and named for the Flemish painter Van Dyck.